Fay turned and descenc  boat. She dug deep into her she now carried with her to t known to all seafarers as "Davy Jones' Locker.

The frigid night air slapped her face as the small boat raced across the flat surface of the night water; sea spray soaked her face and hands. She squinted and fixed her gaze on the wall of black now standing before her. *I'm going to need severe beauty salon time when I get back to civilization,* she thought.

Shortly after, the boat arrived at the prescribed dive location. The dive team donned their facemasks and tested their gear—then, one by one, the divers rolled backward from the boat and into the water. Fay was last to leave the safety of the small boat.

The cold salt water stung her skin momentarily, until the thin layer of water between her skin and her wetsuit warmed to a tolerable temperature. She bobbed on the surface for a moment, then flicked on her underwater torch. Fay then slipped beneath the water's surface and began her descent toward the bottom.

The wreck was ninety feet below. The *Carr* came to rest upright on the edge of a reef. The ship had not completely settled and was subject to shifting with each tide change. All good reasons for her to exercise extreme caution.

Praise for Norm Harris

"Norm Harris' book grabs the reader with its first sentence and holds the reader throughout with its fast-paced action. Dialogue is always the hardest to write, but Harris has captured the art and with his writing keeps the reader turning pages, his ability to heighten the intrigue keeps the reader on the edge of his or her seat throughout the story. Strongly recommend the book…"

~ CAPT David E. Meadows, US Navy, author of numerous military thrillers such as Sixth Fleet, Seawolf, and Tomcat.

"A great read with a stunning finish… A good and recommended read."

~ Advocate, Narayan. -- Picturing Justice, The On-Line Journal of Law & Popular Culture, published by the Faculty of Law, University of San Francisco.

Fruit of the Poisonous Tree

by

Norm Harris

*Spider Green Mystery Thriller
Series, Book One*

Fruit of the Poisonous Tree

Cover Art by *Diana Carlile*

The Wild Rose Press, Inc.
PO Box 708
Adams Basin, NY 14410-0708
Visit us at www.thewildrosepress.com

Publishing History—First Edition, 2022
Trade Paperback ISBN 978-1-5092-4099-9
Digital ISBN 978-1-5092-4100-2
Previously Published in 2002 by Author House & Published in 2003 by Futami Shobo in Japanese

Spider Green Mystery Thriller Series, Book One
Published in the United States of America

Dedication

For my son, Kristopher-Kent Herbert Harris, with love and amazement.
IN MEMORY
Josephine Hindman, Gladys Richardson, Nell Gelis, Eunice Harris, and Jack Brix.
Many thank yous to those who made this book possible, be it for your technical advice or moral support.
Jeanette Lundgren, Captain David Meadows US Navy, Carolyn Starr, Marki Hocking, and Sheriff Jack Gardner.

A special thank you goes out to Kathleen Jackson and Mom and Dad. Thank you all for both your inspirations and your valued friendships.

Words cannot express my gratitude to Editor Carolyn Shafer for her professional advice and assistance in polishing this manuscript.

Chapter 1

Awake at the first knock, Simon Linn sat upright in his bed as the continuous hard knocking sent the framed photograph on the wall by his bedside crashing to the floor. The glass in the frame exploded, spraying shards across the bare hardwood. Any slumber deeper than a catnap could cost him his life in his business.

"Beat the damn door down, why don't you," he yelled. "Hang on! I'm coming, damn it!" He cinched a pair of blue jeans around his waist. "It's three-thirty in the damn morning." *Who could that be?*

With instinctive caution, he cracked open the door, careful not to step onto the broken glass with his bare feet. He left the security chain in place. The bright lights from the hallway stung his dilated eyes as they strained to focus on the man standing at his door. As his eyes adjusted to the light, he could distinguish a large man dressed in a dark green trench coat. Simon thought he looked like a cop.

"Whadda ya want?" Simon asked warily.

"You Simon Linn?" the man asked. His voice was deep, surly, and demanding in tone.

"I'm Linn. Who the hell are you?"

"Detective Farmer, Seattle Police Department." The man displayed his shield. "Open the door."

Linn focused his eyes on Farmer's gold badge and sighed. He closed the door, slid the chain latch, and then reopened the door.

With their weapons drawn and pointed directly at Linn, Farmer and two uniformed police officers bullied their way through the doorway.

"Hey, hey, hey!" Linn protested. "What's this all about?"

Detective Farmer surveyed the room. He seemed satisfied that Linn was alone and motioned to the officers to holster their weapons. "Mr. Linn," Farmer announced, "I'm arresting you for the murder of Paul Charma."

"Paul?" Linn was puzzled.

"Hands behind your head," Farmer ordered. "Legs apart."

Linn responded without protest but glowered at Farmer while one of the cops searched him. Starting at his ankles, the cop systematically worked his way toward Linn's waist.

"You have the right to remain silent," Farmer said. "If you give up the right to remain silent, anything you say can and will be used against you in a court of law. You have the right to speak with an attorney and to have the attorney present during questioning. If you so desire and cannot afford one, an attorney will be appointed for you without charge before questioning. Do you understand each of these rights I have explained to you?"

Linn nodded and continued to stare directly into Farmer's eyes.

"Do you wish to give up the right to remain silent?" Farmer asked.

"No."

"Do you wish to give up the right to speak to an attorney and have him present during questioning?"

"No," Linn responded.

Farmer ordered, "Get dressed."

Linn grabbed a black sweatshirt off a nearby chair and pulled it over his head. He then sat in the chair and slipped on a pair of black socks and black loafers.

"Cuff him," Farmer said to one of the cops.

The cop took little care when he clamped the black handcuffs tightly around Linn's wrists. He was ushered to a waiting police car without a further word spoken.

****

Navy Captain Vern Towsley was cursing his favorite professional basketball team's ineptitude, as recorded in the morning edition of the Seattle online newspaper. The sharp ring of his telephone interrupted his morning solitude. He reached for the phone.

"Vern Towsley," he answered.

The caller identified himself as Brandon May. Towsley knew May, an old friend; they had worked together several years prior as agents for the Naval Criminal Investigative Service. Admiral May was now the Commander of the U.S. Special Operations Command.

"Admiral, good to hear from you," Towsley said in greeting.

"Vern, I wish I had time to chat. I'd like to ask a favor of you." Without waiting for a reply, May continued. "Marine Sergeant Simon Linn, one of my men, was arrested this morning. The Seattle police have detained him for additional investigation in the death of a Navy SEAL. I'd like you to get him out of jail."

"How can I help?" Towsley immediately responded.

"I'm not at liberty to give you a lot of details on this," May said. "Much of what I'm dealing with right now is top-secret UMBRA. This is a need-to-know matter—classified. I want Sergeant Linn out of jail—ASAP."

Towsley knew a top-secret UMBRA designation meant that whatever Admiral May was dealing with was only known to the President and a small handful of his military advisors, which obviously included May. Carefully choosing his words, he said, "The Seattle Police Department has the right to hold Linn for seventy-two hours without filing charges. I'm not sure how I can help your man."

"I can't wait seventy-two hours, Vern," May insisted. "I want someone to collect Linn for me—now. We'll grease the skids for you. It's an election year, so I'm sure the Seattle District Attorney will cooperate once someone from the Justice Department explains it to her."

"Have you notified the NCIS?" Towsley asked.

"I've talked to the Naval Criminal Investigative Service. Their Terminators are tied up. Which brings me to my second request."

"There's more?"

"Your office will conduct a preliminary investigation into the death, with Lieutenant Commander Green as lead investigator," May instructed.

Towsley rubbed pensively at the side of his neck with his free hand. "Green is an exceptional lawyer, Admiral," he acknowledged, "but lacks experience in death investigations."

"I'm aware of Green's background," May said. "Green will be your lead."

Towsley glanced at his watch. "Green will have your man in Navy custody by twelve hundred hours, sir."

"Thanks. And Vern?"

"Yes, sir?"

"This is a need-to-know assignment," May stated firmly. "Green is not on my need-to-know list."

****

Lieutenant Commander Faydra Green liked to wake up slowly: hit the snooze alarm a couple of times, shower, and drink one (but more often two) strong cups of "Seattle's Best Coffee." Then, her day could start.

But before the sound of her alarm had awakened her entirely, the phone began ringing. Groggy and annoyed, her first impulse was to pick up the cell phone and beat the alarm clock with it.

Blinking at the clock face and noting the time - 06:15 hours - she shut off the alarm. "Good morning," Fay said, hoping the insincerity of her greeting was not noticeable. She cleared her throat. "Fay Green speaking."

"Lieutenant Commander," the voice said. It was the voice of a person who had been awake much longer than she. "This is Vern."

She sat up in bed. "What can I do for you, sir?"

"I have an urgent matter for you to attend to. Can you be at JAG Corps in one hour?"

"Aye, sir. One hour."

Her curiosity growing, Fay stepped in the bathroom and turned on the shower, adjusting the temperature of the water. Closing the shower curtain behind her with a quick jerk, she stepped into the hot rushing water. The shower was short, but she felt invigorated. Snatching a sizeable fluffy towel from the bar next to the shower stall, she dried the moisture from her skin and brushed her hair.

The tall, athletic blonde brought an almost clinical method to applying her makeup. Appearances mattered in society. It was a fact of life—not necessarily fair, but true. And she tended to her appearance the same way she would research or try a case, with as little personal involvement as possible.

Some mornings, she would look for small lines on her otherwise smooth and spa-tanned complexion. It was now she realized her neck was too long and her cheekbones too high, too strong. Her eyes curved slightly upward at the corners to meet the sweep of gracefully arched brows. "These are proud features," her mother would say. She sighed. Mom was right, of course. Without rechecking her appearance in the mirror, she dropped the hairbrush into the basket of makeup and walked back to her bedroom.

A short thirty-minute drive brought her to her office. Fay was out of breath when she entered the JAG's office. A submissive nod conveyed her apology to Captain Towsley for keeping him waiting. She stood at his desk, waiting for permission to sit.

"Good morning, Miss Green." His greeting was immediate and seemed to express a sense of urgency and concern or irritation; she could not tell which. "At ease, Lieutenant Commander. Please…have a seat."

Towsley took a file from his desk and handed it to her. "This is a fax copy of Marine Master Sergeant Simon Linn's service records," he said. "Early this morning, the Seattle Police Department arrested Linn. He's being held in the Seattle City jail. I want you to collect him on behalf of the Navy."

Fay affirmed the request with a quick nod and took the file from him. "Why was he arrested, sir?"

"He's been implicated in the death of a SEAL."

"Homicide?" Her eyes widened. "You are assigning

me to an investigation involving the death of a sailor? Sir, I don't—"

"Affirmative, Green." He nodded toward the file she held in her hands. "I suggest you review Linn's service record and get to Seattle ASAP."

"Yes, sir."

"And before you ask," Towsley said, "page thirteen of his service records has been censored."

"Sir, no duty assignment history?"

"Linn is a shadow warrior. Spec/Ops chose not to share his duty status with us."

Fay's eyebrows arched. "He is an operator? Need-to-know, sir?"

Towsley nodded. "I want you to retrieve Sergeant Linn from the jail and conduct a preliminary investigation." He gave her a reassuring smile. "Dust off your JAGMAN, and if you run into any trouble, I'm here to help. Any further questions?"

Yes, she had many questions but asked only one. "Will I need a Shore Patrol detail, sir?"

"That won't be necessary. Sergeant Linn is a suspect, not a convict. All you have to do is escort him back to Bremerton and confine him to quarters."

"Aye, aye, sir."

Fay returned to her office to review Linn's service records. Bosnia, Desert Storm, Afghanistan—he had served in them all and had been awarded almost every service medal known. He had been wounded in action during one of his three tours of duty in Afghanistan and saved four Marines' lives. *A regular hero*, she thought. *What reason would a war hero have for killing a SEAL?*

Consulting her ferry schedule, she noted the next boat was scheduled to leave in forty minutes. Fay stuffed her *Manual of the Judge Advocate General (JAGMAN)* and Linn's service records into her briefcase and dashed for the ferry terminal.

The commute to the Seattle City jail would take almost two hours. The one-hour ferry ride was an excellent time to think; she often took her work with her for her ferry commutes.

Fay bought a cup of strong coffee and moved to one of the upper decks. She knew the wind off Puget Sound in the late fall months was brisk, so she chose a chair on an enclosed deck.

She had a deep appreciation for the Washington State ferry system. Even the smaller ships were huge by any (except perhaps Navy) standards. As with all boats, the ferries had names; many were Native American words for famous Indian chiefs and beautiful places: *Walla Walla* (place of two rivers), *Spokane* (children of the sun), *Kaleetan* (arrow), *Chelan* (deep water). She pursued an interest in learning the meaning of each name. She liked to find out what things meant; mysteries intrigued her. Any mystery beckoned her, like a clam closed tightly, and she brought a sea otter's ambition and patience to cracking one open.

The weather was nice. Fay chose to walk the one-mile distance from the ferry terminal to the Public Safety building. After signing in with the jailer, Fay was asked to wait. Thirty minutes later, a man in uniform escorted her to the holding cell containing Sergeant Linn.

The jangle of the jailer's keys grated on her nerves as he unlocked the heavy, gray steel door. He swung it open, allowing her access to the small and barren cell; it seemed stuffy—the overhead lights far too bright.

Sergeant Linn snapped to attention. When

reviewing the service records, Fay had noted he was tall. Yet, she was taken aback when he uncoiled his large torso from the bunk on which he sat. His massive body seemed to occupy the entire cell. True to his strict military discipline, he remained at attention as she crossed the floor to greet him.

"Master Sergeant Linn, I am Faydra Green, JAG Corps." She flashed him a smile and said, "At ease," as she extended her hand.

Sergeant Linn's handshake was firm. He seemed to relax.

"I am sorry I couldn't get here any sooner," Fay said apologetically. "It is a long haul from Bremerton to Seattle." She had been expecting a fierce and surly warrior but instead found a vivacity and radiant ruggedness in his dark eyes. She cleared her throat. "Okay, Master Sergeant, what is going on?"

Tiny beads of perspiration formed on Linn's brow and shaved head. "They say a man has died and I'm responsible."

She thought for a moment. "I am here to see if the SPD will release you into military custody. I am meeting with the arresting officer. What is his name?" Fay inquired.

"Detective Farmer."

"Farmer," she noted. "Sit tight. I'll be back, Sergeant Linn."

"Thank you, ma'am."

Fay had little trouble locating Farmer's office, where she was asked to wait. A woman in uniform showed her to a small room. It, too, felt warm and stuffy.

"Wait here," the woman said.

She surveyed the room—posters of various wanted

criminals decorated the light-gray walls. Several worn vinyl chairs lined the perimeter of the room. A table strewn with an assortment of year-old, dog-eared monthly news and sports magazines, much like those found in hospital waiting rooms, dominated the center of the room. She picked up a magazine, flipped through several pages, and then put the magazine back onto the table.

A water-cooler stood at the far side of the room, although the cup dispenser appeared empty. Condensation glistening on the outside of the bottle caught her attention. The water looked cold and refreshing. She stared at the little chilled rivers forming on the glass. Her throat felt dry, her mouth as if were stuffed with a wad of cotton. Her train of thought was broken when a man entered the room.

"Lieutenant Commander Green?" he asked.

Fay smiled and nodded. "I am she."

The man returned her smile and extended his hand. "Sorry to keep you waiting. I'm Detective Frank Farmer."

"Hello, Detective." She firmly shook his massive hand, which was warm and smooth. "It is a pleasure to meet you."

Farmer wiped his brow with the back of his hand. "The air conditioner must be broken again. Please, Lieutenant Commander, this room seems stuffy. Let's go down the hall where it's cooler." He smiled. "We can talk there." He glanced at Fay. "Would you like a cup of water?"

"Yes, please," she said, hoping she did not sound desperate.

Farmer's smile had genuine warmth. He walked to

the cooler and banged the top of the cup dispenser with his hand. A paper cup appeared. "Dang thing sticks." He filled the cup and handed it to her.

As they walked along the hall, Fay sized Farmer up. She decided she felt comfortable with him. Detective Farmer was a large but not a tall man. His hair was graying, and aside from the detective's belly, he appeared physically fit. An aura of confidence surrounded him. She was sure, in his day, he had been an exceptional sleuth. But she saw a hint of retirement in his eyes. He most likely carried a well-worn brochure for his dream RV in his jacket pocket, next to his detective shield and police revolver.

It was a short walk. Detective Farmer opened the door, gesturing for her to precede him into the room. Like the other room, this one was decorated with worn vinyl chairs. A wooden table dominated the center of the room. Two straight-back oak chairs faced each other from opposite sides of the table.

He walked to one of the chairs, pulled it away from the table, and said, "Please, have a seat."

Fay felt too keyed up to sit but sat anyway.

Frank Farmer walked to the other side of the table and sat down. He studied her for a moment. "Let me get right to it," he finally said. "I'm sure you know we've arrested Sergeant Linn for the murder of Paul Charma. Are you Linn's attorney?"

"Detective Farmer," she began, "I—"

"Frank."

"Pardon me?"

"My name is Frank." He smiled. "Please, call me Frank."

"Thank you, Frank. My name is Fay." She could not

help but return at least some of his warmth. "As I was about to say, I am not Mr. Linn's attorney. I am a Judge Advocate...a Navy lawyer."

"A JAG?"

"In military law, I am an officer assigned to the Judge Advocate General's Department," Fay explained. "I serve as legal adviser to Captain Vernon Towsley of the U.S. Navy."

"I used to watch that program on television," Farmer replied. "It was called JAG."

"Fortunately, just like movie cops, JAG is nothing like it is made out to be," Fay joked.

Frank shook his head and gave her a knowing chuckle, then recapped the sequence of events leading up to the arrest of Simon Linn. "Charma's body was discovered at ten twenty-five last night," he recounted. "Charma was stabbed in the neck—we presume with a knife—and left dead in an alley near Jillian's Pool Club in downtown Seattle. Someone saw Linn in the club earlier that night talking with Charma. The conversation escalated into an argument. About an hour later, a witness saw Linn running from the alley where Charma's body was found."

"You have a witness?" Fay interrupted.

"We have a man who places Linn at the scene, and his observation coincides with the time of death."

"I assume Linn was arrested without a warrant?" Fay knew, without the warrant, Frank would not have been allowed to search Linn's home for evidence.

"That's right," the detective confirmed. "We did make a warrantless search of the immediate area, which, as you know, we are allowed to do."

"Tell me," Fay leaned forward, "what about the

knife?"

"No physical evidence, if that's what you're asking. What I've got are a body and a suspect. Our suspect, at this point, doesn't seem to have an alibi."

"No alibi… Where did Linn say he was at the time of Mr. Charma's death?" Fay asked.

"Linn hasn't said much," Farmer said.

"Did he waive his right to remain silent?"

"He says he won't answer any questions until he talks to an attorney."

"Has he said anything at all?" she inquired.

"He admits he was in the area at the time Charma died. And he denies he had anything to do with it." Farmer shrugged. "That's all I've gotten out of him so far."

Fay offered a judicious sigh as her only response.

Frank sounded apologetic when he said, "I'm afraid it doesn't look good for Sergeant Linn, Lieutenant Commander."

"Afraid?" Fay repeated.

"In my business, I meet all types of scum and vermin. I think I've seen it all, rapists, muggers, murderers." He clasped his hands behind his head and tipped back in his chair. "I think I'm a pretty good judge of character, and I'll bet you are too." Farmer paused as he studied her. There was a quizzical look on his face - that look most people seemed to have as their brain began the recall process leading to the inevitable question, *Aren't you Faydra Green, the daughter of?* To her surprise, he instead said, "I don't see it. Not with Simon Linn anyway."

They sat in silence for a moment, before Fay spoke again, "Frank, I appreciate your candor. It sounds like you have voluntary manslaughter here. Am I correct?"

"That's what we've determined." Frank pointed toward her crumpled cup, which she did not recall crumpling. "More water?"

"Yes, thank you," Fay said as her fingers fumbled with the cup in a pathetic attempt to reconstruct it. "I would like to borrow a minute from y'all to think, if it is okay."

He rose from his chair without a word and walked to the door. Fay heard the door quietly close. With a sigh of relief, she slumped back in her chair. *What now?*

Frank was gone for ten minutes. When he returned to the room, he walked over to her with the water. "Forgive me for taking so long," he apologized. "I ran into my supervisor in the hall. He had a few questions and—"

"I understand. Thank you for the water." Fay sipped from her cup and then said, "I was wondering…" She felt a stream of perspiration race down from the pit of her right arm and stop at her bra band. She knew the Seattle Police Department had the right to hold Linn for seventy-two hours, but there was no harm in asking. And a good lawyer never asked a question she did not already know the answer to. "Would it be possible to have Sergeant Linn released to military custody? You have my assurance as a naval officer and a lawyer I will be fully responsible."

Frank gave a hearty laugh. "And as the daughter of a former President of the United States?"

He had recognized her after all. Few Faydra Greens were running around this country. It was a curse, something that had plagued her for most of her life. Never knowing whether she had accomplished something on her own merit or because she was Faydra Green, former President William Green's daughter.

"No sir, not as my father's daughter," Fay replied, "but as an officer of the United States Navy. I will accept full responsibility for Sergeant Linn."

Farmer was still chuckling as he shook his head. "All right. That's what I was speaking to my supervisor about. We've received word from the District Attorney to release Sergeant Linn to the Navy with discretion. The supervisor and I agree with the DA. We'll let you have Linn. I recommend he be confined to his quarters at the base, pending our investigation."

Unusual, Fay thought to herself. "That seems reasonable," she said. "Thank you." Without waiting for any further explanation, she gathered up her briefcase and pocketbook. She bolted for the door, intent on clearing the area before Frank changed his mind.

"Lieutenant Commander Green," Frank called after her. She turned. "Win this one."

She winked. "I intend to, Frank," she said and whisked out of the room.

She was escorted back to Linn's cell. Once again, Sergeant Linn snapped to attention as she approached.

"Mr. Linn, good news!" Fay announced. "They have agreed to release y'all."

Chapter 2

Fay waited in the lobby while Linn was processed for release. After surveying the hall, she chose what looked to be a reasonably clean chair and sat down. She sniffed. She must have another cold. It was not surprising, considering the Pacific Northwest climate's interminable dampness. Six hours into the day, and she felt spent. Perhaps a cold virus was gnawing at her strength—plus the stress she was feeling about her new assignment. She wrapped the strap of her pocketbook tightly around her arm and clutched her briefcase in her lap. Willing to risk a possible mugging in exchange for a few precious moments of rest, she leaned her head back and closed her eyes. She must be tired and headed for a severe illness, if she could nap in the city jail lobby.

She was dozing when her cell phone chimed. Startled, she focused her eyes on the screen.

When Fay put the call in, the phone rang twice on the other end before being picked up. "Good mornin', United States Navy, Judge Advocate General, Lieutenant Commander Green's office. Petty Office Pearce speakin', how may I help you?" a voice queried.

Pearce's uncanny ability to make the entire greeting sound like a single word, combined with her soft southern drawl, amused Fay every time.

"Hi, it's me. What's up?" Fay responded.

"Hey, ma'am! How's Seattle?"

"I'll tell you all about it when I get back this afternoon," Fay assured her.

Pearce seemed satisfied with the arrangement and then said, "Okay. Captain Towsley called. A special delivery priority document from Admiral Wallace arrived for ya, and when will y'all be back?"

"About four."

"Ma'am?" Pearce sounded hesitant.

Oh, God, what else could happen? "Yes, Pearce, what is it?" Fay said aloud.

"Will ya pick up a turkey sandwich for me from that sandwich shop near the ferry terminal? Extra mayo on wheat bread, please."

Fay breathed a sigh of relief. "You got it, sailor. Anything important going on?"

"No, ma'am. Just the sandwich."

"How did ya know I was in Seattle this morning?" Fay wondered.

"Towsley told Don. Don told me, ma'am."

"I see." And she did see. Fay knew in the Navy, bits of information filtered from the bottom, the enlisted ranks, to the top, the officer ranks. Those same bits of information then recycled through the system, filtering from the top back down to the bottom in the form of new and original ideas. She had long ago stopped wondering who was in charge at the JAG offices. She knew it was Petty Officer Pearce and her cronies. The officers were there merely to give official direction and provide comic relief to the actual idea people and decision-makers, the office support staff.

"See ya in a couple hours," Fay said. Pearce was one of a kind. She wondered if this information flow worked the same way on a surface vessel. Pearce charmed her;

nonetheless, Fay had great respect for Pearce. As she hung up the phone, she saw Sergeant Linn enter the lobby with the jailer. "Y'all ready to go, Master Sergeant?"

He nodded. "Yes, ma'am."

Fay took a pair of sunglasses from her pocketbook. "Let's get a cab to the ferry terminal," she said as she walked toward the door. "We'll grab a sandwich at the ferry terminal if you are hungry."

She felt the radiant warmth of the midday sun as she walked out of the Seattle Public Safety Building and onto Second Avenue. As it typically did, the wind gusted through the concrete canyons created by Seattle's tall office buildings. It is a true challenge for a lady with a hat, a dress, a briefcase, and a handbag.

The wind made a mischievous attempt to snatch her hat from her head. "Mercy! I have only got two hands!" Fay said, while at the same time, the roguish wind filled her skirt like the sails on a schooner.

Linn came to the rescue. In one quick motion, he snatched the briefcase away from her and hailed a cab.

It was a short ride to the terminal where the ferry was about to leave. The two had just enough time to buy their sandwiches and sprint for the dock.

"Just made it!" Fay said, huffing for breath.

As for Simon, it appeared it would have taken another 5K sprint before he would have run out of breath. This did not surprise her. A Marine like Simon would be in excellent physical condition.

The two people found a bench seat near a stern window and sat down.

Fay asked, "Hey, Sergeant, how about a cup of coffee? Cream and sugar?"

"Yes, ma'am." Simon nodded. "Thank you, ma'am."

She stood; so did Simon—he, again, at attention.

Fay, standing five-foot-eleven in pumps, looked up into the eyes of the man who towered above her. She asked, "Marine, have y'all ever disobeyed an order?"

"No, ma'am."

She did not think he had. "Okay, Linn, I have one for you. Master Sergeant Linn, you are at this moment issued a permanent at ease when in my presence. And the name is Fay. Understood, mister?"

Linn smiled and relaxed. "Understood."

The two sat in silence while they ate. When both finished eating, Fay asked, "Did the SPD tell you why they were detaining you, and did they advise you of your rights?"

"Yes."

"I've been assigned to conduct a preliminary investigation into the death of Petty Officer Charma," Fay informed him. "Detective Farmer was required by civilian law to advise you of your rights. *Article thirty-one* of the UCMJ gives you those same rights. I would like to ask you some questions, but I want to advise you that you have the right to remain silent. That means you have the right to say nothing at all. Any statement you do make, either oral or written, may be used against you in a trial by courts-martial or in any other proceedings. You have the right to consult with a lawyer before any questioning. And to have a lawyer present during this or any other interview. You can have military representation free of charge. In addition to military counsel, you are entitled to civilian counsel at your own expense. You may request a lawyer anytime someone is interviewing you. Have you requested counsel?"

"No," Simon replied.

"If you decide to answer my questions or anyone else's questions, you can stop the questioning at any time," Fay explained. "Do you understand your rights as provided by *Article thirty-one*?"

"I do."

"Do you want a lawyer at this time?"

"No," Simon responded. "My CO told me I was to talk only to you, Lieutenant Commander."

"You've talked to your commanding officer?"

"My first and only phone call was to my CO. He told me to talk only to you."

"Are you willing to answer my questions then?" Fay asked.

"As best I can," Simon said with a sigh. "I left home about eighteen-thirty, caught the nineteen-ten ferry to Seattle. I planned to meet Sergeants Philip De Vinsone and Peter Wu at Jillian's Pool Club. It was twenty-fifteen when I arrived. Wu and De Vinsone were already there. We drank a few beers, shot pool, and watched part of the Seattle Kraken hockey game on TV."

"So far, so good," Fay said encouragingly. "Then what?"

"I struck up a conversation with a sailor," Simon recounted. "The conversation evolved into a discussion of military life. Which branch of the service, Navy or Marines, is more significant. Usually, when a squid and a jarhead take up that topic, either they get into a heated discussion, or a fight breaks out."

"You had an argument?" Fay asked.

"A friendly argument."

"Was the sailor Mr. Charma?"

Simon gave a slight nod. She caught a hint of sadness in his eyes.

"I meet sailors like Charma all of the time," Linn said.

"Where were your buddies at the time?" Fay pressed. "Were they with you?"

"No, they were shooting pool with two other guys. Charma left the club, so I rejoined De Vinsone and Wu. I was tired. So, I said goodnight and left. It was around twenty-two fifteen. I took a cab to the waterfront. I was thirty minutes early for the next boat, so I got something to eat. I watched some fishermen jig for squid off a nearby pier while I waited for the ferry."

"You have a clear account of the evening's events. You did not see or talk to anyone after you left Jillian's, did you?"

"I didn't talk to anyone except the cab driver," Simon confirmed. "I brushed by a man in the alley behind the club. He was entering the alley as I was exiting."

"Thinking back to the moment of your arrest, Simon, did the police physically search you?"

"They did."

"Did they take scrapings from under your fingernails?" Fay asked next.

"Not in my home. They did later, at the jail."

"When the police searched your home, did they search any area of your home other than the area immediately surrounding you?"

"No."

"Do you recall if the SPD took any photographs of your home while they were in your home or if they removed any items from your home?" inquired Fay.

"They did not."

Their conversation was interrupted by the loud, deep blast of the ferry's horn, signaling their arrival at the Bremerton dock. The walk from the ferry to Fay's car was three blocks. By the time she and Simon reached her car, the ferry's horn was blasting again, signaling another departure to Seattle.

Simon paused to admire the low, white BMW roadster. "Sweet ride," he said appreciatively. "Is it new?"

"I bought it a year ago," Fay replied. "I thought it was time to reward myself for all my years of toil. It's a great little buggy. I love it. And I got it for a song."

"That doesn't surprise me," he chuckled. "I'd imagine you wield a mean club at the bargaining table. The dealer probably didn't stand a chance."

"I reckon they practically gave me the car," she said with a sly grin.

Simon laughed. "It's my impression having you on my side will be a good thing, Fay."

Fay unlocked and opened the car's door and dropped down into the roadster's leather bucket seat. She flicked the ignition key as the tall Marine folded himself into the passenger seat beside her. The car's powerful engine roared to life. She gunned the engine once. The tires leaped from the asphalt, and the car rocketed across the parking lot and onto the nearby freeway access ramp.

Simon casually grasped the passenger door handle with his right hand. "You drive the car as if it were a Navy jet." He cleared his throat. "I was wondering…" He cleared his throat again. "I was wondering—"

"You were wondering if I am going to be your lawyer?" Fay guessed.

"Is that possible?"

"At this point, I do not think so. If you are indicted for the murder of Mr. Charma, it will be at the discretion of the civilian court. That is not my province. You will need a civilian lawyer to represent you." She brought the car to a slower pace. "I am to deliver you to the base and to begin a preliminary investigation in the matter of Paul Charma. Beyond that, I do not know." Fay softened her tone. "Relax. They don't award the death penalty for manslaughter."

"I know. What I mean is the Marine Corps is my life. I don't know anything else. This will be the end of my career. I don't hold much hope for a black man in the white man's court."

"You from the South, Simon?"

"Yeah."

"Me as well, but you know, Sergeant, our civilian court system may not be perfect; however, unlike the military courts, it is at least a democracy."

"Unfortunate but true," he said.

Fay said quietly, "I move in a world where winning is everything. People depend on me and my ability to win, win and keep on winning. Yet I play in an arena where I am not always allowed to win, even though I may clearly be the strongest and most skilled competitor. That single truth is the most exasperating thing I have to deal with as a Navy lawyer." She looked at Simon again, thought for a moment, and then said, "I have a civilian friend. The guy is an excellent trial lawyer. I will call him for you. In the meantime, I will speak to my CO and see how I can help." She put her hand on Simon's forearm. "Okay?"

Simon Linn nodded. "I appreciate your concern."

"The man I spoke of is very good at what he does. You will be in good hands with him." As the roadster arrived in front of Simon's base housing, she said, "I would imagine y'all have a knife."

"I have three, stored with my field gear in my locker here on base."

"When you get a chance, send me the knives."

He nodded, before opening the car door and unfolding his large frame from the small car.

"One more thing, Simon. Would you mind if I took a look-see around your apartment?" Fay offered him a smile. "I do not have a warrant. But I think it could be helpful if I could look around."

"Sure." He thrust his left hand into his pants pocket and produced a key. "Here ya go. Just be careful of the broken glass on the floor, near the door."

"Broken glass?" Fay repeated, confused.

"Yeah. Detective Farmer was beating on my door so hard he knocked a picture off the wall."

"Thanks for the warning. I will be mindful. Where's the apartment located?"

"It's called Spinnaker. About two miles south of the base. Apartment D."

"I know it. Here is my card," Fay said, handing him her business card. "Call me with your phone number."

Simon stiffened and snapped a salute. "Yes, ma'am."

"And, Sergeant Linn," she said. "Try to be cool, man."

It was 16:30 hours when Fay arrived at her office. Entering, she called to Pearce, "Hey, sailor! Got your dinner! I'm sorry I'm so late at getting it to y'all."

She kept a list of pet names she used to address

Pearce—*kiddo, honey, darlin', sailor, JP*, and so on because Pearce had a great dislike for her first name and let it be known. *Pearce* seemed to work for both of them.

"Did anyone call for me?" Fay asked as Pearce bit into her sandwich.

"Yes, ma'am. Captain Towsley called."

"I'll go call him. Then I will return and tell you about Seattle."

The conversation with Captain Towsley was short. He wanted to know what was going on. Fay agreed to meet with him at 08:00 the following morning. She then returned to spend the next forty-five minutes bringing Pearce up to date.

Chapter 3

Fay arrived, barely on time, for the 08:00 briefing with Captain Towsley.

"May I get you a cup of coffee, ma'am?" Petty Officer Winslow called out when she whisked past his desk.

"Please," she called over her shoulder as she cleared the doorway leading into the Captain's office. Towsley was on the phone and motioned for her to enter and sit down.

Captain Towsley does usually have a pot brewing in his office, Fay wondered, *so what is the difference between his pot of coffee and the one from which Winslow was serving me? Perhaps it gives Captain Towsley purpose?*

Don Winslow entered with her coffee. The portly young man moved as if everything he did was of great importance. He was one of Pearce's buddies. Winslow stood five-foot-five. On the other hand, Pearce was a statuesque six feet two or more inches tall. They were the best of friends, and their differences made them seem more like a matched set, in a whimsical way.

Fay chatted with Winslow while Towsley spoke on the phone. Winslow was somewhat pedantic, so it was not difficult for her to find a conversation topic with him. Towsley finished his conversation and hung up the phone. Winslow dismissed himself.

Nodding toward the closing door, Towsley said, "Don is a great kid."

"I enjoy him, sir."

He looked at her and asked with a hint of concern in his tone, "How are you, Faydra?"

"Fine, sir." She sniffed. "I seem to have a mild cold virus. Although lately, it seems I have been going from one illness to the next."

"I'm not surprised to hear you say that."

"Why?"

His expression took on the look of a country doctor consulting a patient. "Could it be you burn the candle at both ends and you are wired on caffeine most of your waking hours?" He thought for a moment, "And you don't sleep?"

"I sleep all the time, sir."

"You sleep when your body finally decides it has suffered enough of your abuse and shuts itself down in self-defense."

She offered a meek glance and said softly, "I know." His assessment was fair, and his concern for her was heartfelt.

"That was Admiral Wallace on the phone. He wanted to know about Simon Linn," Towsley said. He stood and walked to the coffee pot located on the credenza at the opposite side of his office. "More drugs?"

She eagerly held out her cup for a refill.

He refilled her cup, then returned to his chair. Tapping his chin with his pen, he asked, "So, tell me about your meeting with Detective Farmer. Did you learn anything from Sergeant Linn?"

She gave the Captain a detailed briefing.

Towsley listened as she spoke. From time to time,

he would make a note. Several times, Towsley asked her to repeat or clarify a point.

When she finished retelling the story, he leaned back in his chair, folded his arms, and frowned. "Hmmm," he said. "Wallace is very concerned. One of his sailors has died. He wants to know what our involvement will be."

"Sir, what can we do?"

"I don't have to tell you this is not our province. While a government-issue Marine sergeant may have assaulted a government-issue Navy petty officer, it didn't occur on a military reservation. Civilian law and civilian justice are in order here. If Sergeant Linn is found guilty as charged, then military law may respond with a court-martial action. I would imagine the court-martial would be cursory, however. I've assured Admiral Wallace we'll do whatever we can, within the bounds of JAG Corps."

"Sir, Admiral Wallace's authority as CO allows him to petition the civil courts, asserting military jurisdiction in cases involving persons subject to military law."

"Thank you. I'll take it into consideration."

"What have we heard from NCIS?" Fay asked.

"Virtually nothing."

"I find it odd, sir. You would think NCIS would be all over this one."

"I find it strange myself. But the local NCIS agent-in-charge has opted to acquiesce to you, Faydra."

She appreciated Towsley's patience. She had admired his professionalism from her first day at JAG Corps. He was firm but supportive, careful not to patronize her, but always willing to offer gentle and constructive criticism. Aside from his warm, curious brown eyes, he reminded her of her father. Both men were compassionate and inquisitive. The Captain, like her father, had a full head of silver-gray hair. Both smoked a pipe, which was one thing she enjoyed about visiting the Captain's office. The aroma took her back to a time when she, as a youngster, sat in her father's den— he working on one of his various projects, and she just content to be near him.

"Fay." Towsley's tone suddenly turned serious. "I'm issuing you a direct order. You are to proceed with caution in this investigation. It goes without saying, this is your first homicide investigation. You are to keep me in the loop at all times. Is that clear, Lieutenant Commander Green?"

"Your order, sir, is received and clearly understood. Are we done?"

"What do you have on your agenda today?" Towsley asked as he surveyed his schedule.

"The usual stuff. Wills, adoption papers, financial planning…" She thought for a moment. "Busier than a cat on a hot tin roof, sir."

Towsley seemed to be contemplating her odd reference.

Fay came to his rescue. "It's a Southern thing, sir."

"Oh!" Towsley smiled. "One more thing." He stood and moved to the vacant chair next to her and sat down. "I know you have a heavy workload. I plan to shift some of your assignments to the other officers." His offer to reduce her workload seemed puzzling. "In all my years in the JAG Corps, I've known of no finer lawyer than you."

"I appreciate your support, sir."

"I'm sending you a yeoman to replace Miss Pearce."

"Sir, you can't take Miss Pearce. She—"

"Miss Pearce isn't going anywhere. The yeoman will free up Pearce's time so she can better assist you with your investigation. Review all I've said and act accordingly." Towsley returned to his own chair and said, "You're dismissed."

As she closed the door behind her, Winslow said, "I've got a couple of messages here for you, Lieutenant Commander."

Winslow handed her two slips of paper, one from Detective Farmer and the other from Sergeant Linn. She called Farmer first.

Detective Farmer had Charma's autopsy report and was willing to share it with her. They agreed to share any information on the case. Frank offered to fax the autopsy report, but she declined. She would have Miss Pearce visit his office to pick it up. She then called Sergeant Linn. He had the knives ready. She told him Petty Officer Pearce would be by to get them.

She returned to her office and briefed Miss Pearce on her meeting with Towsley.

"Sergeant Linn has some knives for us," Fay said. "Will you pick them up?" She handed Pearce a slip of paper with Linn's address written on it. "Here's the address. But wait a minute." She dashed into her office, retrieved her car keys from her pocketbook, and returned to the doorway separating her inner office from her outer office. "Here are the keys to my buggy," she tossed them to Pearce, "and how about picking up lunch?"

Pearce said nothing. She did not exactly catch the keys; she snatched them out of the air, barely looking at them, made a thumbs-up gesture, grabbed her hat from the hat rack near the door, and swooped out of the office.

Fay laughed. What a source of joy Pearce was.

Fay phoned Ford Clay, attorney at law. He agreed to rearrange his schedule to meet in her office at 11:00 on Monday.

Pearce returned one hour later.

"I'm starving!" Fay said. "What did you bring for lunch?"

"Dolphin sandwich." Pearce held up a fat sandwich wrapped in waxed paper. "I also got ya some grits. I know ya been missin' them." Pearce smiled. "I'm just messin' with ya on them grits."

"A dolphin, huh?!" Fay smiled and took a hearty bite. "Umm, you know, they're not even fish, really; they're mammals. Now tuna," she was talking and chewing, "that's a fish—"

Appearing as if she had heard enough of Fay's impromptu marine biology lesson, Pearce interrupted. "Oh, I brought ya that set of steak knives." Pearce lifted a gray sports bag. "Sergeant Linn says the two that look the same are Ka-Bar knives. The other is a bayonet."

She put her sandwich down and took the bag from Pearce. "My word, these are heavy." Before unzipping the bag, she swiveled around in her chair, opened a drawer in the cabinet behind her, withdrew two latex gloves from a dispenser box, and pulled the gloves onto her hands. She then unzipped the bag and carefully extracted one of the Ka-Bar knives.

On assessing the knife's massive blade, Pearce melodiously remarked, "Rambo!"

At that precise moment, a petty officer chose to enter the office. He observed the knife made a quick about-face and left the office.

Fay and Pearce looked at each other, laughed, waited for the door to reopen, and then, when it did not, shrugged and went back to eating their sandwiches.

Fay said, "I have an errand for you to run. Other than a pile of hush puppies on a Sunday mornin', there is nothing more enjoyable for you than a trip to Seattle. I would like for you to pick up Charma's autopsy report from Detective Farmer." She knew she could ask Frank to fax the report. It would be faster.

She might as well have asked Pearce to go to one of those kids theme parks. Pearce looked as if she had won a contest. "I've got a ferry schedule in the top drawer of my desk. I'll go first thing in the mornin'. I'll take my packsack to get some things at the Elliot Bay Market. I hope it doesn't rain!"

Fay removed another Ka-Bar knife from the sports bag, turning her attention to more serious thoughts.

Captain Towsley phoned her. "Yeoman Rayzon will report for duty at fifteen-thirty hours. Will either one of you be there to greet him?" he asked.

Seaman James Rayzon was punctual to the minute. Although she thought Rayzon pleasant, Fay did notice his gaze seemed distant. It struck her as similar to the look in Sergeant Linn's eyes. Perhaps an equal to Sergeant Linn concerning stature, the tall, blonde, and fit sailor seemed exceptionally bright. She wondered how Pearce and Rayzon would work as a team. Fay's team seemed to be taking on the demeanor of a basketball team of late.

"I'm a ninety-watt person operating in a one-hundred-watt world," Pearce often said, thinking herself not a smart woman. Still, Fay noticed Pearce, more often than not, got the correct answer to a problem faster than most people would.

Pearce and Rayzon worked well into the evening.

Despite the physical drain from the cold virus she was battling, Fay offered to take them to dinner. It was partly a team-building tactic and somewhat because she appreciated their dedication.

On her way home from dinner, she stopped by the Spinnaker apartment, Simon's home. She knew the two-story gray building well. Most likely built in the late 1980s to house the constant stream of military personnel, both Navy and Marine, stationed at the Puget Sound Navy Yard, Spinnaker was clean, modern, and cheap.

She found apartment D. She unlocked and opened the door using Linn's key. Quietly, Fay slipped into the dark apartment and - *Crunch!* - stepped squarely onto the broken glass Simon had warned her to watch out for. "Oh, crap." To plan her next step, she looked down at her feet and noticed a framed photograph lying near her left foot. She stooped down and picked up the photo. Locating the light switch next to the door, she flicked the light on.

As she searched the wall for the photo's original location, she glanced at the image. Six rugged, smiling men stood in what appeared to be a desert - that or a sand trap at a golf course. She chuckled. No, it was definitely a desert, and the men were obviously commandos. They held a flag she recognized as Arab by the flag's symbols. She drew the photograph close to her face to read the hand-printed message written across the flag's bottom. She squinted but realized the print was too small for her to read.

She placed the photograph on a small table near the door. The search for the broom and dustpan took much longer than her search of the spartan apartment did. She did locate the broom and the dustpan. Still, she found nothing else in the apartment interesting other than the photograph.

It was 20:15 when she arrived at her home. Her orange-and-white cat, Barnacle Bill, greeted her with an impatient growl. She stooped down to rub the cat, which had rolled over onto his back, on his belly.

"Oh, Billy, quit complainin'," she said. "Are you hungry, cat? Of course, you are." She opened the refrigerator door and surveyed the shelves. "Huh. Oh, here's something for you. How about pizza?" She looked at the cat, who responded with a blink. "It's pepperoni!"

The cat blinked at her again.

"You might be interested to know your buddies, the feral cats who live in Rome's Colosseum, eat pizza. You could go live there." Fay shrugged her shoulders and sighed. "You're more difficult to please than I am. All right. The only other thing I can offer you is cat food, I'm afraid." She popped the lid on a can of something called "Seafood Delight" and scooped the contents of the can onto a plate with a fork.

The cat purred with the resonance of a chainsaw.

"What do you see in this stuff, anyway?" Fay placed the dish of food in front of the impatient animal, wiped her hands clean, and then proceeded to the living room.

She glanced at the canvas sports bag containing the knives she brought home with her. Recalling the size of the blades, she said, "You know, Billy, something tells me this isn't all as simple as it appears to be. What do you think?"

Chapter 4

A warm sunny morning greeted the throng of Bremerton commuters waiting to board the ferry MV *Sealth,* bound for Seattle. Petty Officer Pearce made her way to the ferry's passenger deck. She recalled Fay telling her *Sealth* was Chief Sealth of the local *Duwamish* tribe, for whom Seattle was named. This was stuck in her mind, whereas most information went in one ear and out the other.

She, like Fay, was a Floridian. After attending a community college for two years, she had joined the Navy. She knew she was not college material, and besides, Pearce had already planned from a young age she would join the Navy, just like her dad. Consequently, she did not put much emphasis on her looks. Her shoulder-length, raven hair and make-up-free face fit the tomboy image she cultivated. This was probably to compensate for a shaky sense of self-confidence regarding a long, jagged scar on her right cheek, resulting from an automobile accident.

Even so, odd as it was, Pearce would have liked her face if it had not been for a mouth she thought much too large. Her tea-brown skin only served to amplify her sky-blue eyes and intensify the whiteness of her teeth to almost embarrassing proportions. Although there was a fair amount of Native American blood coursing through her veins, she often thought she appeared more gypsy-like, which, in her opinion, ruined everything.

A brisk walk of several blocks from the ferry terminal brought Pearce to the Public Safety Building and Frank Farmer's office. An amiable one-hour conversation with Detective Farmer ensued. After obtaining the coroner's report, she escaped to enjoy the ambiance of downtown Seattle before she returned.

The Elliot Bay Market on the waterfront, in particular, always attracted her. The aroma of fresh produce, fresh fish, and fresh brewing coffee was akin to an ascent to heaven. She savored the sound of vendors spraying mists of water on fresh produce and hearing the catch-of-the-day tossed onto large beds of ice. Artists, artisans, and musicians all brought this fantasy world to her; hours passed by before she returned to the ferry terminal. Clutching the autopsy report under her arm, Pearce arrived at the JAG offices in the late afternoon.

Fay found the report disturbing. The medical examiner had determined Charma had been assaulted from behind. Charma had died from a single fatal blow from a sizeable sharp instrument, probably a knife. The entry point was on the left side of his neck, where the neck met the shoulder, severing Charma's larynx and his internal carotid artery. As his heart had continued to pump, blood had filled his lungs via his severed larynx. The cause of death was drowning. There were some gruesome pictures of the wound as well.

A single methodical stroke. A quick and fatal jab administered by someone with skill. *This slaughter was a macho thing*, Fay thought. *Boys play so deadly at these games girls choose not to play*. Was Sergeant Linn capable of this? He was certainly strong enough. She was confident he had killed people in the line of duty throughout his military life, but for Sergeant Linn to commit this atrocity was difficult for her to comprehend.

Based on Charma's size and the location and direction of the wound, the coroner felt his assailant would have been over six feet tall and left-handed. Fay recalled Simon was left-handed.

The report recorded the contents of the victim's stomach and the condition of other internal organs. No evidence of alcohol or drug abuse was indicated. Artifact notes listed two antemortem lacerations. One was located on the victim's right leg and one on the victim's left leg. Each tear was professionally repaired—one as recently as thirty days ago. The coroner had also noted a tattoo on the victim's right forearm; a photo of the tattoo was included.

Fay slipped the report and the photographs back into the eight-by-eleven manila envelope she had received it in. She printed the words: "CAUTION, CONTAINS GRAPHIC PHOTOGRAPHS, VIEWER DISCRETION WARRANTED" in large letters on the front of the envelope. In passing, she wondered why Simon Linn, a Marine, would have an alliance with Wu and De Vinsone, both Army. She likened the partnership to a dog befriending two cats. The three men's relationship seemed an unnatural affinity, at best.

****

Ford Clay arrived at 10:45 Monday morning. Clay, a Native American, wore his long, flowing, jet-black hair neatly combed back.

"Hello, sweetheart," he called to Pearce as he entered the office. His greeting prompted Rayzon to glance up from his work. "How's my favorite girl?" Clay asked.

"Hey there, handsome," she called back. Clay's athletic build and aerodynamic hairstyle made an impression. "It's so good to see you again. Lieutenant Commander Green is expectin' you," she said, ushering him toward Fay's office.

Sergeant Linn arrived at 11:00. "Mornin', Master Sergeant," Pearce greeted him, striking a cheerful tone. "They're expectin' you. Y'all can go on in." She motioned toward the door.

Simon opened Fay's door slowly.

"Oh good, you're here," Fay said. "Miss Pearce, would you come in here, too?" she called through the open doorway. Fay was upbeat and in charge. "Simon Linn, this is Ford Clay." The two men shook hands, quietly exchanging hellos.

If the two men were trying to size each other up, it was not noticeable. "Ford is an old friend," Fay said. "He will be able to help you." She motioned for him to sit next to Ford.

Pearce entered the office with her notepad and quickly sat down.

Fay briefly looked at everyone. "Okay, we are ready. Feel free to begin, Mr. Clay."

"Sergeant Linn," Ford Clay said, "I understand, from Lieutenant Commander Green, you have been advised of your rights, both by the SPD and by Miss Green."

"I have, sir."

"Have you changed your mind about your willingness to answer our questions?" Clay asked the other man.

"No, sir. I've been advised by my CO to cooperate with both you and Lieutenant Commander Green."

"I'd like to have you recall the events of the evening of Paul Charma's death," Ford said. "Give us as much detail as you can."

Simon drew a deep breath. "Well, sir, I'd made plans to meet two of my associates, Philip De Vinsone and Peter Wu, at Jillian's Pool Club. I got there about twenty-fifteen. We shot pool, drank beer, and watched a little round-ball and a hockey game on television." He paused to take a sip from a glass of water Fay poured for him. "Anyway, I was talking to Mr. Charma."

Ford said, "Please describe the man."

"He was about five-eight. He had black hair, like yours." Simon indicated Ford's straight hair. "I'd say he weighed around one hundred seventy pounds. I believe he was Hispanic."

"Sounds like Charma," Fay confirmed.

"Anything else?" Ford asked.

Simon thought for a moment. "The man had a tattoo on his right forearm. That's what started the friendly argument."

"Describe the tattoo," Ford said.

"An eagle perched on an anchor. The eagle held a trident in one claw and a pistol in the other."

"Is there any significance to the tattoo?" Ford inquired.

"Special warfare insignia, SEAL team," Pearce volunteered.

Linn nodded in agreement.

"Forgive a civilian," Ford pleaded. "Can you explain?"

"SEAL is an acronym for Sea, Air, Land team," Simon said. "The man was a SEAL."

"Is the tattoo unusual?" Ford asked. "I would

imagine a lot of the sailors have tattoos, don't they?"

"They do," Pearce offered. "In fact, I've got one on my left…" She abruptly stopped talking. "Never mind."

Fay snickered. She had seen the tattoo Pearce referred to.

Sergeant Linn continued. "I spoke with Mr. Charma for a time. He said he had someone to meet. He left, and I rejoined Wu and De Vinsone. I got tired, so I left." He paused as if to organize the following sequence of events. "I believe it was between twenty hundred hours and twenty-fifteen. I looked for a cab but didn't see one, so I double-timed it toward the ferry terminal."

Ford laughed. "You ran. Right?"

"Yes, sir. I ran until I found a cab. The cab took me the rest of the distance to the ferry terminal."

"Okay, Sergeant. Let's back up." Ford glanced at his watch. "I have a phone call to make. Why don't we take a five-minute break? Then I want you to tell me about your jog to the ferry."

"You can use the phone on my desk, Ford," Pearce offered.

"Thanks. But I'll use my cell." He smiled and left the office.

Simon excused himself and left the office as well.

Fay asked Pearce if she had obtained Charma's service records, but NAVSPECWARCOM (Naval Special Warfare Command) had not sent the documents.

"Have you talked to Admiral Wallace's office, Miss Pearce?" she asked quietly.

"They're claimin' they don't have the records," Pearce whispered.

"That doesn't surprise me. I suppose you've tried to access the file online?"

"Access denied, ma'am."

"Keep after it," Fay said.

Simon and Ford returned. The meeting resumed.

"Sergeant Linn, tell us what happened after you left Jillian's. I want every detail," Ford instructed.

"I couldn't find a cab, so I ran to the ferry terminal. I took the most direct route I could," Simon answered.

"That route included the alley where Paul Charma was found?" Ford asked.

"Yes, sir. I understand I ran through that alley. I don't recall seeing anything except what I assumed to be two bums lying near a dumpster. At the end of the alley, I passed by a guy heading into the alley. Later, I heard he was the guy who found Mr. Charma. He must have been the man who identified me."

"We want to talk to the man who placed Sergeant Linn at the scene," Ford said to Fay, without looking up from the notes he was scribbling. "If one of the people whom Sergeant Linn thought was transient was really Charma, then we still have one transient who may know something about the murder. We'll want to find that person."

"I'll find out from Detective Farmer who his witness is and contact him. Detective Farmer may have something on the other person in the alley as well," Fay said.

Ford motioned toward the gray sports bag on Fay's desk. "Fay, I understand you have the Sergeant's knives?"

She handed the bag to him along with a new pair of latex gloves.

Holding each knife at the butt and point as carefully as possible, Ford examined each one before replaced them in the bag. "We're all in agreement these are not the murder weapons, I assume?"

Fay nodded.

Ford asked Fay, "Were any of Sergeant Linn's Fourth Amendment rights violated?"

"No, sir."

"I understand," Ford said, "the SPD obtained a search warrant for Sergeant Linn's off-base home but not his quarters on base."

"That's right," Fay replied. "They searched his apartment over the weekend. Frank Farmer said they did not find anything."

"Simon," Ford said, "could you possibly have had an opportunity to transfer these knives from your apartment to your on-base housing?"

Simon shook his head. "Lieutenant Commander Green took me directly to the base from the jail."

"His only window of opportunity would have been between the time of Mr. Charma's death and the time he was arrested by the SPD," Fay said. "I checked the Shore Patrol's base sign-in log. Sergeant Linn did not go on base during that time."

"Let's photograph the knives before we hand them over to the SPD." Ford spoke dispassionately, as if these were all just eventualities or obstacles to simply overcome, one at a time. "The SPD can run their forensic tests on them. If they're clean, then I suspect the SPD will relax. If not," he paused and looked at Simon, "they'll have their indictment." He turned toward Fay. "Either way, you've ingratiated yourself with the SPD. That can only help us."

All were silent for a moment.

"So, where are we?" Simon asked.

"Unless something substantial turns up in the way of physical evidence, the SPD will proceed with caution. I think even in a worst-case scenario, and should we go to court, I would be able to convince a jury there is reasonable doubt. I don't think the district attorney feels she has a strong case. Otherwise, the SPD wouldn't have released you so quickly, and they would be pressing for an indictment," Ford observed. "What they do have is a dead sailor, a suspect who has probable cause, which is flimsy at best, and a witness who places you at the crime scene. What they don't have is a murder weapon." Ford turned to Fay. "Would you concur, Fay?"

"Completely. I think Seattle Police will continue to try to link you to the murder, Sergeant. The knives will keep them busy for a while. Simon, I am going to see if I can get you released from restriction." She turned to Ford with a warm smile and said, "Thank you so much."

Ford nodded as he stood and walked toward Pearce. He embraced her and whispered, just loud enough for Fay to hear, "Take good care of your sister, JP." He kissed Pearce on the cheek, turned, waved, and was gone.

Both Fay and Pearce stood looking at the door through which Ford Clay had departed. "He sure is a great guy," Fay said.

Pearce sighed. "He sure smells good, ma'am."

Fay glanced at her desk. "I have something for you, Simon." She walked to her desk, opened the bottom left drawer, and extracted the photo she had taken from his apartment. She glanced at it and then handed it to him. "Here, I stole this from your apartment."

Simon gave her a grateful look and accepted the photograph from her. He quickly admired the photo before saying, "You replaced the glass."

"I did?"

"You did. Your kindness is deeply appreciated."

"I was wondering what the words said." She pointed at the photo. "There, on the flag." Petty Officer Winslow had told her the flag was Iraqi, typical of the flags flown at the many palaces of Saddam Hussein.

"It's a slogan. Honor in the highest sense of the word." Simon admired the photo again. "It meant a lot to me when I was awarded the Purple Heart. But this," he said, displaying the image to Fay, "means more to me."

"I assumed the men in the photo to be your team members. Was the photo taken during the Gulf War?" Fay asked.

"Right on both counts. The why's and where's behind the flag are still classified. The team presented the photo to me in recognition of service above and beyond the call of duty."

"Like saving a life?"

Simon nodded and smiled. "Three or more lives might qualify. The words on the flag say, '*Hear ye, one. Hear ye, all. Hear ye, and know the talk. That by this way, a hero did walk.*' It's a poem, I guess?"

Fay sniffed. "It's a poem, and it's beautiful, Simon."

"OH…GEEZ!" Pearce suddenly exclaimed. She had been sitting still without saying a word. "I think I've got it!"

"Got what, Miss Pearce?"

Without hesitation, Pearce recapped Sergeant Linn's story. "Sergeant goes to a pool club to meet his buddies. He meets a tadpole—"

"You mean Frogman or SEAL?" Fay asked.

Pearce nodded. "He gets into an argument, but the

guy leaves. Later, Sergeant's got to catch a ferry. He shortcuts through an alley and runs right by the dead tadpole. A witness sees Sergeant Linn runnin' away. He thinks Sergeant Linn has killed the man."

Fay patted Pearce on the shoulder. "Good job, Miss Pearce."

"Excuse me, ma'am. There's more," Pearce insisted. "I reason the second person in the alley is really the killer, maybe an operator like Mr. Charma. The killer meets Charma in the alley, where he knifes him. Tadpole Charma croaks. The killer hears Sergeant comin' along, so he lies down and plays possum. After the witness passes by, the killer wiggles away into the darkness. I'm done." Pearce sat back in her chair, gave a quick smile, crossed her legs, and folded her arms.

Simon seemed stunned, and if the truth were known, so was Fay. Pearce's version seemed plausible. Another operator could have killed Charma. If the murder weapon proved to be a military knife, such as a Ka-Bar or a bayonet, Pearce's theory had merit.

"A brilliant bit of deductive reasoning, Miss Pearce," Fay said.

"Murder case—like donut, has hole. Optimist only see donut, pessimist see hole," Pearce replied.

"Confucius?" Fay asked.

"No. Chan."

Chapter 5

Lieutenant Commander Green spent a good portion of Tuesday morning briefing Captain Towsley on her meeting with Ford Clay and Simon Linn. Miss Pearce's version of the events had merit.

Towsley said, "There's something very troubling about this. Assuming Mr. Charma was killed by another operator, then we have a case of botched wet-works."

"Botched wet-works, sir?" Fay repeated, confused.

"A bungled hit. An assassination. It's messy." Towsley rose from his chair and walked over to his office window. He paused, then pointed towards the numerous ships moored in the harbor. "We've got over two thousand five hundred Marine and Navy operators out there. They're the cream of the crop. Among them are some of the most elite fighting men in the world. What concerns me is somewhere out there, we may have a loose cannon." He hesitated for a moment, then turned back toward her. "Or..." he briefly pondered, as if he were still contemplating his next thought, "or, we have a mechanic at work."

"A clean-up guy, sir?"

He nodded. "Wet-works mechanics don't make mistakes. If everything went as we now assume, a mistake was made when Mr. Charma's body was left in that alley—a big mistake. Sergeant Linn blundered into it. If the killer thinks Linn saw something that could link him to the crime, Linn is in danger. If a mechanic dropped Paul Charma, then I'm deeply concerned."

Fay understood the concern in his voice. "Sergeant Linn is an operator, sir," she offered. "He must know what the dangers are."

"I'm sorry to say Mr. Linn knows the danger all too well. The Sergeant can take care of himself." Towsley leaned forward in his chair, the look of worry evident in his expression. "You, on the other hand, can't take care of yourself. If the mechanic realizes you are investigating the death, then you, too, are in danger."

The hairs on her neck tingled; she felt as if someone were sneaking up behind her.

"Fay, you're the best I have." He stroked his chin with his left hand. "I'm going to assign the rest of your workload to the other lawyers. We need to put this one to rest ASAP."

"I will give it my best shot, sir."

"Go slow," he cautioned. "And keep me in the loop at all times. If things get too hot, back away. Is that understood?"

"Clearly understood, sir."

Towsley continued, "Admiral Wallace asked me if we can release Sergeant Linn from base restriction. I told him it was the investigating officer's call."

"I do not have a problem with it, sir. I will clear it with Frank Farmer and notify the Shore Patrol."

"Thank you. You're dismissed."

As Fay left Towsley's office, Petty Officer Winslow came around the corner under a full head of steam. The two almost collided head-on, mid-channel.

Fay skillfully maneuvered out of his path. "Mr. Winslow," she said.

"Yes, Lieutenant Commander," he puffed, "what can I do for you?"

"Can I have a word?" Without waiting for a reply, she guided him to his desk. "What can you tell me about the SEALs?"

"What would you like to know, ma'am?"

"I wondered how many are stationed in Bremerton?"

He thought for a moment. "Approximately forty-one, most in training."

"That's all?"

"There are only about one hundred seventy-three in the entire Navy," he said. "There are MEUs here too, close to seventy-three, I'd say."

"What's a MEU?"

"Marine Expeditionary Unit, Commander. The Marine equivalent of a SEAL."

"All in training?"

"Either training or war games. It's their job. Unless they're on a mission, they train."

War games, Fay thought. *Only a man could make a game out of war.* "Tell me, mister. Where do these guys hang out when they're off duty?"

"The Wog. Actually, it's the Pollywog. South of the base. Near the wharf."

"I know of the Wog. It has a reputation for being a rough place."

"A rough place for dangerous men, ma'am. Not a place for a lady," he replied.

Fay thanked Winslow and returned to her office. As she entered, she could hear Pearce on the phone trying to reason with someone. She did not seem to be making any headway.

"I know, sir. I understand, sir. I will see if I can, sir." Pearce looked visibly exasperated with the caller. Suddenly, while in mid-sentence, she put her finger on the hang-up button of the phone. As she did, she exclaimed, "Oops! Disconnected!"

Witnessing this exchange, a look of concern appeared on Fay's face. "Who was that, sailor?" she asked Pearce.

"Ma'am, it was that no-load, butthead Lieutenant Junior Grade Rollie. What a geek. He's upset he's been assigned to some of your workloads. Rollie has a question on one of his new assignments." Pearce sighed, frustrated, before shaking her head and saying, "He don't got no class, ma'am."

"Don't got no." Fay shook her head. "That's a double negative, sailor."

"I reckon ma'am. I'm sorry. I shouldn't use butthead and geek in the same breath."

Fay smiled. She had heard it all before. Lieutenant Junior Grade Rollie was a young Navy lawyer. He was bright, arrogant, and dashing. It was Pearce's opinion Mr. Rollie thought he was the Lord's gift to all women. Based on this assumption, Pearce had come to the conclusion the *JG* part of the Lieutenant's rating meant "junior geek."

"Miss Pearce," Fay asked, "when did the Navy add the rank of 'no-load, butthead lieutenant junior geek' to the officer ratings?"

"Just about the same time Mr. Rollie got his commission, ma'am. All I know is the love of my life is on his way over here, and he's madder than a swamp bee trapped in a box a' grits." Pearce looked at her watch. "Oh! Lunchtime. Bye!" She promptly stood up, grabbed her hat, and left the office.

"Lunch. Very convenient," Fay muttered. "Now, why didn't I think of it first?"

"Lieutenant Commander, are you talking to me?" A voice from a corner of the office interrupted her.

Rayzon's voice had startled her. "I thought you left before Pearce," Fay said.

"No, Commander, I was filing." James pointed to one of the lower filing cabinets.

She got an idea. "Listen, there's a Lieutenant JG Rollie on his way over here. I've got like ten things I have to do before I can even begin to think about the ten things I need to do. So, I don't have time to screw around with him. Could you talk with him, make sure he gets what he needs? You know where everything is. Make a note of anything I may need to tell him, and I'll call you when I get to Seattle to answer any questions."

"Happy to," Rayzon said.

Fay knew Mr. Rollie would go easy on Rayzon—he was a man. That alone would cut the question-and-answer time considerably, if not eliminate it altogether. Her quick footsteps echoed through the long hallways as she practically ran from the building.

Chapter 6

It struck Fay as peculiar that although Detective Farmer had seemed pleased to receive the knives, she sensed the SPD was backing away from the case. There appeared to be a lesser sense of urgency on Farmer's part for the time being.

"Frank," she asked, "were you aware there was a second person in the alley at the time of the murder?"

"Howard Carney, the man who found Charma, mentioned it to me," Farmer responded. "I know the other person was gone by the time we arrived. We couldn't find anyone, but I sure would like to talk to them."

"My assistant has suggested the other person might be the killer," Fay said as she searched his eyes for a reaction.

Frank did raise his eyebrows, but beyond a slight sigh, there was little else to indicate this surprised him. "You know," he said, "sometimes, things can be as simple as that." Frank picked up a file from his desk and pushed it toward her. "Howard Carney's statement. Take a look at it. His address is in there."

She leafed through the statement. "Mr. Carney has Sergeant Linn described accurately." She noted the address, closed the file, and dropped it on Frank's desk. "How about Carney? Is he a suspect?"

"No, he checked out. He'd just said goodbye to

some friends before he entered the alley. He had little time, nor did he have a motive. But," Frank said with a shrug of his broad shoulders, "check him out. I'm not going to discount your assistant's theory. Our killer could be the other person in the alley."

"I am on my way to visit the ME. I will keep you posted." Fay stood and extended her hand. "Thank you."

Frank clasped both of his hands over her hand. A warm smile came to his face. "As always, Fay, it's been a pleasure to talk with you."

Dr. Don Griffin, the medical examiner, met Fay in the morgue's lobby, and they proceeded to his office. Griffin resembled someone she knew, but she could not place the face. The journey took them through a large room, with eggshell-white tiled walls and two rows of stainless-steel tables set in the room's center. To her, the morgue looked much like a giant public restroom. A large bank of drawers was on the left wall, one of them likely containing Paul Charma's body. She felt cold and rubbed her arms briskly as she walked through the room. Fay thought, *A wall full of dead people generates little warmth.*

"Have a seat, Lieutenant Commander," Dr. Griffin offered as they entered his cluttered office. "I trust you had an opportunity to review my report?"

"I did, Doctor," she said.

"Then how can I help?"

"Your report detailed the wound, Paul Charma's physical description, and the time of death. I was curious about the knife. What kind of knife was it?" Fay asked.

"I would describe the instrument to be heavy in nature. It would have a large blade, at least six inches long. The blade was serrated because there was a lot of tearing on the wound's backside. It was evident Charma was struck from behind." He demonstrated a downward motion of his left hand. "This was all in my report," he said, with a hint of irritation now evident on his face.

Boris Karloff. Griffin resembles Boris Karloff. Fay pushed the mental image of the famous nineteen-forties black and white movie ghoul out of her mind. She asked, "I am sorry, but I was wondering specifically, would the wound be consistent with that of a military knife—such as a bayonet or a Ka-Bar?"

Griffin appeared to briefly consider a thought before saying, "Most likely a Ka-Bar, Lieutenant Commander."

"May I see the body?" Fay could not think of any logical reason why she needed to see the corpse, but she was curious. Maybe it was Dr. Karloff's charm that made her feel a bit ghoulish. Whatever the reason, looking at the corpse seemed the logical thing to do.

"Of course you could, if it were here." He had a puzzled look on his face. "You must be aware Mr. Charma's remains have been claimed?"

"What? No!" Fay cleared her throat, and in a calm voice, asked, "Mr. Charma's remains are not here?"

"One of your people came here Saturday with the proper releases. Charma's remains are gone."

"Who presented the release, Doctor?"

"A major from the Marine Corps had all the necessary documents ordering the release and disposal of Paul Charma's remains. The gentleman signed the document I presented to him. W. Irving was the man's name," Griffin said. "I'm sorry, I have nothing more for you."

"How would you describe Major Irving?"

"Male, Caucasian, approximately six feet tall,

muscular build, short blonde hair. About thirty years old, I'd say."

Her mind was racing. "Ah…thank you, Doctor. Thank you for your time."

She heard him say, "You're welcome," as the door swung closed behind her.

While Fay walked toward the exit, she called her office. At the sound of Pearce's voice, she said, without letting her give the whole greeting, "Hi, kiddo, it's me. Listen, I'm in a hurry. Did we get Mr. Charma's service records yet?"

"No, ma'am."

"Call the personnel people. Strongly inform them we are formally requesting the records be made available to my office by thirteen hundred hours tomorrow by order of the Judge Advocate General. And if that does not do the trick, otherwise, they will have to deal with me. And they are not gonna like it."

"Aye, aye, ma'am," Pearce replied.

Fay said, "And Pearce, I need to know who W. Irving is. I reckon he would be a Marine major connected with the Naval Special Warfare Command."

"I'm on it."

Fay smiled. "Did Mr. Rollie talk with Rayzon?"

"Apparently, Mr. Rollie stayed about one minute once he found out we weren't here."

"Talk with you later," Fay said.

Next, she placed a call to Ford Clay. She estimated she would complete her duties in Seattle around dinnertime. She hoped he would be free. As luck would have it, he was.

Her next stop was the home of Howard Carney, who was a student at the University of Washington. The distance from the morgue to Carney's apartment, near the university, was about four miles. She hailed a cab.

Carney's apartment was located on the top floor of an older brick building. Fay asked the cab driver to wait for her. The building did not have an elevator, and she found the trek to the third-floor exhausting. It made her realize it had been a while since she'd had a good gym workout. She knocked on Howard's door several times, but there was no response. As she turned to leave, a young man came bounding up the stairs.

As the man reached the top step, he noticed her and asked, "Can I help you?"

"I'm looking for Howard Carney," Fay told him.

"I'm Howard," he said as his gaze blatantly surveyed the length of her torso from toe to head, lingering at her legs then finally settling on her breasts.

"I'm Faydra Green with the Navy Judge Advocate General Corps," she said, presenting her identification to him.

Carney carefully studied her identification and then said, "I see. You're here about the sailor, aren't you?"

"I am. I've got a few questions to ask you. Do you mind?"

He nodded, preceded to the door, and unlocked it. "Come in. The place is a mess, I think."

As she entered, Fay scanned the room. Carney was obviously a bachelor, the tip-off being the numerous posters of scantily clad women adorning the walls.

"Please," Carney said, motioning for her to sit on a well-worn green sofa, "have a seat. Can I get you a soda, or do you want to use my bathroom or something?"

Howard sat opposite her on a skillfully patched recliner.

It was apparent horny Howard had few female guests. "No thanks, Howard. I'm fine." Fay sat forward on the edge of the cushion. "I'm investigating the death of a man named Paul Charma on behalf of the United States Navy." She took a notepad from her pocketbook. "You were the one who found the body?"

"Correct. I'd just said goodbye to my friends. When I was walking through the alley, a black guy came running past me. Almost knocked me down! I continued along the alley and almost tripped over the dead guy."

"Was the dead person lying in the middle of the alley?"

He gave her a quizzical look. "No, he was off to one side."

"How was it then you would have almost tripped over him?"

"I had a lot of beer to drink; the alley was dark. So, I stopped to take a pe—."

She cut Howard short. "I get the picture. Did you see anyone else in the alley?"

"There was another person further along the way. Possibly a drunk, I thought."

"Did you approach the other person?"

"Not on your life. I was scared shitless."

"Go on," Fay prompted.

"Anyway, I was standing knee-deep in a pool of blood. I yelled for help."

"What happened to the other person?"

"Don't know." He thought for a moment. "Come to think of it, when I looked again, they were gone."

"Did you know Charma?"

"Never seen him before." Howard seemed apprehensive and glanced at his watch.

"What is your major at the university?" Fay asked him.

"Pre-med." He looked noticeably uncomfortable now. "Look, that's all I know."

"I presume the alley was dark?" Fay continued.

"No streetlights, if that's what you mean."

"It was dark. How is it you could identify the man who ran past you?"

"I got a good look at him. Close up. He almost knocked me down," Howard replied defensively.

"What would you estimate the distance to be, in feet, from the point where you first entered the alley to where you found the body?"

Howard thought for a moment. "I'd say about twenty-five feet. Thereabouts."

"And you met the man who ran into you at the entrance to the alley?" Fay asked.

He gave her a confirming nod.

"Did you notice if the man who ran into you had anything in his hands?"

"I did notice his hands. He used both hands to push me out of his way. I saw a hulk hurtling toward me, and I remember thinking about the physics involved. All I could come up with was a collision that would rival the *Titanic* and the iceberg."

"What did you do, Howard?"

"What could I do? I screamed. I prayed." He shrugged his shoulders. "At least he said 'excuse me.'"

"He excused himself?"

"Yeah. Real polite about it. The dude even asked if I was all right, as he hurried by me."

"How would you describe him?"

"Like I said, a hulk," Howard replied. "A huge black

man, muscular, like a pro football player, Mrs. Green. I saw him well enough. Anyway, he dropped his ID card. The collision must have jarred it loose from his pocket. I saw it lying at my feet; I knew he dropped it and called after him. But he didn't hear me. Later, I gave it to the police."

At a distance of twenty-five feet, Simon would have had little time to dispose of a knife and gain a full head of steam before Howard had spotted him. The SPD would have found the blade, had Simon tossed it. And had he sheathed the knife, there would have been at least a drop of blood somewhere on Linn's shoes or clothing. And then for Sergeant Linn to slaughter Charma one minute, only to concern himself whether Howard was "all right" in the next minute, seemed illogical. Fay wondered how the police had found Linn so quickly.

She handed Howard her pen. She already knew his phone number; it was on the statement Farmer had shown her. "Would you mind if I called you if I have any further questions?"

He took the pen. "Don't mind." He wrote his name and phone number and handed the pen and phone number back to her.

He's left-handed, Fay noted. "Thanks, Howard. You have been very helpful." She stood. "Oh, how tall are you?"

"Six feet." Howard was leering again.

She smiled. "Good luck with your studies."

Carney saw her to the door. She left his home feeling in need of a shower.

Why did he abruptly become nervous? Fay mentally replayed her interview with Carney as she rode in the cab to the city.

Chapter 7

The cab driver's route skirted Lake Union, south along Eastlake Avenue. As they neared the south end of the lake, Fay realized she was not more than a quarter of a mile from Jillian's and the crime scene. She asked the cab driver to divert to the Westlake Avenue address.

For her to visit the crime scene at this late date seemed pointless; her curiosity was drawing her there more than anything else. The rain was coming down in buckets as the cab pulled up in front of the pool club. Again, she asked the driver to wait for her. Wishing she had thought to bring an umbrella, Fay flipped up the collar of her raincoat, opened the door of the cab, and darted for the shelter of the club's front-door alcove.

The entire event took less than fifteen seconds, yet when she arrived at the door, rainwater was already dripping from the ends of her neatly trimmed hair. She brushed away a significant drop of water from the tip of her nose. She imagined she must look like the proverbial drowned rat. "Bad hair day gone sour," she muttered to herself.

On entering the club, Fay marched directly to the restroom. Grabbing a wad of paper towels, she managed to dry her hair. A quick brushing helped. She had given her appearance her best effort. When she had entered the restroom, she had looked like hell. When she left the restroom, she looked like heck. It was an improvement.

Jillian's Pool Club was much larger than she had imagined it would be. The club was housed in one of Seattle's many historic, two-story brick buildings. She quickly walked the length of both floors, noting approximately fifty pool tables. A video arcade, several bars, and fifteen monitors showed various sporting events. A respectable club—a fun place—one she might visit again, although the scent of an exotic blend of burning cigarettes and greasy hamburgers that filled her nostrils convinced her perhaps fine dining would be found elsewhere. She returned to the waiting cab.

Fay had intended to walk the alley where Charma died. Still, she reasoned the cab driver could drive her through it, saving her another drenching. She was not looking for clues that would eventually lead her to the killer. It was not her job. Her job was to recommend that the investigation extend beyond the preliminary inquiry level or to conclude that an investigation was not required.

Fay glanced at the cab driver's registration card. "Arnold, will you drive me through the alley behind the building? Slowly, please." Arnold had been driving like a crazed Paris taxi driver since she had first hired his cab. She wanted to see the alley, not experience it as if it were a special effects scene from a sci-fi space movie. But who was she to criticize the man? She, too, drove like a crazed Paris taxi driver. She admired Arnold's skill.

Arnold was not a talkative man, although he did manage a "yeah" as he wheeled the cab around the corner and into the alley at a blistering five miles per hour.

The temperature of the cab quickly turned from warm to cold. "Arnold, will you turn up the heat a little?" Fay asked.

"Yeah."

As the cab rolled through the alley at the speed of a funeral procession, she caught the aroma of aftershave. It was a scent familiar to her. She could not recall where she had experienced it before. And she had not noticed it in this cab until now. It was after she asked Arnold to turn up the heat; then she had noted the scent.

"Excuse me, Arnold. What aftershave do you wear?" Fay inquired.

"Yeah," he replied. And with that, the cab accelerated.

"Thanks." She liked the fragrance and made a note to pick up a bottle of *Yeah* aftershave someday.

"Where are you from, Arnold?' she asked.

"You-crane."

"Ah. Welcome to America," she murmured.

Arnold dropped her at Nordstrom, where she made a quick call to Pearce. No word had been received regarding Charma's records. "Okay," Fay said in an irritated tone. "They've had their chance. First thing in the morning, I will eat their young. The bitch is back. Oh, and make a note to get ahold of one of those *Long Distance Death* shirts for me."

"Ma'am?" Pearce said hesitantly.

"What is it, sailor?"

"I will give you my shirt, but I don't think an angry officer descendin' on them people like an insane banshee from hell will accomplish much. Besides, those guys are my friends. I'll lose my cred with them. Like they say, 'Squeaky wheel—most desirous of grease—sometime experience unpleasant application of same.'"

"Okay, I get your point." Fay smiled and asked, "Chan?"

"No. Pearce, ma'am. But I do have an idea."

"Let's hear it."

"I'm goin' to the hockey game tonight with my friend Davy. He's Admiral Wallace's aide. Anyway, let me ask him about the files. Away from the office," Pearce suggested. "I'll find out what's causin' the hold-up, ma'am."

Fay agreed and asked, "Have I been a bitch lately?"

"I won't mince words with you, ma'am. You're quickly getting' there...ma'am."

Fay smiled. She appreciated Pearce's unfailing honesty. "Ah... good. I haven't lost my charm. See ya later."

While at Nordstrom, Fay purchased a dress and a pair of shoes. Before leaving the store, she stopped at the men's department to search for a bottle of *Yeah* aftershave. After sampling twelve different ones, she discovered her fragrance. *Arnold was wrong.* The aroma was *L'Observe*. She purchased a bottle, thanked the attentive salesperson for her time, and left the store.

Fay arrived early at the Four Seasons Hotel Seattle. Her intention was to duck into a restroom to repair her makeup and change out of her wet uniform and into the dress. As she skirted the outer edge of the lobby, trying to remain as inconspicuous as she possibly could, she passed by a huge flower arrangement placed near her restroom objective. Noting it appeared to be almost the size of her car, she let out a low whistle.

"Faydra?" a familiar voice called from the other side of the flower arrangement.

Oh crap. It was Ford.

"I'm sorry, I didn't see you there," Ford said as he

appeared from the opposite side of the massive flower arrangement. "If you hadn't whistled, I would've completely missed you."

Fay greeted him with a sheepish smile.

He looked as dashing and as handsome as ever. He was holding a small bouquet of beautiful peach-colored roses. "Faydra, you look extremely radiant this evening."

"I do?" Did he, perhaps, mistake the look of radiance for something else? Fay embraced him. The closer she got to him, the less he could see of her. "Hi, handsome. Long time no see."

He smiled and handed her the flowers.

"Thank you." She brought the roses to her nose and inhaled deeply, a tactic designed to hide her face from him. "Umm…these are exquisite," she said.

Ford took a step back. After carefully surveying her from head to toe, he said, "You look ravishing."

"Oh, come on!" More than two years of friendship, and he still knew how to turn on the charm. Ford was a gentleman, he was a lawyer, and he was a big liar.

She excused herself to the restroom to make repairs.

Later, Ford and Fay were seated in the exquisite Georgian Room restaurant.

Ford ordered a bottle of wine. "How's my girl Pearce?" he asked.

"JP is fine. She's at the Seattle hockey game this evening with one of her pals," Fay said. "You know she has a mega crush on you, don't you?"

"I didn't know that. I know someday JP will find a guy who can see what a catch she is. He'll be one lucky guy. He won't be as lucky as I am, but he'll be lucky."

He held his water glass in a toast, and they clinked glasses for luck.

"I worry about JP," Fay said. "She has so little confidence in herself."

"What about the guy she's going to the game with?"

"Davy is a buddy. I don't know why they're not dating."

The waiter arrived at the table. Fay waited for him to pour the wine and move away from the table before continuing. "I do know she loves ice hockey," she said. "Land sakes, she can holler."

Ford's mood changed. "How's your investigation going?"

"Don't ask." She sipped at her wine. "I am concerned, of course. I am getting stonewalled on getting Charma's records." Leaning closer to him, Fay whispered, "His remains are gone. The SPD seems to be backing away from the case, and when I visited Howard Carney, the man who found the body, he acted strangely. Speaking of Howard Carney, now there's a character who has a story I'd like to read someday."

"I agree; the whole thing sounds strange. I'll have a private detective check out Carney for you."

"Miss Pearce thinks Charma was killed by one of his own." Fay took another sip of wine. She held the glass to her lips, gazing at some distant object. "At this point, I am beginning to think JP is right. Oh! And I got something for you." She handed the small gift bag to him.

Ford smiled. He removed the aftershave from the bag and examined it. "You chose it. It must be the best."

"It has become one of my favorites of late."

Ford reached across the table to grasp Fay's right hand. "Thank you, my dear. Now I have a small bit of news."

"I am sorry, Ford. I have been so absorbed in my own troubles; I haven't given you a chance to get a word in edgewise." Fay returned her wineglass to the table and focused her attention on him. "C'mon…tell me!"

He held up his hands in mock surrender. "Okay, okay! It's not that big of a deal." He paused for a moment and then said, "Senators Marsh and Anderson have nominated me to fill a vacancy in the federal court."

Without saying a word, Fay rose from her chair, moved around the small table to Ford, embraced him, and then returned to her chair. "It is a huge deal! I am so happy for you. Ford, you will make an excellent federal court judge."

"Well," he said, "President Ross does have to approve the nomination first."

"Nonsense. Armand will approve it." She knew Armand Ross would embrace the idea of having a Native American serving on the federal bench. While she was overjoyed at the news, she also knew Ford's announcement sounded the death knell to their relationship, given the busy and demanding schedule of a new federal court judge.

Fay and Ford spent the following two hours eating the wonderful meal and celebrating. The restaurant was its own world; they found it hard to leave.

Ford offered to drive her to the ferry terminal. They were early for the next boat, so he elected to wait until the passengers began boarding.

"Faydra," Ford said, "I'm concerned. This has all the makings of a dangerous case. I think you should get help." Ford leaned over and kissed her.

Every phase of a relationship had its own kiss. Theirs was the kiss mirroring the different points they were at in the relationship, he more involved than she. It would have been okay to freeze the situation just where it was indefinitely. But Fay knew—sooner rather than later—she would have to make a decision. She was unsure when it would be or exactly what it would be, but she did know it did not have to happen tonight.

"Thank you for the wonderful dinner." She sniffed the roses again. The flowers were releasing a heavenly scent, sending a wave of optimism over her. It was suddenly tempting to think Ford was somehow wrong about the case's danger - tempting to accept his offer to get her help and compelling to let him further into her heart. Perhaps it was years of training as a professional or years of practice as a woman moving through life looking for the right situation, but still, something made her think better of giving in to any of the temptations.

"Goodnight," she whispered and walked down the ferry's passenger boarding ramp alone and onto the ferry. In the darkness, the blast from the ferry's horn was deafening. Fay felt the deck shudder as the ship's massive propeller began to churn the black water of the Puget Sound. The boat quickly pulled away from the dock, and Ford grew smaller in her sight and soon disappeared from her vision altogether.

She arrived home late. The cat was pouting once again. She had just finished feeding her pest when her cell rang. Fay remembered she had promised Ford she would call the moment she got in. Picking up the phone quickly, she said, "Hi, honey. I got home all right."

"Different honey," the voice replied. "It's JP." She was excited. "Davy told me Charma's records have disappeared. Several people were inquirin' about the records, but they can't be found. To top it off,

NAVSPECWARCOM has never heard of Major Irving."

"Why is a little voice in my head saying, 'I knew it, I knew it?'" Fay asked. "Okay, thanks, sailor. See ya tomorrow. Oh hey, Pearce. Are you in the market for a cat?"

"Nope."

Fay clicked off the cell and picked up Mr. Bill. As she rubbed his head, she said thoughtfully, "I've got to find out what's going on. Who croaked poor Paul Charma, cat? Why did they do that? Huh?"

Chapter 8

Fay spent most of the following day trying to locate both Charma's records and the mysterious Major Irving. She did not have any luck on either account, and she was not particularly surprised at the results of her efforts.

Her day also included another meeting with Captain Towsley.

"Admiral Wallace is pressing me on the investigation," Towsley said to Fay. "What do we know?"

"I met with the ME yesterday. It so happens a representative from the Marine Corps authorized the release of Charma's remains." Fay reached into her briefcase and extracted a file folder. "Here is the autopsy report on Charma," she said as she handed the file to him. "There isn't anything more than what I have already briefed you on, sir."

Towsley frowned. "You say the Marines claimed Charma's body?"

"Yes, sir. W. Irving had the release."

"I think I know the answer to this but clarify it for me. Why is the Marine Corps claiming the remains of Navy personnel?"

"That question occurred to me as well, Captain. My supposition is since Charma was a SEAL, his duty assignment fell under the MEF. The Marine Expeditionary Force is made up of about fifty thousand personnel. About two thousand five hundred of those are Navy people."

"Did you check with the MEF people on Major Irving?" Towsley asked.

"I did, sir. Like Paul Charma, they have no record of him. In fact, I have searched every possible resource I can think of and could not find him." Fay sighed. "I feel like I'm not making any progress. So, I've decided to visit the Pollywog tonight to see if I can find anything there."

"The Wog is a dangerous place, Fay."

"So I hear. But don't worry, sir. I've asked James Rayzon to meet me."

Towsley's eyebrows arched. "Rayzon?"

"I do not know why, but I feel absolutely safe with James, sir."

"Back to Major Irving. It would seem our Major Irving is lost somewhere in the system. Not only has he disappeared, but he's taken Charma with him."

Fay knew operators were often involved in missions officially that did not exist. It did not surprise her Irving and Charma did not exist either.

"Sounds like a cover-up," Towsley said. "Major Irving could very well be our mechanic. It's possible Irving killed Charma and has done a nice job of tidying up by erasing Charma and his records."

"If Pearce's theory is correct, I would suspect it, sir."

Winslow entered the office. "I'm sorry to interrupt. Mr. Clay is on the phone asking for Lieutenant Commander Green. He asked if he could interrupt. He said it was important."

Fay looked to Towsley for his permission to take the

call.

"Yes, Mr. Winslow," Towsley decided. "Miss Green will take the call in here." He motioned for her to use the phone on his desk.

She listened intently as Ford delivered his message. After a brief conversation with him, she hung up the phone. Fay smiled. "Ford had some information on Howard Carney. He had a private investigator watch Carney. It did not take the investigator long to discover he is not only an amiable student but a drug dealer as well."

"He's working his way through medical school selling drugs?"

"So it would appear." Fay sat down. "I knew he was up to something." She looked out of the window. "I think we have just added a third suspect to our list."

"You think Carney had a motive?"

"I do." Fay looked at Towsley. "A drug deal gone bad? Perhaps Charma stiffed him for some cash? An acrimonious Carney killed him?"

"In retrospect then, Sergeant Linn is a victim of circumstance," Towsley theorized. "He passes the killer, who's on his way to meet Charma. Charma is still alive but hiding because Charma hears Linn coming. He then meets Carney, who, after realizing he has been stiffed, kills Charma. Carney then calls for help, hoping to implicate Linn in the murder." Towsley sat back in his chair and removed a pipe and a pouch of tobacco from the top of his desk. Carefully, he packed the tobacco into the pipe's bowl, lit it with a wooden match, and snuffed the flame with a flick of his wrist. Smoke curled slowly from the pipe. "Who was the other person in the alley?"

Fay loved the cherry smell of Vern's pipe tobacco.

"A transient? Carney's backup?" she proposed.

"We're getting quite a list here." Towsley rocked forward in his chair. The look of concern returned to his face. "All along, I've been warning you to move slowly and cautiously on this investigation. Sergeant Linn seems to be moving farther and farther away from the spotlight. I want to caution you again, don't let your theory on Linn bias your thinking toward him. He may not be Charma's killer, but he is still a dangerous man."

"You are trying to scare me, aren't you, sir?"

"Maybe. My point is, don't let your heart fool your common sense into letting your guard down. Not for an instant, Fay."

"I will remember what you said, sir."

Fay returned to her office to ponder the latest twists in her investigation. "What do you have planned for this evening?" she asked Pearce.

"Tonight is my Tae Kwon Do class."

"I'm meeting James at the Pollywog tonight. I wanted to call you afterward."

"Stop by my apartment. I should be home by eleven," Pearce said. As an afterthought, she warned, "The Wog is a rough place, ma'am."

"So I have been warned. Thanks." Fay shut herself into her office for the rest of the afternoon. By the time she left for home, Pearce and James had left for the day.

Fay spent about half an hour going through her closet, putting together the perfect outfit for the evening. She wanted something to attract attention—that way, she would have an opportunity to meet as many men as possible. Perhaps a short skirt or yoga pants with a tight sweater? A lot of legs and a little cleavage. Not so much as to look like a hooker, but enough to be interesting. She finally decided on a short, tight-knit dress with a V-neck. She wriggled into the dress, put on a pair of sexy pumps with a gold ankle bracelet as an accent, and checked the result in the full-length mirror in the hall. *This will get attention. This little dress could almost be classified as a strategic weapon.* She had bought the dress on a whim months before. She and Pearce had been shopping at the Nordstrom store in downtown Seattle.

The minute she had emerged from the dressing room, Pearce had said, "Wow, whatever it costs, slap it on your credit card if you have to, but don't go home without it."

Fay put the finishing touches on her transformation from naval officer to vamp. Adding a little more eye shadow than she would typically have used and a much redder lipstick, the change was dramatic. She then treated her ash blonde hair to a generous amount of hairspray—lots of volume.

"There," Fay said, posing for Mr. Bill. The cat watched her from the hallway. He stared blankly at her as she asked, "What do you think, cat?" *I gotta quit talking to the cat,* she noted.

The air outside smelled fresh; it always did after rain. The raindrops on the roadster sparkled, reflected in the streetlamps. It was dusk.

Fay hoped to meet someone who knew Charma, nothing more. It was a quick twenty-minute drive from her home to the Pollywog. She arrived in the parking lot at 20:05 hours and immediately searched for James Rayzon. The parking lot was full of cars, but she eventually spotted him standing near his vehicle.

She would enter the club alone. James would hang back in the shadows, ready to come out should things get out of hand. She felt completely safe with the plan.

While they walked toward the door, James explained how to identify a MEU or SEAL from the predominantly military crowd. "Marine and SEAL operators often wear their hair much longer than the average male military person. The idea is to look more like a civilian to better blend in with the civilian population. You can also identify an operator, possibly, by the MEU tee shirt. It'll have the words *Long Distance Death,* their slogan, printed across the front, or you may see a tattoo with the same slogan."

"Gee, they sound like a violent group," she said with a shiver. "And what if I should meet a mechanic, Mr. Rayzon?"

"You won't meet a mechanic." His voice expressed the chill of an Arctic blast. "Mechanics are not party-type guys. But if it were your misfortune to meet a wet-works mechanic, you'd be dead before you could say, 'Hi, nice to know ya.'"

The tone of James' voice changed. It had a reassuring manner to it when he said, "Just stay cool, girl. Remember, these guys are still Marines and sailors. And they're more than just lethal." He shrugged. "They're lethal Americans. And they're on our side." He laughed. "After all, you're an officer and their superior. You can order them to do whatever you want them to do."

"Power!" Fay entered the club first, with James trailing about a minute behind her. She sat at the bar while he went to the video games.

Fay ordered a rum and fruit punch-flavored sports drink, her own unique concoction, and then surveyed the area. *So, this is the infamous Wog,* she thought. It wasn't what its reputation made it out to be. She did not recall ever seeing a nightclub as large as this one, either. She noted twelve pool tables and a dance floor. The Wog must have been a supermarket at one time, judging by its size.

The bartender placed her drink down on the bar in front of her. "That'll be two-twenty-five," he said.

She handed him three dollars. "Keep the change."

"What do you call your drink?" the bartender asked.

"An Okeechobee gator-punch." Fay felt proud for coming up with that one, right off the top of her head.

"I'm not sure I know how to spell that," he said as he wrote on a small notepad. The bartender seemed to take her seriously.

Even more daunting than having to actually spell Okeechobee was trying to sit in her little dress while maintaining some semblance of being a lady. The best she could do was tug it down to about mid-thigh.

Her squirming must have inadvertently drawn the attention of the young man sitting next to her. He swiveled on his barstool to face her. "Hi, I'm Rick."

"Hey, Rick. I'm Faydra," she said, heaping on her best southern drawl.

"Where y'all from?" he asked. "Unusual name," he added.

"I'm a Florida gal. I thought y'all could tell." She fluttered her eyelashes for effect and smiled. "My mom wanted to name me Faye, after her mother. My dad wanted to name me Zandra after his mother. They were both stubborn people. Hence, Faydra. A simple concoction, I think. How about you? Where y'all from?"

"A real concoction. Kind of like that drink of yours." Rick laughed. "I knew you were from Florida. I heard you explain the Okeechobee thing to the bartender." He smiled. "And Faydra is a pretty name. I'm from Nebraska. Near Lincoln. I'm stationed here with the Navy. How about you?"

"Navy. I do administrative things at the Thirteenth Naval District offices. What do you do?"

"I'm a torpedoman's mate. I'm based at the Bangor Sub base."

"Cool! Boomers?"

"Yeah, the nukes are easy duty," he replied. "I like it." Rick's face looked as if something caught his eye across the room. "Hey, listen. I gotta go. Nice to meet you."

He offered his hand. They shook hands, and he left.

Well, that seemed short-lived. Not a SEAL. Fay took a sip of her drink and looked around the club once again. The next young man she met looked to have more potential. He had the long hair, anyway.

"Can I buy you a drink, Miss?" he asked.

"I'm gonna nurse this one for a while, sailor, but thanks." Fay patted the top of the barstool next to her and said, "Y'all can sit down and keep me company, though."

The young man sat down slowly, never taking his gaze off her. "I'm Jason Welsh. I'm a Marine, not a sailor."

"Hi, I'm Faye King, and I am a sailor." A Secret Service agent had come up with the alias Faye King, years ago, as a variation on the word "faking." "Pleased to meet ya."

"Do you come here very often?"

"Not often. I'm here lookin' for a friend," she offered vaguely. "What do you do in the Marines?"

"I'm with the MEU. Do you know who we are?"

"I do." She acted impressed. "In fact, the person I'm lookin' for is a SEAL. Maybe y'all know him? His name is Paul Charma?"

Jason's eyes looked straight into hers. "I don't know Charma. I gotta go. Nice talking to you, Faye King." He said her name deliberately as if he were committing it to memory. It sent a wave of goosebumps across her skin.

When he'd gone, Fay rubbed her arms briskly. *Must have hit a nerve with that guy.*

The band began to play. It turned out to be a western music band, Fay's favorite kind of music. Several men asked Faye King to dance for the next hour, but none knew Charma. It seemed like a dry well to her. She had just signaled James they should go when a young man nonchalantly approached her.

"Excuse me, ma'am," he said. "You're an officer, aren't you?"

"Busted! Do we know each other?"

"I visited your office the other day. You were just about to fillet some poor petty officer with a Ka-Bar when I walked in."

"Oh, that was you?" She laughed. "I remember. Y'all darted in and out of the office so fast we didn't have time to explain."

While he did not offer her a reason for his aborted visit to her office, the man did offer her his name. "Andrew Lawrence, Lieutenant Commander." He extended his hand. "I hear you've been asking about my friend, Paul."

Turning off the drawl, she said, "Faydra Green," as she shook his hand. "Yes, I've been asking about Paul Charma. Are you a SEAL?"

"Affirmative, ma'am." Andrew seemed nervous. "Will you meet me outside?"

"Sure, see you there." She glanced to the corner where James sat at a video game. He appeared to be concentrating on the screen, yet she knew he had all eyes on her. She flipped her hair by quickly moving her head in the direction of the door and picked up her pocketbook. The moment she made a move, James stood up slowly and began moving casually toward the door.

Chapter 9

It had rained again, although Fay could see a wall of dense fog rolling toward her from the west side of the parking lot. A deep breath of the fresh night air cleansed her smoke-filled lungs.

Through the gathering mist, she could just make out James lurking in the shadows. His presence gave her comfort; she began searching for Andrew Lawrence.

"I'm over here," Andrew said.

With apprehension, she walked toward his voice. The sound of the parking-lot gravel crunched beneath her feet with each step she took. Sounds always seemed much crisper, much clearer in the fog. Her heart pounded against her chest, now audible enough for her to hear. Her imagination took over, bringing with it the thought of a foggy London night. Jack the Ripper lurked just around the next corner. *That damn Towsley*, she thought. *Was Andrew Lawrence perhaps Paul's killer?*

Fay heard a car squeal its tires, startling her. She snapped her head toward the direction of the sound. *Probably some military in a hurry to get back to base.* As she turned back around, Andrew Lawrence appeared out of the fog, like an apparition, directly in front of her.

Fay brought her hand to her chest and gasped. "Mercy! You scared me!"

"I'm sorry." Andrew looked around as if someone

might be watching them. He looked back at her. "You're shivering, ma'am."

"I am?" She rubbed her arms briskly. "If I thought I could trust you, I'd invite you to sit in my car where it's warmer." According to James, she would be dead if Andrew were a mechanic.

Andrew held up his hands in an arresting manner. "You're safe with me. I just need to talk to you."

They walked toward her car. She had a flannel-lined raincoat in her vehicle; she put it on as they got into the roadster. "Okay, Mr. Lawrence," she said, shaking off the chill. "What about Charma?"

"Paul was my buddy. We were members of the same team," Andrew explained.

"So, Paul Charma is a real person. I was beginning to wonder if he really did exist."

"He did exist, although my guess would be all trace of him has been erased by now."

"What was Paul involved in?"

"Paul died for what he knew. For what we all know."

"What did he know?"

"I'm not allowed to say, ma'am. If I told you, you'd be in danger." Andrew Lawrence looked out of the car's window. "We're being watched."

Fay felt a chill race up her arms. "Where?" He pointed in James' direction. "Relax. That's my backup. Now, about Paul Charma. Do you know who killed him?" She held her gaze where she thought James was hiding, but she could not see him. For that matter, neither could Andrew have seen him; he had merely sensed someone was there.

"I don't know who killed Paul." Andrew was visibly

shaken.

"You really are frightened, aren't you?" She instinctively put her hand on his shoulder.

"I can take care of myself, ma'am." He turned his head away, again looking out the passenger window. He turned back toward her. "Look, I just wanted to warn you. You don't want to know anything about Paul Charma."

Without hesitation, Fay asked, "Will you talk to me tomorrow?"

"What time?"

"How about nine hundred hours?"

Andrew nodded. "Goodnight, ma'am." Andrew shook her hand and opened the car door. She thought he smiled at her as he waved before disappearing into the fog.

She got out of the car when she saw James approaching. "Bingo," she said. "I think we're done here. I'll fill you in later."

A dry smile came to his face. "Drive safely, ma'am. The roads are dangerous tonight."

"Thanks, James," she said with a warm smile. She slid behind the steering wheel of the roadster. "Goodnight."

Arriving at Pearce's apartment, she knocked on the door.

"Who is it?" Pearce called from the other side of the door.

"It's me. Your favorite sister."

Pearce opened the door. "Come on in. And FYI, I have only one sister."

Fay slipped through the doorway and immediately shed her raincoat. "Well, here is an FYI for you. It's raining cats and dogs."

Pearce's apartment was small but immaculate. The furniture was new; everything was color coordinated in tangerines and grays. "Sweet baby Jesus!" Pearce exclaimed on seeing Fay's dress. "Look at you, girlfriend! You probably need some kind of permit to wear that outfit in public. How'd it go?"

"Better than I'd hoped. I'm onto something."

"Hey, I made coffee and tea." Pearce motioned toward the kitchen counter. "I didn't know which you'd be in the mood for."

Fay kicked off her shoes, tucking her legs beneath her as she sat down on the couch. "The tea would be fine…as long as it's chamomile."

"Hungry?" Pearce called from the kitchen.

"No thanks. But I do have something to bounce off you."

"Go ahead, bounce away." Pearce returned from the kitchen and set a delicate English teacup in front of Fay. "I'm listenin'."

"What do you think of this? Paul Charma stiffs Carney for money he owed him for drugs. They argue. Carney kills him," Fay proposed.

Pearce dropped a large pillow on the floor and sat down on it. "I think it's possible, but I'm more comfortable with my theory."

"I met a SEAL at the Wog tonight who knew Charma," Fay explained. "He said he knows why Charma died. Although he wouldn't tell me why."

"Y'all think Paul Charma and Howard Carney had some kind of drug deal goin'. Why?"

"I don't know," Fay replied. "I have a feeling Carney is involved in this somehow. Yet, the guy is a goof. So, I'm conflicted at the moment."

"Dad use to tell me when I ran into a difference of opinion, I should consider a compromise."

The look on Fay's face changed suddenly from thoughtful to pained. She looked away from Pearce to some distant point. "I used to get the same advice," she said. She turned her attention back to Pearce. "And how would you compromise on this?"

"Try this," Pearce offered. "Another SEAL murders Charma. That's my part of the equation. The motive: a drug deal gone sour. That's your part of the equation."

"It may explain why Andrew Lawrence, the SEAL I met tonight, seemed so frightened. He knows the killer is an operator." Fay sat up and searched for her shoes. "You're going to be at the office by seven-thirty tomorrow, aren't you?"

"I always am."

"Petty Officer Lawrence is coming in, and I have a Seaman...ah—?"

"Lewis."

"Right. Lewis, coming in for assistance with his will. How about you take Lewis while I talk to Andrew Lawrence?"

"No problem. I'll have Mr. Rayzon pick up some of my duties tomorrow," Pearce replied.

"Having James' help has been a blessing, hasn't it?" Fay asked.

"He's been great, ma'am. He's a pecker, though."

"A what?

"A pecker. James uses the hunt and peck method when he types." Pearce appeared to reflect briefly. "I don't know how he ever got to be a yeoman. You know, I don't know why, but James strikes me as someone who could have been an officer or something rather than an administrative assistant."

"I had not thought about it." Fay found her shoes and slipped them on. She looked at Pearce as if she were admiring her. "Tell me, sweetheart, why aren't you dating Davy? He's such a sweet guy."

"Fayzie, Davy Cane is a good guy, but in case you haven't noticed, he's none too bright. There should be at least one smart one in every relationship. It would concern me if I found myself in a relationship where I was the smart half."

****

03:20 hours, U.S. Navy frigate Jonathan Carr, the Yellow Sea, Pacific Ocean

"Captain Nevada, the North Koreans have given us thirty minutes to abandon ship."

"So be it, Mr. Kim," Nevada said to his Korean interpreter. Nevada stared blankly into the coal-black night. He reconsidered his options. "I don't see we have any other choice. Tell the North Koreans we will comply."

Nevada sighed and turned to his X-O and said, "Give the order to all hands, Commander Nathan. Abandon ship."

Chapter 10

"Vern, this is Brandon," Admiral May said over the secure phone line. "Things are heating up between the North Koreans and the United States."

There was a silence. Then Towsley said, "It leaves Green exposed."

"I know, I'm exposed as well. I gave both you and Bill Green my word E-Team would be available to ensure her safety while she conducted her investigation." May sighed. "I can no longer provide it. You will have to reassign her. NCIS will bring in the Cold Case Squad to take over the investigation."

"I'll take care of it." Towsley's voice was barely audible. "How much time do I have?"

"I need Captain Rayzon and his men in Chinhae in four days."

****

It had rained throughout the night. The rain was still coming down hard, with a gusting wind, when Fay arrived at the JAG offices. For a moment, she sat in her car, watching the windshield wipers slap at the raindrops cascading down the glass, seeking the courage to brave the torrent of rain.

With a sigh, she turned the car's ignition key off, opened the car door, and stepped out into the cold, wet morning. She opened her umbrella and snatched her briefcase and pocketbook from the back seat. She slammed the door with more force than usual. Then she dashed to the JAG Corps' main entrance, trying to avoid the numerous puddles of water dotting the parking lot. It proved to be an obstacle course, hopping and jumping over the larger pools of water, but more often splashing down into smaller ones in the trade-off. By the time she reached the entrance, her shoes were soaked, and rainwater splattered her legs to mid-thigh, even under her skirt. "It's the weather like this that proves God isn't a woman," she muttered under her breath as she pulled open one of the two double glass doors.

Inside, Fay noted the warmth of the main lobby. It was a significant improvement. She darted into her office, flung her raincoat and hat onto the nearest chair, then sprinted for Towsley's office.

On seeing her, he smiled and gestured toward the vacant chair. "At ease." Walking to the coffee pot, he asked, "Need a fix?" knowing full well her answer.

"Maybe I should just throw the first cup on myself."

Towsley poured two cups. He put one cup down and picked up the pot. Holding it in one hand and the cup in the other, he asked, "Do you want the cup, or should I just give you the pot?"

Her evaluating eyes darted back and forth between the two choices before Fay said, "I'll take the cup this time, sir."

Towsley smiled and returned to his desk with the two cups of coffee. Her eyes were fixed on the two cups as he approached her. Towsley gave her a fatherly smile and set one of the cups on the desk in front of her. He raised his cup in her direction before sipping.

Fay smiled and picked her cup up with both hands, huddling around its warmth as if it were a campfire on a cold night.

Rubbing the palms of his hands briskly together, Towsley said, "Now, let's dig into this investigation. He looked warily at Fay and asked, "Are we ready?"

"We are ready, sir," she said

"I acted on your suggestion that Admiral Wallace's authority, as base commander, allows him to petition the civil courts, asserting military jurisdiction in cases involving persons subject to military law."

"I did tell you, sir."

"Wallace petitioned the Seattle District Attorney to have Sergeant Linn bound over to military jurisdiction. I advised Wallace if the authorities refused to surrender Linn, the proper procedure would be to refer the matter to the Adjutant General."

"The A.J. would then request to obtain custody through *habeas corpus* proceedings. Correct, sir?" she replied.

"That's the direction I advised Admiral Wallace to take. I think the District Attorney won't take the time or the trouble to fight us on this one. My hunch was they have other fish to fry, and they'd see this as an opportunity to have us lighten their workload."

"So, essentially, we set up a smokescreen."

"Correct," he replied as he pawed through the mound of papers scattered across the surface of his desk. "Ah, here it is." Towsley picked up his pipe with a look of satisfaction and began to pack the bowl with tobacco. "This is a win/win/win situation for the SPD, the Marine Corps, and the Navy."

"How so, sir?"

Towsley placed the stem of the pipe in his mouth. He again rearranged the papers on his desk as he searched for what she presumed to be a match. He patted his shirt pockets. "The last thing we need—any of the services need, for that matter—is another nasty public relations issue."

Fay reached into her pocketbook. "Here, I have matches, sir." She tossed them in the direction of the appreciative captain.

He caught them, removed a match, and lit his pipe. Drawing in that first puff of smoke seemed to relax him. "The Tailhook scandal was years ago, and it's still haunting the Navy today."

"Unpleasant public relations issues," she said.

"For the Navy and the Marine Corps, getting Sergeant Linn away from the Seattle Police Department allows us to keep Charma's death from attracting media and public scrutiny. Wallace granted the petition late yesterday afternoon; Sergeant Linn is now ours."

"Congratulations, sir."

Towsley smiled. "Once again, your precognition was dead center. The SPD practically tripped over themselves in their hurry to accede."

Fay felt a sense of gratification welling within her. The game, now rescheduled, had given her the home-court advantage—a court on which she seldom lost. "Has Wallace informed us of his intention to convene a court of inquiry?"

"Not yet. Wallace is still waiting for your recommendation, based on your preliminary investigation. But he's heading in that direction." There was a sense of urgency in Towsley's voice. "It's crucial we move swiftly and keep Wallace informed."

"I promise I will move quickly."

"Good enough. The catch, as you know, is if Linn

were to go to courts-martial, as the investigating officer, you would be prevented under military law from being appointed counsel for the defendant. Linn could request Ford Clay as his attorney, since opting for a civil lawyer is his right. Otherwise, he'll have to opt for whoever is assigned. Probably Rollie."

"Rollie? Rollie would be a good choice, sir, but Sergeant Linn does have the right to request the investigating officer as his counsel."

"True. I can't appoint you to defend Linn, but he can request for you to defend him," Towsley replied. "Linn may request defense by either his accuser or by the investigating officer."

"I think we have been fortunate so far." Removing the Charma file from her briefcase, Fay handed it to him and waited while he reviewed it.

"You've been very thorough, as always. I'll forward this to Admiral Wallace."

"Pardon me, sir. Before you do, I would like to interview Mr. Lawrence," Fay requested. "I met him last night at the Pollywog. He claims to have known Paul Charma."

"Very well." He handed the file back to her. "Have a good day, Faydra. By the way, Wallace has reassigned Rayzon. You've got him for two more days."

"Thank you, sir. We have appreciated having his help. We will be sorry to see him go."

Petty Officer Lawrence was waiting for her when Fay returned to her office. She smiled at him, then turned to Pearce and asked, "Any messages for me?"

"No, ma'am."

Fay wiggled her finger at Lawrence. "Okay, Mr. Lawrence, come with me." As they entered her office, she gestured toward the chairs facing her desk. "Please, make yourself comfortable, Mr. Lawrence." She waited while he sat. "Tell me about yourself."

Lawrence cleared his throat. "Well, I joined the Navy about seven years ago. After basic training, I requested SEAL Team training. I've been a SEAL ever since."

"Where do you call home?"

"San Francisco, ma'am."

"It's one of my favorite cities." Fay purposefully slowed her pace to a more relaxed tone. "I was thinking," she said, "about our conversation last night. Of course, I am concerned for your safety. I am also concerned about Paul Charma's death. Any information you can provide will be beneficial. Would you mind if I made a few notes while we talked?"

"No, ma'am."

"Call me Fay." She smiled. "Was Paul a close friend of yours?"

"I'd say so. We've been members of the same platoon for the past two years."

"How many men are there in your platoon?"

"Twelve. Comprising two squads of six men each."

"What is your present duty assignment?"

"Training."

"Have you been issued a Ka-Bar?"

"Yes, ma'am. I have two."

Fay paused, recalling her conversation with Andrew the previous evening. "Was Paul Charma involved with drugs?"

"Certainly not, ma'am."

"Who killed Paul, Andrew?"

"I don't know."

His body language suggested he knew more than he was telling. "Did Paul ever mention the name Howard Carney?" Fay continued.

"No."

"Are you right-handed or left-handed?" She purposefully picked up the tempo of her questioning.

Andrew looked at both of his hands. "It's odd with me," he said. "I write with my right hand, but when I use tools, I use my left. Don't know why."

"What mission are you training for?"

"We're focusing on ship seizures. The training involves nighttime boarding and seizing of ships."

"What's your objective once you seize the ship?" Fay paused. "I want to apologize to you, Andrew. I invited you here today for a meeting. Not an interrogation. Please forgive me."

Andrew smiled. "It's okay, ma'am." He continued, "To secure the ship, its cargo, and crew until the Marines arrive."

"I've always admired you SEALs. My passion is scuba diving, so we have something in common." She smiled. "I should have pursued a career as a SEAL."

Andrew smiled.

"It must take a tremendous amount of courage and strength to do what you do, day in and day out," Fay said.

"It's a job." His ego seemed to swell. "We enjoy what we do." He hesitated for a moment. "They call me Timmy."

"Oh? A nickname? You will have to explain it to me. Nicknames fascinate me." With military professionals, the awarding of nicknames had been a badge of honor.

"It's a long story, but the name evolved from

another nickname given when I first joined the SEALs," Andrew explained.

"Which was?"

"I was referred to as 'Intimidator.' As time went by, the nickname took on a nickname; it was shortened to 'Timmer,' then 'Timmy,'" he clarified.

Fay chuckled. "Andrew, is there something wrong?" That look of anxiety she saw on his face the previous evening had returned.

"Paul's skill is stealth—he was an accomplished assassin. He'd be on his guard, especially in the dark. To kill Paul, the killer would have to be as good at his job, or better, than Paul was."

"You mentioned Paul was an accomplished assassin. An executive order, signed by former President Reagan, stopped assassination by government personnel. How is it he would have those skills?" Fay wanted to know.

"There are many things in an operator's world that 'don't exist.' We conduct numerous missions in the name of national security never mentioned." Andrew took a sip of water. "No SEAL has ever been captured. No SEAL has ever surrendered. No SEAL is left behind."

No SEAL is left behind, Fay wrote on her notepad.

"Paul's assassin is good at what he does," he continued. "If he can get to Paul, then he can get to any of us."

She rocked forward in her chair. By her assessment, Andrew Lawrence was an honest man, a brave, patriotic young sailor. Yet, there was something about his demeanor that left her wanting more. "You believe another operator killed Paul."

91

"Or a mechanic or a sweeper," Andrew added.

"Sweeper," Fay repeated. "I've not heard the term before."

"The guy they would hire if they found it necessary to terminate the mechanic. A mechanic's mechanic, if you will," Andrew explained.

"Heavens." Fay emitted a nervous chuckle. "He sounds like a noxious sort." She made a note and then said, "You and Paul were friends. I assume you know where he lived?"

"Paul had a room in one of the temporary duty barracks. Building three, room two ten."

"I appreciate your help this morning, Andrew. I have one more question. Do you know of Marine Major W. Irving?"

He thought for a moment and said, "No. He's not a part of our team."

"Andrew, what about you? Is there anything I can do for you?" Fay asked.

"I can take care of myself. My concern, Fay, would be for you. Be careful."

Fay dismissed Andrew "Timmy" Lawrence. He knew why Paul was dead, and he knew who had killed him—maybe not who precisely, but he knew the killer was an operator. He pretended to be frightened but admitting to the nickname "Intimidator," and her intuition, said he really felt otherwise. His mission was to warn her, nothing more. She duly and gratefully noted his concern.

Fay watched as Andrew walked through the outer office. Petty Officer Rayzon made a comment to him as he passed by. Andrew nodded without looking at James. There was no other exchange between the two sailors.

Chapter 11

Fay's plan for the afternoon included a visit to Charma's quarters. The parking lot adjacent to building three was vacant. It was duty hours; naturally, the building's residents would be away. The single gray main door to the building squeaked as she pulled open the door. Room two ten would be on the second floor of the two-story wood structure. The building had probably been built to house sailors during the Vietnam War and was in excellent condition. The stairway to the second floor ascended on her immediate right. The first step groaned as she stepped onto it. The noise reverberated down the long hallway. She tiptoed up the remaining steps to the building's top floor.

The second floor mirrored the first, a long hallway with the same number of doors along either wall. The building seemed as quiet as a church mid-week. Fay tiptoed along the hallway to room two ten, fearing the noise created by the hard heels of her shoes on the linoleum floor would make a racket akin to a cattle stampede.

Fay arrived at the door, knocked softly, waited for a moment, and then knocked again, louder the second time. She twisted the doorknob, expecting it to be locked. She glanced both directions up and down the hall, as one would look up and down a busy street before crossing. She shrugged her shoulders and sighed. "Damn!" she said out loud. Out of frustration at the events in general, she kicked at the door with her right foot.

To her surprise, the door swung open. *Huh.* Once again, Fay looked up and down the hall, then quickly slipped through the door. She did not think anyone, including the SPD, would have visited Charma's room. After all, not many knew of the man's existence. Her gaze swept the room, taking everything in. But to her surprise, Charma's quarters were vacant—except for a bunk, a desk, and a chair.

She dropped her pocketbook onto the desk and walked to the only closet in the room. When she opened the door, she found the closet's interior to be the same as the room: barren. Being a tall woman, she could see along the top shelf's length by rising on her toes. There was nothing there. She closed the closet door and continued to search the room. Someone had recently cleaned the room —there was no dust on the blinds and a slight hint of fresh floor wax lingered in the air.

Sailors tended to hide things, a skill they learned in basic training. You had your inspection razor, and you had the one you shaved with every day. The one you shaved with was hidden in a light fixture or the bunk tube frame, anywhere a drill instructor would not think to look for it. Although the DI had been a recruit once herself, so it seemed illogical she would not have thought to look in these places.

Fay sat down on the bunk, again surveying the room and thinking about these possible hiding places, glancing at each location as it came to her mind. *Why not start by looking under the bunk?*

She was on her elbows and knees, looking up at the underside of the bed's springs, when she sensed she was not alone in the room. She froze and held her breath. She looked back at the floor behind her. In the reflection of the floor's high polish, she could see the shape of a human form. She cursed herself for getting out of arm's reach of her pocketbook and the derringer tucked in its side pocket. She would never make it to the bag.

Then, as quickly as it had appeared, the form disappeared. Fay released the air she had been holding in her lungs, relaxed the tension in her muscles, and gingerly backed out from under the bunk. When her head cleared the frame of the bed, she rolled over into a sitting position and rested on the bed frame, quickly surveying the room. Satisfied it was empty, Fay lunged for her pocketbook, opened it, and withdrew her derringer. She then stood up fully, cocked the derringer's hammer, and inched her way across the polished floor toward the door.

Gingerly, she opened the door with the toe of her right foot. With caution, she poked her head out into the hallway. No one was there. She sighed in relief. Whoever it was had gone.

She slipped back into the room. She noticed the reflection from the nearby window cast light across the polished floor, revealing the track of her footsteps. She blinked her eyes. There were only her footprints. No one else had been in the room but her. The slight hint of perfume had replaced the smell of floor wax. No, on second thought, it was aftershave. *L'Observe*. Paranoia was getting the better of her. Was the scent coming from the ventilation system?

There was no time to ponder this curiosity. Fay's head snapped back toward the door when she heard the entrance door on the first floor—the door she had entered through—squeak. Had someone left the building? Then, the first step leading to the second floor groaned under the weight of an intruder. All the terms she heard over the past several days - *assassin, mechanic, sweeper, psychopath, Pennywise* - flooded her mind. She could feel the hairs on the back of her neck tingle as she faded back behind the open door and held her breath.

Like those of a large stalking cat, soft, almost inaudible footsteps approached room two ten. Fay's right hand tightened on the derringer's grip. The stalking cat stopped at the door. She fought the temptation to wipe off the tiny beads of sweat that formed on her brow. Not daring to breathe, she waited.

"Ma'am?"

She knew the voice, but did she trust the person who spoke? She took in a quick sip of air and remained silent.

"Lieutenant Commander, are you armed?"

No sound.

"Is everything all right?" the voice persisted.

Fay had trusted the man before. She now would trust him again. She relieved the tension on the derringer's hammer and exhaled. "Yes, Timmy," she said. "Come in."

Andrew Lawrence eased his head around the edge of the doorjamb. "Lieutenant Commander," he said, "I wanted to see if you were all right."

Emerging from behind the door, Fay exclaimed, "Heavens! You startled me!" She looked down at the weapon in her hand. "I'm sorry. But I'm fine."

"I saw the roadster outside and figured you'd be up here."

"What are you doing here?"

"I live here, ma'am." He pointed directly at his feet. "Downstairs."

"Well, I do appreciate you cared enough to check on me." She glanced over her shoulder, back into the room. "Did you see anyone leave the building?"

"I arrived just after you did. I didn't see anyone go in or out of the building."

She glanced back into the room once more. "Everything seems to be in order." She paused. "Andrew, why did you think I may be armed?"

He looked at the derringer she held in her hand. "I've been trained to be cautious. And I can smell a weapon from a mile away."

"Amazing," she said. "Should I call the Shore Patrol?" she wondered. "They will search the building, find no one, ask many questions I do not want to answer, and take up a lot of my time."

Still deciding, Fay closed the door to room two ten, and Andrew escorted her back to her car in the parking lot. Yes, this incident would go unreported.

Was it a coincidence Andrew had arrived at Charma's quarters when he did? It was duty hours. He should have been at work - if one were to call it "work."

****

Fay felt her stress level escalating by the day. It was time for a break. "JP, I'm going to take a drive out to the ocean after work," she said. "To clear my head and reset my bearings. Would you like to join me?" She knew Pearce would enjoy the diversion.

"Yes, ma'am."

A ninety-minute drive brought the women to Ocean City, a town on the shore of the Pacific Ocean, just as the sun touched the horizon. The chill of the westerly ocean breeze penetrated Fay's thin windbreaker. Pearce built a small bonfire for warmth.

Fay said, "Considering what Andrew Lawrence told me, he seems to think someone more powerful than Howard Carney is responsible for Paul's death."

"Who would've had access to Paul's records or his body?" Pearce asked. "Unless the killer was someone with the power to access records and release remains?"

"Something Andrew Lawrence said to me, 'no SEAL has ever been left behind,' I'm sure it is true. Paul's records disappear, Paul disappears, and we have what is beginning to look like a cover-up," Fay noted.

Pearce poked at the fire with a stick. "Too bad we didn't think to bring marshmallows." She sighed. The orange glow of the fire reflected on her face. "That thing that happened to you today in Paul's room. Jesus, Joseph, and Mary, what was that? Creepy."

"I saw an apparition," Fay said softly. The fire was beginning to fade, along with the late afternoon sun. The cold ocean air was becoming uncomfortable. "Let's go."

Pearce put out the bonfire. As the women waded through the cool sand on their return to the car, Fay stopped, turning back to face the ocean for one last look. She held back the loose strands of her wind-whipped hair from her face and reflected long ago, back to when she had been a young girl sitting on a similar St. Augustine beach, mesmerized by the sea. A girl who had dreamt of someday becoming a part of its tremendous power and beauty. She recalled how she had felt that day—so full of hope, full of dreams, convinced she would make a difference.

Now, some thirty years later, those hopes and dreams made up the reality of things as they were. It was now a different ocean, a different life, and—sadly—the girl was gone. The woman watched the sea through now-jaded eyes. After all, the world was not so wonderful, and she knew she had not made the slightest difference. She wondered where the innocence of childhood ended and where the guilt and burden of adulthood began. Pearce had managed to hold on to her childlike innocence; Fay admired her for that. How she wished for the simple life, the life she had envisioned for herself.

"How can this be?" Fay asked. "A brave young man is dead—a man who pledged his life to defend the honor of his country to the death. Ironically, the same country who once embraced the man as its son may well be the one who betrayed him in the end."

Pearce listened but remained silent.

"Oh, to be a child again," Fay said distractedly. "Times were so much simpler then."

"I know what ya mean, ma'am. Used to be, when I was small, it was a big deal to finally be tall enough to ride the 'big people' rides at one of those kids theme parks."

Fay laughed affectionately. "Well, you do also recall at age twelve, you were almost six feet tall."

"Yes, I recall," Pearce replied. "I was hideous. Pardon me for sayin' this, but I think somewhere along the way, as you were travelin' down the freeway of life, your karma must have run over your dogma. And left y'all in a rut or somethin'."

Fay was not entirely sure if what Pearce said made complete sense, but it did sound funny. "Thanks. I was thinking about something you said. Something about the tadpole croaking?"

"Ma'am. If Paul were a rat instead of a frog," Pearce said, "what would he have done?"

"He would have eaten cheese or squealed?"

"What if we're just about to sail right into the murky backwaters of the U.S. government's dirty dealin's? Paul squealed about somethin' those government guys didn't want nobody knowin'?"

Fay felt cold. "It would tie into what Andrew Lawrence said about Paul dying for what he knew. He told someone what he knew."

"Either that, ma'am, or someone thought Paul was about to tell someone. I would bet the tadpole who killed Paul was a bullfrog," Pearce speculated.

"You mean an officer? Someone like W. Irving. Right?" The thought had crossed Fay's mind.

"That's right," Pearce replied.

Chapter 12

North Pacific Ocean, 18:10 hours—second dogwatch, naval vessel DDG59

Guided-missile destroyer U.S.S. *Nalon Vet* had been pounding heavy rollers for the past two hours with Captain Egan Fletcher on her bridge for most of the day. The wind maintained a steady fifty-six knots—about ten knots below the classification hurricane force at seventy-five miles per hour.

Captain Fletcher's concern for his crew and ship went with the territory. If the blow kept up, it would mean a long and sleepless night for him. "Right fifteen degrees rudder," he patiently ordered. "Steady on course zero-seven-zero."

"Right fifteen degrees, aye," the quartermaster replied. "Steer zero-seven-zero, sir."

Fletcher stared through the spray-spattered glass of *Nalon Vet's* bridge window into the closing darkness. He could see the ship's bow disappear each time the destroyer knifed through another wave, up one side and down the other.

Quartermaster Striplin was Captain Fletcher's favorite helmsman, perhaps because he enjoyed Jeffrey's upbeat, boisterous personality or because Striplin reminded him of his own son, Kristian. It made no difference because Fletcher always looked forward to his watch with him. "Jeffrey, do you think we could sneak in a 'gar before they douse the smoking lamp?"

"I think so, sir."

Egan Fletcher reached into his shirt pocket, producing a small box of cigarette-sized cigars. After offering one to the others on the bridge, he handed one to Striplin. "Here, son. I have a light."

"Thank you, sir." Striplin placed the small cigar in his mouth. Fletcher lit it for him. His cheeks drew the cigar to life.

Fletcher lit his own cigar, then ordered, "Ease your rudder to five degrees."

"Ease to five, aye."

"Nothing to the right of zero-seven-zero, sailor."

"Aye, aye, sir. Nothing to the right of zero-seven-zero."

"Mark your head, Mister," Fletcher said.

"Zero-seven-zero, sir. Steady as you go. Course zero-seven-zero."

"Keep her so, helmsman." Fletcher took a drag on the cigar. "This damn weather. I'd like to have a calm sea for our last night out."

"Yes, sir."

"What plans do you have for your leave, Mr. Striplin?"

"After being at sea for a month, I plan on getting reacquainted with my family. My wife is the most beautiful woman in the world."

"You've been married for seven years, and you still feel that way about her," Fletcher said. "I admire you, son."

"How about you, sir?"

"I'll take my son to Hawaii for a sun break." Fletcher continued to stare out into the black and stormy

Pacific Ocean night. The orange tip of his cigar reflected in the dark glass of the *Vet's* bridge, a burning eye glowing in the dampened night. Fletcher's thoughts were somewhere on a Hawaiian beach.

The U.S.S. *Nalon Vet* had been on sea trials for twenty-eight days. The modified Burke-class guided-missile destroyer had initially been designed as a predecessor to the *Zumwalt* stealth ships. She had been refitted in the Todd Shipyards in Seattle to modernize her Integrated Power System. The Navy had added some experimental radar jamming electronics and new radar-reflecting, stealth hull paint. The ship's black hull was more reminiscent of a submarine than the standard gray of other surface vessels.

It was not up to Captain Fletcher to wonder what plans the Navy had in store for the *Vet*, as she was affectionately called. His concern was for a safe test with no life or property loss. He did know some of his crew consisted of MIT brainiacs, now gainfully employed by the National Security Agency. The NSA was charged with snooping into everyone else's government affairs worldwide. The agency was affectionately known in the intelligence world as "No Such Agency."

Like the Air Force stealth bombers, should *Nalon Vet's* electronics and radar reflecting paint testing prove a success, the *Vet* would be invisible to any radar.

How fitting, Fletcher thought. *The proverbial ghost ship.* For centuries, mariners had told the tale of a mysterious vessel that appeared from nowhere, only to disappear as mysteriously as it had first appeared. He likened himself to a ghost ship's captain, his crew salted with spooks from "No Such Agency."

****

20:00 hours

"Good evening, Captain," Lieutenant Commander Caldwell said. "Commander Martin sends his respects and reports the hour of eight o'clock. I have our position report and equipment status report. Request permission to strike eight bells on time, sir."

"Permission granted, X-O," Fletcher said. "Why don't we see if Cookie left us something to eat in the galley? You can brief me there."

"Aye, Skipper," Caldwell responded.

"The OOD is Commander Walker," Fletcher announced to those on the bridge. "Heading zero-seven-zero, Mr. Walker."

"Zero-seven-zero, Captain," Walker confirmed.

"Have a good night, Mr. Striplin," Fletcher said.

"Aye, Skipper," Striplin said, accompanied by a slight two-finger gesture that was half salute, half-wave.

Throughout the night, *Nalon Vet's* electric engines propelled the destroyer through the foam-tossed sea. Fletcher awoke at 03:15. The ship had stopped bucking, indicating the storm had passed. He picked up the phone near his bunk and rang the bridge.

"Bridge, Commander Martin on, sir."

"Good morning, Mr. Martin. I trust you are well."

"Exceptionally well this morning, sir. We're making good time, now the wind has died."

"Will we make the Washington State coast by twelve hundred hours, Mr. Martin?"

"Affirmative, Captain. We're on schedule."

"Thank you, Commander. Have a pleasant morning." Fletcher replaced the phone and returned to his nap.

"Six hundred hours reveille. Up all idlers," were the

next words Captain Fletcher heard.

"Six hundred hours. Weather, partly cloudy," the voice blared over the ship's speaker system. "Wind fifteen knots. Sea is calm."

He enjoyed every aspect of his job. It was traditional for Captain Fletcher to eat the last breakfast of the cruise with the enlisted men. He loved to interact with his crew. Fletcher showered, dressed, and went to the galley. As he entered, someone called the room to attention and a chorus of "For He's a Jolly Good Fellow" began. He felt the honor of having his crew's admiration, definitely one of his job's non-monetary rewards.

After making a brief speech about pride and patriotism, Fletcher wished the crew well. He told them he hoped he would have the honor of serving with them again. It was an emotional moment for him. It always was and always would be.

Following breakfast, Fletcher stepped out of the galley and into the salt-laced morning air. He thought the dawn magnificent. He paused to watch the early sunlight as it sparkled in the foam created by the ship's wake. Sea birds whirled and dove off the fantail as if to salute the ship's arrival into Washington State coastal waters. Satisfied all was in order on the bridge, Captain Fletcher went to his quarters to prepare for the *Nalon Vet's* arrival at Puget Sound Naval Shipyard.

He later returned to the bridge for the noon reports. "The quartermaster sends his regards to the Captain. He reports twelve o'clock," the OOD said. "Chronometers wound and compared, request permission to strike eight bells, sir."

Fletcher caught his first glimpse of the Washington coastline through an early afternoon mist. "Cape Flattery light to starboard, Captain," the navigator report.

"Noted," he confirmed. "Thank you."

No matter how many times he had gone to sea, to Captain Fletcher, the sweetest sight of all was the first sight of land. Especially when it was his home state. He realized how much he was looking forward to seeing his son, Kristian.

The wide channel separating Washington State from British Columbia, the Strait of Juan De Fuca, was active with vessels of all shapes and sizes—tankers and cargo ships, fishing vessels, pleasure craft, and military ships—U.S. and Canadian. It had been a long time since a Navy vessel had severed a fishing skiff. It would not happen during his command either. Fletcher spent the balance of the day preparing for port arrival while the *Vet* slowly traversed Puget Sound.

****

Fay arrived at her office that morning feeling apprehensive. The scale of this investigation was changing too fast. She had an increasing feeling much more was involved in this whole thing than she had first assumed. Pearce's words kept replaying in her mind.

Fay placed calls to Frank Farmer and Ford Clay. She was particularly interested in getting any feedback Frank had on Howard Carney. She learned Farmer's men had watched Carney for four days but had observed nothing suspicious. She concluded the private investigator Ford Clay had hired to tail Carney must have alerted him.

****

The phone rang in Vern Towsley's office. "Vern," Admiral May said, "I would like you to meet *Nalon Vet* when she makes port. It looks like we're going to need the services of Hurricane Fletcher. And I understand Lawrence contacted Faydra."

"Mission accomplished," Towsley confirmed.

****

It was 13:30 hours when Fay returned from her lunch.

"Ma'am, Captain Towsley left a message for y'all," Pearce said as Fay entered the office. "He requests your presence dockside this evening for the arrival of the *Nalon Vet*."

"What time?"

"Twenty-one hundred hours, ma'am."

"Do you have any plans?" Fay asked.

"Sweet! I suspect I'm dockside at twenty-one hundred hours."

Fay laughed. "Tell Towsley we will join him."

****

The *Vet* loomed so quickly out of the darkness, its sudden appearance took Fay by surprise. It took forty-five more minutes for the *Vet* to moor and disembark her crew. The docking area was filled with laughter and shrieks of joy as individual crewmembers were reunited with their families and friends.

She spotted Captain Fletcher descending the gangplank. He was about forty yards away from her when she noticed a young man run up to greet him. They embraced one another and chatted excitedly for a moment. Fletcher then pointed toward his personal effects, piled neatly on the dock, and then toward Fay. The young man nodded and walked toward the luggage. Fletcher turned and walked toward her. As he approached, Fay recalled their first meeting. It had been at Admiral Wallace's Christmas party almost one year earlier. He was as she remembered: rugged, handsome, and confident.

The Captain had a stocky build and was approximately her height, although neither fat nor overweight. On the contrary, he had the appearance of a pro football linebacker. She thought back to the party. When she had learned Fletcher was single, she had attempted to flirt with him several times. He had seemed aloof but not rude, as if he simply had not noticed her. She had decided he probably had a woman in his life.

She had made it a point to find out the origin of his nickname, "Hurricane." Several versions of the story had been offered to her at the party. One version told of Captain Fletcher saving three Marines' lives during a street brawl in a Persian Gulf port city. It was said a band of Arabs had descended upon three unsuspecting Marines. The Marines, badly outmatched and in need of help, had been rescued when Fletcher drew his sidearm. The body count had been nine dead Arabs, shot by Fletcher, with three more dispatched by his bare hands when his weapon had run out of ammunition.

Fletcher himself had told her the story grew in proportion with each telling. He had claimed the story's true count included one Marine with a broken leg, three middle-aged and overweight Arabs, high on hashish, and an inebriated Fletcher. The legend had grown out of the embellishment of the story. The "Hurricane" nickname had resulted from the fury he had supposedly unleashed on the multitudes of Arabs lain waste in the path of "Hurricane" Fletcher. He seemed to her to be a modest man. And after hearing his telling of the story, Fay had not known which version to believe. *Well, here he is again. Hurricane Fletcher.*

The trio saluted as Fletcher approached them. The

salutes were crisply returned. "Lieutenant Commander Green," he said with a smile, extending his hand. "It's a pleasure to see you again." He turned toward Vern Towsley. "Vern, good to see you again." Next, he turned to acknowledge Pearce, whom he had not met before, by bringing his right hand to the bill of his cap and nodding with a smile. "Evening, ma'am."

Fay extended her hand. "The pleasure is mine, Captain Fletcher," she said. "I am flattered the gentleman remembered me."

"How could I forget the most elegant officer in attendance at the Admiral's Christmas party?" Fletcher was sincere and smooth.

Pearce sighed.

Fay turned toward her protégée. "This is my Legalman, Petty Officer J. Pearce," she said proudly. "Meet Captain Egan Fletcher."

"I'm honored to meet you, Miss Pearce," he said as he shook her hand. "I'm sorry to hold you up, Lieutenant Commander." He pointed toward the young man. "That's my son, Kristian. He came to meet me and to help me with my gear."

Vern Towsley asked Fletcher if he would meet with him the following day.

Captain Fletcher told Vern he had a debriefing scheduled the entire day with Admiral Wallace and some government people. Still, after that was wrapped up, he would meet him the following day. "Your office, nine hundred hours, your coffee? Vern. Miss Pearce." Fletcher smiled and nodded again in Fay's direction. "Miss Green." He shook her hand more slowly, thoughtfully this time. "Have an enjoyable evening."

Fay watched as Fletcher returned to the waiting

young man. He placed his arm around the young man's shoulder as they walked away.

"What a hunk," Fay whispered to Pearce.

Chapter 13

Admiral May seemed stern. He said, "Captain Fletcher, five days ago, the frigate U.S.S. *Jonathan Carr* was sunk in North Korean provincial waters." May sipped at a cup of hot chocolate. "I don't have a lot of details, Hurricane, but I need your help."

A puzzled look crossed Fletcher's face. "I'll do whatever I can, Admiral. Strange, I hadn't heard about this." He looked at Vern Towsley, who was sitting at his desk, facing the two officers.

May replied, "North Korea and the United States have managed to keep a lid on it, so far."

"We're not at war?"

"Not yet. We're not ready to go public on the incident."

Fletcher sensed the Admiral had something to tell him but was waiting.

May sipped at his hot chocolate and then said, "I have been given permission to brief you and Vern on this, Hurricane." He paused to loosen his necktie. "Five weeks ago, Defense Minister Park Seung He, North Korea's number one man, defected to South Korea. Park arrived with the aid of a secret American commando team assigned to my department."

"A counter-proliferation team?" Towsley asked.

"That's right," May confirmed.

"Was the *Carr* off course?" asked Fletcher.

"No," Admiral May replied. "She had the North Koreans' permission to be there."

"Odd. Then why did the North Koreans sink her?" Fletcher asked.

May shrugged his shoulders. "It remains a mystery. I suppose the captain of the *Carr* knows why, along with our President and the North Korean government. I do know I need your help. President Ross has ordered my operators to Chinhae." He frowned. He took a deep breath and said, *"Nalon Vet* has been dispatched to Chinhae as well. She left port the day following your arrival in Bremerton."

"This comes as a shock, Admiral," Fletcher said. "Do we have any other details?"

"We're still sorting this thing out. We know Captain Matthew Nevada was given thirty minutes to abandon his ship before it was torpedoed and sunk. One life was lost."

"I…" Fletcher paused.

"I know you are the one man I can count on, Hurricane."

"What can I do, sir?"

"I've put together a team made up of much the same men who extracted the defense minister from North Korea," Admiral May explained. "If you agree, we will meet tomorrow at zero-eight hundred in the Tac/Log Center briefing room at Joint Base Lewis-McChord."

"I'll be there."

"Good," Admiral May said and then turned toward Towsley. "I'd like you to be there, Vern. I can use your help as well."

"Of course, Admiral," Towsley replied.

As Egan Fletcher walked toward the JAG office's

foyer, he passed the office of Lieutenant Commander Green. He could see Petty Officer Pearce through the window in the door. He entered the office. She seemed startled to see him, lurching to the required position of attention before greeting him.

Egan said, "Good morning, Miss Pearce. At ease."

Pearce relaxed. "Mornin', sir. Lieutenant Commander Green isn't here." She pointed over her shoulder, indicating the conference room's general direction. "She's in the conference room."

"Thanks, but I wasn't looking for Lieutenant Commander Green. I happened to see you through the window and stopped by to say hello. Anyway, I don't want to disturb you. Carry on."

"Thank you, sir. Y'all weren't disturbin' me. I wasn't doin' nothin'. Well…I mean, I was doin' somethin', but—." Pearce blushed and seemed to be at a loss for words. "Can I help you with somethin', sir?"

"No, no. Carry on."

Fletcher's route toward the building's exit took him past the conference room. Through the door, left ajar, he could see Fay sitting alone at the end of a long conference table. He eased his head just inside the doorway and said, "Hello, Faydra."

She looked up from her work, quickly removed her reading glasses, smiled, and said, "Oh…hello, sir!" With a motion of her right hand, she said, "Please, join me."

Egan entered the room. "I just wanted to say hello."

She stood and pulled a chair away from the table. "Please, have a seat, Captain. Is your meeting with Captain Towsley over?"

He sat down. "We just finished up." He sat motionlessly.

She asked, "Is something wrong, sir?"

"No…nothing wrong. I was heading home, saw you through the doorway, and thought I'd pay my respects."

"I am delighted you did, sir."

Pearce entered the conference room with a large manila envelope tucked under her arm. "Excuse me, ma'am. This arrived for y'all via mail carrier." She laid the envelope on the table in front of Fay, smiled at Fletcher, and left the room.

Fletcher's eyes followed Pearce from the room. "She's a very charming woman," he observed.

"Do you live near Bremerton?" Fay asked.

"I live on a small farm east of Seattle. Near the city of Maple Valley."

"Does your son tend to the animals while you are at sea?"

"He's a full-time student at the University of Washington. Ronda watches the place while I'm away." Egan drummed his fingers on the arms of his chair.

"Is Ronda your wife, sir?"

"I suppose I would marry her if she would wait for me." He chuckled and relaxed for a moment.

"How so?"

"Ronda is my seventy-year-old housekeeper. I've told her many times if she would hold at seventy until I caught up, I'd sweep her off of her feet."

Fay laughed. "Captain, pardon me for asking, but how is it there is no Mrs. Fletcher?"

"My wife died eight years ago."

"I am so sorry I asked. Forgive me for the asking."

"I'm fine. Life has been good to me. I have a great son and a fine career." He sat back. "When the time is right… You were married at one time, weren't you?"

"Briefly, a long time ago," Fay replied. "Anyway. In the end, the entire mess did not amount to more than a hill of beans."

"A hill of beans," Fletcher said thoughtfully.

"It's a Southern thing, sir. You know, why I reckon if I had my druthers and was fixin' to get hitched again, I'd have to be livin' in the high cotton," she said.

Fay had said it so matter of factly, Egan laughed. "You will remind me if I ever travel to the South to take a translator with me."

"Sho' nufff," Fay said with a giggle.

Egan glanced at the assortment of papers scattered across the table. "It looks like the law business is booming."

Fay surveyed the table, shook her head, and sighed. "I'm investigating a homicide."

"A homicide?"

"Yes, it is out of the ordinary. Normally I defend, prosecute, or investigate the inconsequential, such as petty theft, sexual harassment, absent without leave, and various misconduct cases. Until now, the Navy has not assigned me to a homicide case."

"How's the investigation going?" Fletcher asked.

"Off the record… it's quite unusual for many reasons. Someone far up the food chain sprung the prime suspect, an operator. A Marine major kidnapped the corpse, and the deceased's service records have disappeared."

"I don't know much about the inner workings of the military justice system, Fay," he offered, "but I would imagine this would be somewhat disconcerting for you."

"Not really, sir."

The conference room's natural light emphasized

Fay's almond-shaped sea-green eyes, eyes of enormous depth and directness, which gave her face an undeniable allure. Fletcher studied her for a moment but remained silent.

A sly grin formed on Fay's full, sensuous lips, and her expression changed to one of mock anger. "But I must admit I'm starting to get up into a hissy fit."

Egan chuckled.

She sighed. "Time for lunch. It's Miss Pearce's birthday."

"Really." He smiled to himself. "Miss Pearce's birthday?"

"I am taking her out for lunch."

****

Several hours later, a flower delivery arrived: six huge, lavender roses. When she spotted the flowers, Pearce said, "Those would be for Lieutenant Commander Green. I'll take them for her."

"I'm sorry, Miss," the deliveryman said, and handed the flowers to her. "I know little about the Navy, but I do know the difference between an officer and a petty officer. I think these are for you. That's if you're J. Pearce?"

"Huh…who, me? Who sent them?"

"Check the card," he suggested.

Pearce thanked him and hurriedly tore open the envelope. How thoughtful of Fay to buy her lunch; the flowers were unexpected.

Happy birthday! The card read. *Please enjoy your special day*! The card was signed by Egan Fletcher.

Pearce was stunned. Running to Fay's office, flowers in hand and a broad smile on her face, she exclaimed, "Zowie!" She held up the bouquet for Fay to see. "They're birthday flowers for me from Captain Fletcher!"

"That is a zowie, alright!" Fay shrieked. "How very nice of him!"

"I guess Captain Fletcher don't worry so much about protocol and regs."

"Oh… I'm sure Captain Fletcher does," Fay replied. "At least the important ones anyway. But just so's ya know, Mr. Fletcher does not come in a pair."

"Then I can keep 'em?"

Fay winked at her. "Of course." She smiled. "Seems you may have an admirer!"

Looking down at the top of Fay's desk, Pearce said, "Ma'am, not to change the subject. I notice the envelope I gave to you this mornin' is still layin' here on your desk, unopened. Wasn't it important?"

"Mercy! In all the excitement, I forgot about it." Fay snatched the envelope off her desk and opened it. Although it had been addressed to her, there was no return address. Immediately, she realized what she was reviewing. As she paged through the contents, a tendril of hair fell in front of her left eye. With a quick puff from the corner of her mouth, the tendril returned to its proper location.

Speaking barely above a whisper, Fay said, "Charma's service records, his wallet, and a pack of cigarettes." She again thumbed through the records. "His records, sans page thirteen."

Chapter 14

08:00 hours, Joint Base Lewis-McChord, Washington

"Gentlemen, thank you for coming," Admiral May said to the men seated around the conference table at Joint Base Lewis-McChord Tactical Logistics Center's planning room. Motioning to Fletcher and Towsley, he offered, "Hopefully, the Captains will agree with me when I suggest we dispense with military formalities this morning."

"I agree, Brandon. And please, call me Egan, gentlemen," Fletcher stated.

Captain Towsley nodded in agreement. "Vern, gentlemen."

"Egan," May said, pointing toward a man seated across the table from him, "I believe you know this man."

"Simon Linn!" Egan said. "Long time, no see!" He recalled he had last seen Simon several years prior in the Persian Gulf port city of Manama. Simon, hobbled with a broken ankle, had evoked the wrath of three knife-wielding Arabs. Fletcher had come along in time to join the melee and save him from further injury. He glanced at the man's left leg. "How's your ankle, Marine?"

Simon smiled. "Never better. Good to see you again, Hurricane."

"Gentlemen, let's begin with introductions," May

said. "To my right is Captain Vern Towsley, former NCIS Terminator, now JAG Corps, Bremerton."

Captain Towsley nodded.

"Next to Vern, Hurricane Fletcher, Navy Special Operations Command and captain of the U.S.S. *Nalon Vet*."

Egan nodded.

"Next to Hurricane," May continued, "are Army Sergeants Peter 'Kimo' Wu and Phillip 'Dah-Vee' De Vinsone, Special Warfare Command, Delta Force."

The two men nodded.

"Next, Marine Master Sergeant Simon Linn, Special Warfare Command, MEU." Simon smiled and nodded.

"Navy Petty Officer Andrew 'Timmy' Lawrence, Special Warfare Command, SEAL Team-ED."

Andrew smiled and nodded.

"Next to Mr. Lawrence, Petty Officer Matthew 'Cupid' Valentine, SEAL Team-ED."

Valentine nodded.

"And Navy Captain James 'Raisin' Rayzon, Special Warfare Command, team leader SEAL Team-ED."

Captain Rayzon nodded.

"ED?" Fletcher asked.

"Executive Detachment," Admiral May answered. "These men report directly to me. In matters regarding these men, I, in turn, report to President Ross. We affectionately refer to these men as E-Team."

Egan had heard rumors of such a team - a team created to conduct missions so secret only a handful of high-ranking officers knew of them.

"Hurricane, you are aware the Special Warfare Command has been training teams of elite operators for counter-proliferation operations."

Egan nodded. He now knew what was about to transpire. In the world of shadow warriors, each man seated at the table were the alpha dogs in the military food chain. Each man's identity was a secret; only the President of the United States and a few select admirals and generals knew of them or their existence. Whatever May was about to reveal was severe in nature—highly classified—and it somehow included Hurricane Fletcher.

May turned back to the men assembled at the table. "The men you see here today represent a culmination of the best operators from their respective branches of service." He smiled. "The *crème de la crème*, if you will."

The smile left May's face. "Gentlemen, I have a problem, and I need your help. The *Carr's* sinking has presented President Ross with many problems, as you can well imagine. The *Carr* incident and the events leading up to her sinking have brought North and South Korea to a crisis: a war, gentlemen, that would quickly draw Japan, China, and the United States into the fray, leaving our friend Taiwan caught in the middle."

May turned to a map hung on the wall behind him, depicting a section of the Yellow Sea. He pointed to pinpoint the location of the *Carr*. "The *Carr* returned the North Korean Prime Minister of Defense to North Korea. The Prime Minister and his family defected, with our help, to South Korea; he brought a wealth of military secrets. Unfortunately, his defection was ill-timed. Shortly after, a U.S. spy plane flying a routine mission over China and North Korea crashed into the Yellow Sea. The plane's crew ejected, landed in North Korea, and were captured. The aircraft and crew, gentlemen, became the focus of an intense series of negotiations between the United States, North Korea, and South Korean governments.

"The North Koreans knew the value of the spy plane, known as *Aurora*," May went on. "The Air Force denies the plane even exists. Needless to say, it's a crucial piece of weaponry. The North Koreans proposed a trade—the aircraft and crew for the Prime Minister. After much deliberation and with the Prime Minister's consent, it was agreed the North Koreans would trade *Aurora* for the Prime Minister. The *Carr* was dispatched to transport the Prime Minister to a rendezvous point in North Korean provincial waters and retrieve *Aurora's* crew. The *Carr* was accompanied by a salvage vessel responsible for recovering *Aurora*."

As Hurricane Fletcher listened, the ramifications of the events quickly sank in.

"The damage is done," May said, his voice disconsolate. "The crew and plane have been returned. What remains is a U.S. Navy man-of-war lying in ninety feet of water at the bottom of the Yellow Sea. In the crew's haste to abandon the *Carr*, sensitive data were left behind—data we badly need. It's also imperative we locate and verify the whereabouts of the crewman who died when the *Carr* sank."

"An easier task," Egan commented, "if the *Carr* were any place other than in North Korean waters."

"Detection by the North Koreans of a U.S. naval vessel in their waters would be viewed as an act of retaliation to the *Carr* sinking. The war we most fear would result." May spoke directly to Egan, "Hurricane, I want you to deliver these men to the *Jonathan Carr*."

****

Faydra Green spread out Paul Charma's wallet's contents on her desk, the sum total of his existence on planet Earth. *Why was the man murdered? Why has the corpse disappeared, and why do I possess his service records and wallet—the only remaining trace of this man? It would be impossible to trace Paul Charma's life in the Navy without page thirteen of his service records. What am I supposed to glean from any of this?* The conclusion she drew was squat.

There was only a wallet, a few dollars, an ID card with Charma's photo attached, and a pack of cigarettes. Fay studied the picture. Paul was a good-looking man, in her estimation. The white book of matches she found wedged inside the cigarette pack's cellophane wrapper was plain. The word *Trance*, embossed in black, was the only label on the book. She assumed it was a business.

As Fay placed the items back in the envelope, her nose itched. When she scratched it, she detected the scent of *L'Observe* on her fingertips. She startled. She had been handling Paul's personal effects before her itchiness. She lifted the envelope from her desk. Drawing it to her face, she inhaled deeply. The scent was gone. Perplexed, she punched the intercom button on her phone. Without waiting for the usual response, she asked, "Miss Pearce, were you able to access the records of Peter Wu and Philip De Vinsone?"

"I tried, ma'am," was the expected reply.

It did not surprise her when Petty Officer Pearce reported De Vinsone's and Wu's records were classified. She had been denied access to them. Fay asked her to try accessing them through Admiral Wallace's office. Forty-five minutes later, Pearce delivered the two records to

Fay's desk.

"How did you do that?"

"Magic, ma'am. Some guy named…" Pearce caught herself, "pardon me. I mean, some flag, ah… an admiral named May authorized it. Don't know who he is."

"Huh," Fay remarked. She pondered the Admiral's name for a moment. Unable to recall the person attached to the title, she said, "I don't know who he is either. Oh well, we've got what we wanted. Good work, JP." She motioned for Pearce to sit while she scanned the men's records. Fay nodded. "Just as I thought. The duty history pages are missing from both records."

"More operators, ma'am?"

"More secret guys, I am afraid."

"What does it tell us?"

"It's what it does not tell us that intrigues me," Fay said as she rocked forward in her chair, placing her elbows on the desk in front of her.

Pearce frowned. The wheels were definitely turning. "Small things tell large stories?"

"Charlie Chan. Right?"

Pearce nodded.

"Think about it for a moment," Fay offered. "Charma, Lawrence, Linn, De Vinsone, and Wu, all classified. No duty assignments. They all must know one another."

Pearce thoughtfully nodded. "One way or another, each of these men is somehow linked to each of the others."

"Right." Fay thought for a moment. "Find out where Wu and De Vinsone are. I want to talk to them."

Wu and De Vinsone were located. Interviews with the two men were scheduled for the following day at the nearby offices of the 13th Naval District.

Chapter 15

A constant stream of military personnel passed through the busy lobby, most carrying briefcases or files. The atmosphere seemed somber. Hushed tones of distant voices drifted up the numerous hallways; occasionally, Fay heard one of many doors squeak and close. Brisk footsteps echoed from the highly polished floors.

Several Army sergeants came into the lobby, looking as if they were searching for someone; none were Wu.

Finally, an Army sergeant entered. He immediately spotted her, smiling as he approached her. "Lieutenant Commander Green?" he asked with a steady gaze, never losing his smile.

She smiled and extended her hand. "Sergeant Wu, I'm honored to meet you."

"Likewise, ma'am," Wu said.

Fay tried to conceal her preconceptions. "An office has been set aside for our use. Let's make ourselves comfortable," she suggested.

A yeoman escorted them to a well-appointed office, including a massive cherry wood desk with an oversized leather stuffed chair located behind it. Two matching leather chairs faced the desk. The walls were decorated with photographs of various naval vessels. The nameplate slot next to the door was vacant.

Fay chose to sit in one of the two chairs facing the

desk, rather than placing herself behind it. She would conduct her interview, but she would not do it from a superior position. She offered the chair behind the desk to Wu.

"This'll be fine," he said, taking the other chair next to hers. "Do you mind?"

"Of course not."

Sergeant Wu was obviously not her idea of the rigid, prototypical Marine. Fay had expected the high and tight haircut and the thousand-yard stare typical of a seasoned combat veteran, similar to the gaze she had noticed in James Rayzon and Simon Linn's eyes. Wu's long black hair was gathered back into a ponytail and stuffed down the collar of his shirt. Along with the constant smile, there was a warm sparkle in his dark eyes. She presumed Wu to be of Chinese-Hawaiian ancestry. He was hardly the dark and sinister operator she had expected—although her common sense told her differently. The proverbial wolf in sheep's clothing was her guess.

"Your excellent tan tells me you might be from the Islands," Fay began.

"Yes, Miss Green." Wu's eyes seemed to reflect happy thoughts of home. "I was born and raised on the Big Island. I'd say, judging from your accent, you're from the South?"

"Northern Florida, near Pensacola."

"Once again, I'm pleased to meet you, Lieutenant Commander Green. What can I do for JAG Corps?"

"You are very perceptive, Sergeant. I am investigating a sailor's death—a man named Paul Charma. Sergeant Wu, I would like to ask you some questions—off the record, so I won't need to advise you of your *Article thirty-one* rights. Is that all right?"

"Go ahead, ma'am," he replied.

"If you change your mind during this interview and wish to invoke your rights, as allowed by the UCMJ, let me know." Fay smiled and continued, "I understand you were with Simon Linn the night he was arrested."

The smile drained from Wu's face. "I was with Simon that night. Although I will say I know the man well enough to know he wouldn't kill unless he were defending himself or his country."

Fay paused, referred to her notes, and then continued. "How long have you known Sergeant Linn?"

"I'd say almost three years, ma'am."

"You've known Simon Linn for three years."

"Yes."

"Have you ever seen him angry? Or seen him lose his temper?" Fay questioned.

"Simon is like all of us. He gets angry, frustrated, disappointed. But where most of us in those situations will lash out or retaliate, Simon will hesitate before he responds."

"How's that?" she asked.

"You may know Simon was born and raised in the South," Wu explained. "He called it the 'Jim Crow South.' I have tried to understand. But what did touch me was something his mother taught him."

"And what was that, Sergeant?"

"She told him to refuse haters and to refuse blanket judgments. Simon is a good man, ma'am."

Fay removed a handkerchief from her pocket, dabbed at the corners of her eyes, sniffed, and then made a note. "I understand a third man joined you and Sergeant Linn at Jillian's that evening."

"Sergeant Philip De Vinsone," Wu confirmed.

"Did you know Paul Charma?"

"Yes."

"Did you see Sergeant Linn talking with a man that night?"

"I did," he replied.

"It would then be Paul Charma. Were they arguing?" Fay pressed.

"I wasn't paying much attention."

"What is your present duty assignment?"

Sergeant Wu offered an apologetic smile and said, "I'm sorry, that's classified."

She wrinkled her brow. "Can you tell me anything about your duty assignment?"

"I'm on training status."

"Do you know Marine Major W. Irving?"

Wu brought his right hand to his chin. He stroked his chin thoughtfully and said, "Can't say I do."

Fay was not learning much. Further questioning seemed pointless. "I have one more question, Sergeant, then we'll wrap this up. Do you know why someone would want to kill Paul Charma?"

Wu shifted slightly in his chair. The movement was slight, but to an astute lawyer, body language spoke volumes. "No," he said, "I've no idea why anyone would want to kill the man."

Fay sensed he did know why. "Thanks, Sergeant. You're dismissed."

The warm smile returned to Wu's face. "By the way, my friends call me 'Kimo,'" he offered.

"My pleasure, Kimo."

Wu paused momentarily, then asked, "Do you have a nickname, Fay?"

She briefly considered his odd question before she

responded. "When I was a child, my parents called me 'Spider.' According to my father, I was all arms and legs. To this day, my sister still calls me 'Spider,' although she's the only one who does."

"Is Simon going to be okay, ma'am?"

"Simon will be fine."

A pleased look came to Wu's warm brown eyes. "*Semper Fi*, Lieutenant Commander," he said.

"Always faithful, Kimo," she responded, translating Wu's Latin words into English. "Sergeant Wu," Fay said as she stood, signaling the end of their meeting. "I'm happy to have met you."

"My pleasure."

Chapter 16

Sergeant De Vinsone proved to be of a much different temperament than Kimo Wu. Where Kimo had seemed warm and friendly, De Vinsone seemed cold and sullen. His intense black eyes had the thousand-yard stare Fay had expected. She felt intimidated.

Sergeant De Vinsone greeted her with a very rigid military salute. Like Simon, it took him some time to relax, even slightly. Her impression of De Vinsone fit the sinister operator she had expected to meet. The new term she had recently learned from Andrew Lawrence, "sweeper," came to mind—the long hair, the goatee, and the earring gave De Vinsone the air of a buccaneer.

"Sergeant De Vinsone," Fay began, "I'm investigating the death of a sailor named Paul Charma. Would you mind answering a few questions for me? Off the record."

A slight grin came to De Vinsone's lips. "Of course, Lieutenant Commander Green." De Vinsone spoke with a distinct Jamaican Creole accent.

"If I ask a question you wish not to answer, tell me so. Understood?"

"Understood, ma'am."

"Sergeant Linn told me he met you and Sergeant Wu at Jillian's on the night of Paul Charma's death."

"That is correct, ma'am. But Simon Linn isn't about killin' someone. Not even a *phoque*."

De Vinsone's dark eyes refocused to meet hers. They were intense and piercing—Fay felt goosebumps on her arms and hoped he did not notice. "I hope you meant *phoque*, the French word for seal, Mr. De Vinsone?" Fay queried.

De Vinsone nodded. "How you feelin' about this, ma'am?" he said, without emotion or expression.

"I agree with you." She felt an urge to look away from his eyes. They were unnerving, an experience she was unaccustomed to, but she did not look away.

Sergeant De Vinsone stroked his goatee. "What is it you'd like to be knowin', Lieutenant Commander?"

"How long have you known Sergeant Linn?"

"Almost three years, ma'am."

"Sergeant, I have a…" She paused, then said, "Please call me Fay."

He nodded.

"On the night of Paul Charma's death, did you see Sergeant Linn talking to a man in the club?"

"I did."

"Were they arguing?"

"I didn't notice. Simon has a lively personality. He always seems excited about somethin'." De Vinsone smiled. "In a good way. You understand."

"What were you doing at the time?"

"I was a-playin' pool with Sergeant Wu and two other gentlemen."

"Who were the two other men?"

"I don't know. The men said their names, but I don't recall what they were."

"What time did you and Sergeant Wu leave the club?"

"Twenty-three hundred hours, Fay."

"You seem definite about the time."

"We had a twenty-three-thirty ferry to catch. So, we were watchin' the time," De Vinsone responded.

"Sergeant, what is your present duty assignment?" Fay knew what his answer would be.

"That's classified."

"Training status then?" *Of course.*

Sergeant De Vinsone nodded.

Fay was done with Mr. Freeze. She sensed getting any information out of this pirate would be more challenging than prying an oyster out of its shell using only her fingernails. Nothing more would be learned from him. She glanced at her fingernails, then looked at De Vinsone and asked, "Sergeant, will you call me if you think of anything else?"

"Certainly," he said.

The expression sounded odd. Usually thrown out by people with enthusiasm, De Vinsone said it with determination—half promise, half threat. As she handed her business card to him, Fay said, "I have one more question, Sergeant." She tried her best to convey a warm smile. "Do you know a Major W. Irving?"

"I know W. Irving," he said with a chuckle.

Shocked would have best described how Fay felt at the moment. *Finally!* "You do?"

"He would be Washington Irving."

"The headless horseman guy?" Fay asked.

"Yeah…Ichabod Crane. I understand government operators," he explained, "find it convenient to use an alias from time to time. You might recall prisoners of war occasionally used that name when their captors forced them to sign confessions. That would be the same W. Irving you seek."

"Government operators find it convenient…" says *the biggest operator of them all*, Fay thought. She chuckled to herself, and then said, as she sank down into her chair, "Don't I feel like a fool. Of course, I do recall now."

De Vinsone's smile broadened. "W. Irving be him. To use a worn-out cliche, ma'am, he does not exist."

Fay thanked Sergeant De Vinsone again. As he left the room, she sank further down into her chair. She did not like the man, no doubt about it, perhaps because she thought she could tell a lot about a person based on the amount of warmth they exuded. Sergeant De Vinsone radiated as much warmth as a frozen Thanksgiving turkey.

Fay returned to her office. On seeing her, Pearce said, "Ma'am, I have a message for you. Captain Towsley would like to meet with you regardin' Sergeant Linn."

Fay looked at her watch. "Towsley wants to be briefed on the investigation. See if eight hundred hours tomorrow works for him." That would give her time to collect her thoughts and prepare a report. "Then come into my office. I'd like to bounce my thoughts off you."

"Aye, ma'am," Pearce chirped. "Be there in a second." She quickly picked up the phone. Shortly after, she entered Fay's office and sat down. "Eight hundred is fine with the Captain, ma'am," she reported.

Fay surveyed her assemblage of notes. "Help me collect my thoughts." Soon, she looked up and smiled. "I find it interesting a significant number of operators have congregated all in one place."

"Kinda like a black ops convention," Pearce quipped.

"Exactly. Except something's missing."

"A keynote speaker?"

Fay chuckled. "Precisely. Something Andrew Lawrence told me. He said he was a member of a team of six men. I presume Simon Linn knows Andrew Lawrence because, to Andrew, Paul Charma was a friend, and Simon spoke with Charma the night he died. I don't think Charma just happened to be at Jillian's on the same night as Simon Linn, Philip De Vinsone, and Peter Wu. It's too coincidental. My hunch is—"

"Excuse me, ma'am."

"—that Linn, De Vinsone, and Wu knew—" Fay continued.

"Ma'am…. hey," Pearce said, accompanied with a short, low whistle.

Fay looked up from her notes. "Did you say something?"

"Yes, ma'am. Will ya hold your horses there for a second?"

"What's that?"

"Will ya repeat those names?"

"You mean, Linn, Wu, Charma—"

Pearce interrupted, "Ma'am. The names with the first names."

"What are you driving at, JP?"

"Humor me." Pearce thought for a moment and then said, "Y'all remember 'The Saint?' Remember, ma'am, how he came up with his various aliases?"

"He used the names of the various saints. And—"

"Say the names."

Fay looked at her notes and read, "Simon, Philip, Peter, Paul, Andrew."

"Is it a coincidence, ma'am?"

"Could be? These are common male names." Fay thought for a moment, then rewrote the names on her notepad. "Could be saints? I'm lost. What are you driving at, JP?"

"Andrew Lawrence told you his platoon numbered twelve and he was a member of a team of six men."

"Yes, he did."

"Those names are five of Jesus's twelve disciples, if I remember correctly."

"It certainly fits. An astute observation, sailor. I am very impressed."

Pearce nodded and smiled. "I know you are, ma'am."

"If you are right, it would mean the five men are indeed linked. But more importantly, it means we do not even know their real names."

"Like stage names. Like actors use."

"Precisely, JP. And it means we have zilch."

"Bogus men, ma'am, with bogus service records. Are we back to square one?"

"Almost, but not entirely," Fay answered. "To finish my original thought, my hunch is Simon, Peter, and Philip must have known Paul Charma would expose a secret. They were at Jillian's that night to talk him out of it. We do not know if they were successful or not. Again, as we have discussed, someone else who did not want the secret told silenced Paul Charma."

Pearce nodded. "That's kind of what I thought. If there was someone named Judas somewhere in the mix, that's where I'd point my finger. If I count correctly, ma'am, there are only five men: Linn, De Vinsone, Wu, Lawrence, and Charma. We're still one can short of a six-pack."

Fay snickered.

"That's my point. Every team has a leader. In this case, an officer," Pearce explained.

"Like Major Irving?" Fay replied thoughtfully.

"Irving, or whatever his name is. Irving could have been the other man in the alley."

"The killer? But consider this," Fay said. "Paul was a valuable piece of Navy property. A million-dollar investment, when you stop to consider all of the training those SEALS go through."

"I see what ya mean, ma'am. It would be expensive to replace him. To kill him would be costly."

"There would have to be a very compelling reason for someone to want to execute him," Fay said. "An argument between Paul and Simon is not a compelling reason, given the circumstances. Otherwise, Simon would be in big trouble with whomever he reports to. And yet he doesn't seem to be."

"Yet, Sergeant Linn has a 'Get Out of Jail Free' card," Pearce said.

"Yes. The Navy knows why and how Paul died."

"Sanctioned?"

"More than likely."

"But why, ma'am, was Paul killed in such a demonstrative way? I mean, you'd think someone would just tag him and bag him and throw him in the trunk of a car. Take him to a wreckin' yard and then turn him and the car into scrap metal. Kind of like they did to Jimmy Hoffa."

Fay wondered where Pearce came up with some of her facts. She felt tempted to ask but decided it would be better to just let it go for the time being. "I wondered about that too," she continued. "Unless someone wanted to draw a certain amount of attention to his death. To set an example for others to see."

"Like leavin' a trail?"

"Accountants call it an audit trail. Paul was a man who lived his life in the shadows, a 'shadow warrior,' Towsley called him. But the way he died placed him center stage and in the spotlight."

"I see what ya mean."

"I do know my meeting with Andrew Lawrence the other night at the Pollywog was not an accident," Fay said. "And I would have never interviewed Wu and De Vinsone unless someone allowed it to happen."

"Admiral May?"

Fay nodded. "I did some checking on Admiral Brandon May, by the way."

"And?"

"Nada. There are several Admirals named May. When I tried to access their records, all were classified. And no one was named Brandon May."

"No surprise." Pearce pondered for a moment and then said, "Interestin'."

"Even more interesting, I did locate a V. B. May. A flag assigned to the Pentagon. His present assignment is classified, but his biography says he was, at one time, a Terminator."

"NCIS!?" Pearce's eyes widened in surprise. "You gotta be kiddin'!"

"His stint with the NCIS coincides with none other than our own Vern Towsley. I find it both interesting and coincidental," Fay remarked.

"Ya suppose Towsley knows May?" Pearce asked.

"I would imagine he does. Two officers serving in the same department at the same time."

"Towsley's the one who assigned y'all to this investigation. Do ya think it was at Admiral May's direction?"

"I do."

"But, ma'am, if they know what's goin' on, why don't they just tell you rather than put you through all of this cat-and-mouse, cloak-and-dagger bull crap? This is startin' to drive me nuts!"

"Look at me, JP. Anyone would be better qualified to investigate this homicide than me. Don't you see? THEY DON'T WANT THIS ONE SOLVED. It's supposed to disappear—like Paul Charma's corpse did," Fay emphasized.

"I suppose with human nature bein' what it is, if someone came out and told you outright what happened, handed it to y'all on a silver platter, so to speak, y'all would tend not to believe it. Or at least you'd be suspicious of it. But if you were led to the same information by little clues planted here and there and you discovered what happened on your own, then y'all would tend to believe it." Pearce sat back, apparently to mentally review what she had just said. She gave herself a confirming nod and said, "Yeah. That sounds right to me." She looked squarely at Fay and said, "Geez. Whadda ya gonna do, ma'am?"

"I'll tell ya what I'm gonna do," Fay said playfully. "I am gonna do my job—the very best way I know. No one ordered me not to investigate. As far as I know, I am supposed to investigate and then submit my recommendation to either continue the investigation or to terminate the investigation." She lowered her voice. "There's one more thing."

Pearce inched closer to Fay's desk to better hear the

confidential message and whispered, "What's that?"

"The U.S.S. *Nalon Vet*," Fay whispered.

"Now there's a ship that's made a serious dent in someone's black budget."

"Was it a coincidence the *Vet* showed up just in time for your so-called black ops convention? I think not. I noticed *Nalon Vet* left port no more than twenty-four hours after she arrived."

"A quick turn around," Pearce observed.

"Too quick. And the ship sailed without its captain."

"Yes. Egan Fletcher is still here."

"I found it curious, so I checked with the harbormaster for other sailings on the same day. As you know, Navy ships normally travel with support ships or battle groups. A supply ship, or an oiler, or ships in escort of a carrier."

"Were there any other ships, ma'am?"

"Not *a* ship. The U.S.S. *Jimmy Carter*."

"Mercy," Pearce gasped. "The spy sub? Another huge dent in the black budget. So, the spy sub and the spy ship are off to ports unknown at flank speed," she said thoughtfully. "Yeowzer."

"Yeowzer is right. Two of the most insidious vessels in the world headed for destinations unknown."

"Two pretty serious weapons, I'd say." Pearce wrinkled her brow. "Used to be, when I was small, a water balloon was considered to be a serious weapon." She shook her head. "The world sure has changed. What does it all mean, ma'am?"

Fay smiled. "You got me there." Her voice changed back to a normal speaking voice. "And I have a feeling I am going to be up half the night working on my recommendations. Why don't we squeeze in a workout this afternoon? Say, five-thirtyish?"

"Okay, but hold up, ma'am," Pearce whispered. "I got one more for y'all. James Rayzon."

"What?"

Chapter 17

Exercise and fitness rated high on Egan Fletcher's list of priorities. He tried to keep a regular workout schedule aboard ship, but his duties often took precedence. He would squeeze in a workout before his departure to South Korea. The Lord only knew when he would see a free weight room or treadmill again.

As he walked toward the locker rooms at the back of the fitness center, he was surprised to see Petty Officer Pearce sitting on a nearby mat, stretching. He made a slight course correction, pointed himself in her direction, and waved as he passed by. "Good evening, Miss Pearce," he called cheerfully.

She smiled and waved. Pointing over her shoulder with her thumb to the locker rooms, she said, "Fay is in the locker room, sir. She'll be out in a minute."

Egan grinned. "I wasn't looking for Faydra. I just stopped by to say hello to you. Have you been here long?"

She glanced at her watch. "Ten minutes, sir."

Egan smiled. "This is a gym. We're off duty. My name is Egan."

She nodded, blushed, and smiled again. Besides thanking Egan for the flowers, she did not seem to have much to say to him.

He recalled a conversation with Faydra regarding Pearce and her shyness around men. "I'm going to change. I'll see you in a few minutes," he said. He continued toward the locker rooms. Several minutes later, Egan emerged from the locker room and noticed Fay had joined Pearce. He again approached the women. "Would you two lovely ladies mind if a tired old man joined you?"

"Please do, sir," Fay replied coyly.

Egan smiled and surveyed the gym. "I'm ready to go," he announced as he turned his attention back to the women. Fay joined Egan for a workout while Pearce worked out alone.

"How old is your son?" Fay inquired.

"Kristian is twenty-one."

"You are very proud of him."

"He's a fine young man." He beamed. "There's a lot of his mother in him."

"You miss her. Eight years is a long time."

"Kristin died eight years ago next month."

"Kristian is named for his mother?"

"It was her idea," Egan explained. "Kristian was one of the *H.M.S. Bounty's* crew, Fletcher Christian. She reversed the name."

"I like it."

"She'd be proud of him if she could see him today," he said. "With him at the university and me at sea, I don't see my son as often as I'd like."

"Will he follow his father's footsteps into the Navy?" Fay wondered.

"He doesn't seem to have an interest in the Navy. He's got his feet firmly planted on *terra firma*."

"How so?"

Egan chuckled and shook his head. "When he was twelve or thirteen years old, I was talking with him about career opportunities. We were at the airport at the time, and a jet was taking off. You know the racket they make. I said, 'Hey Kris, how about a career as an airline pilot?' He replied, 'No way, Dad. Those things aren't safe.' I started my Navy career as an aviator; I suspect his mother had a hand developing his thinking along those lines. She was deathly afraid I'd go flying one day and never return. So, I gave up flying and went to sea."

"And you told your son air travel is safer than driving a car?"

"I told him, but it didn't seem to matter to him."

"How did he take his mother's death? I ask because I lost my mother at a young age as well," Fay continued.

"Naturally, it was very hard on him. I took a two-month leave. He finally did adjust." Egan looked away from Fay, searching the floor for nothing of consequence. He grew solemn. "There was a time when he wouldn't let me out of his sight. I suppose he was afraid I'd leave him too." He saw the sympathy in her eyes when he turned his gaze back toward her. "Oh, don't feel sorry for me," he said. "As I said, I have a great life. It can get lonely from time to time. But I have a woman in my life. She is wonderful and gives me great peace of mind."

"Who is the lucky gal?"

"Pacific, Atlantic, there are so many," he said, smiling again. "I learned some years ago the female human is a jealous creature. The sea can show her rage, but never jealousy. If I have to choose, I choose the sea."

"I have known that about sailors. It is easy to understand. There are not many women who are willing to share their man with another woman." Fay was silent for a moment and then asked, "Do you miss flying?"

"Very much. It was my second love, next to my family. Tell me about you, Faydra."

"What would you like to know?"

"Where are you from?"

"Pensacola, until I attended Brigham Young University. I received my *Juris Doctor* from Texas. I was married to a sailor for a short time. A Navy lawyer like myself—but as I said before, it did not work out. No kids. But I love children. Pets, not so much. Like Kristian, my mother died—I was twenty at the time."

"At any age, it's horrible to lose a parent."

A single tear raced down her cheek. Fay stopped its progress with a swipe of the back of her hand. "Dad was driving. He lost control of the car; the car veered off the interstate and struck a tree. The crash killed my mother; my sister was badly injured. Dad, to this day, has not forgiven himself."

"I'm sorry."

"About six years ago, the guilt and the loneliness got to Dad, and he started drinking." It was Fay's turn to turn away. "I told him if he did not stop drinking, I would not speak to him until he did."

"Did he stop?"

She cleared her throat. "I have not spoken to Dad since, and I have not forgiven him for what he did to our family."

"Then he's lost a daughter as well."

"He did, but he made his choice. It's a shame, however. I think it's a pretty crummy trade. I miss him very much. He is one of the most important people in my life. I think about him every day." Fay looked at Egan. "I love the great man he was, not the drunk he has become. Well! What a happy conversation we are having," Fay said. "Forgive me. I've been rambling. Do you feel like running?"

He agreed. They moved to two vacant treadmills.

"So, who are the other important people in your life?" Egan asked.

"My bubba and sissy. My brother is a nurse; he lives in Florida."

"Is there a special man in your life?"

"For a while, I was serious about an attorney in Seattle. The relationship is cooling off, however. His name is Ford."

Egan turned his gaze toward Pearce. "How about Miss Pearce? You seem very close to her."

Fay responded with a puzzled look on her face. "I love her more than anything in this world. By the way," she said, lightly touching his arm, "the flowers were wonderful. You made her entire week. Thank you so very much."

"That's nice to hear. It seemed to be the right thing to do at the time. I've been watching Pearce lift weights. She's a powerful woman."

"Yes, she is strong," Fay agreed. "With her weight training and martial arts skills, she seems almost superhuman to me. She was at one time a Florida State amateur kickboxing champion. Those abnormally long legs were registered with the Department of Revenue and Taxation as a lethal weapon. Now she is military, she no longer needs to register."

"Now, wait a minute. I recall reading somewhere your sister was a kickboxing champion?"

Fay laughed. "Okay, now I know why you had a puzzled look on your face a few minutes ago. JP is my sister, Egan! My sissy. I thought you knew."

"I didn't realize until just now. That little kid I would see on television? Your sister? No kidding!"

"I would have mentioned it if I thought you didn't know. I guess I assume everyone knows JP and I are sisters."

"How did you manage to have your sister work under you?"

"Sometimes, being the daughters of a former Commander-in-Chief has its privileges. To make it simple, JP reports to Admiral Wallace. I report to Vern Towsley," Fay explained.

"I've been a bit dense these past few days. I didn't make the connection, that's all. How is it JP's last name is Pearce and not Green?"

"You may recall my parents adopted a baby girl near the end of my dad's first term in office," Fay replied.

"I recall that."

"The official story was the President and the First Lady wanted more children. For my mother, childbirth was out of the question. My parents adopted JP into the first family. She was two years old at the time. To honor her natural mother, she recently changed her name to her mother's family name."

"I remember reading about it in the news," he said.

"The media bought the story about the adoption. The truth was," Fay divulged, "my dad had fathered an illegitimate child. The administration knew if my dad hoped to see a second term in the White House, the American public—and the Democrats for that matter—could never know the truth. So, to avoid a scandal, they concocted the adoption story. And to this day, the ploy has worked. I felt and still do feel very bad for my mom. To her credit, she accepted JP into our home and our family as if she were her daughter. Even more amazing, Mom forgave my father for his indiscretion. I wouldn't have."

"I had no idea," Egan said.

"Her biological mother, Candice Pearce, died when JP was two, hence the adoption. At least my dad did the right thing. Later, Dad told JP the true story. For a time, she was known as J. Green-Pearce. Soon, it dawned on her that her new name sounded like an environmental group, and she dropped the Green."

"Green-Pearce," Egan thoughtfully repeated, then chuckled.

The workout ended, and none too soon, as far as Egan was concerned.

Fay patted a small amount of perspiration from her brow with a towel. "We had a good workout," she huffed. "Let's do this again!"

"I don't know, Faydra," he puffed. "I must admit I find it difficult to keep up with you. For many different reasons."

She laughed. "Do you have time for a bite to eat? My treat."

"I'm sorry. Forgive me; I have a long drive home ahead of me. And I have to pack."

"Packing?"

"I'm flying tomorrow afternoon. Can I have a rain check?"

"Sure. Some other time."

Egan said goodbye to Fay. As he walked toward the locker room, he stopped to chat with Pearce for a moment. Several times, she laughed at his humor. Several times, he laughed at her humor. He then wished her well, patted her on the shoulder, and disappeared into the locker room.

Chapter 18

Fay had been sleeping for little more than an hour when she was awakened by the ringing of her cell phone. With her face buried deep into a large soft pillow, her left arm flailed for the cell. She located it on the fourth ring. "Faydra Green," she croaked into the mouthpiece.

"I'm sorry to wake you," the familiar voice said. "Can we talk?"

"Of course," she whispered. The caller now had her undivided attention. "Where? When?"

"Right now," the voice replied. "I'm outside."

Many people would have been irritated to be awakened, and had it been someone other than Vern Towsley, Fay would have been annoyed as well. She cleared her throat—and her head. "Give me a moment." She clicked off the phone.

She sighed as she threw off the warm covers and sprang from her bed. She again found herself fumbling in the dark, this time searching the bathroom wall for the light switch she knew must be there. It seemed to move around on the wall just to annoy her. She was sure of it. Finally locating the switch, she flipped the light on. The light stung her eyes for an instant as her dilated pupils adjusted to the light's harsh glare. *When will I learn not to look directly at the light to confirm it has come on?* She hastily brushed her hair, added a quick dab of makeup to her eyes and lips, brushed her teeth, and returned to her bedroom to grab a jogging suit to cover her now-chilled body.

Fay hopped on one leg through the darkened condo in response to the rapping sound coming from her entry door, struggling between hops to pull the pants on. By the final hop, she managed to tug the last leg on, only to find herself stumbling headfirst into the door. With a resounding "thump," her head and protective forearm greeted the door. Rubbing her forehead, she peeked through the peephole to confirm it was indeed Captain Towsley at the door.

A rush of cold sea air blasted her face as she swung open the door. "Hurry, Vern," she said. "Get in here before you freeze your butt off."

"Thanks, Faydra," he said, brushing a few droplets of rain from the shoulders of his raincoat. He stepped through the doorway and into the welcome of the warm home. He looked thankful to be in a more hospitable environment. "What was the bump I heard?" he asked with a look of mild concern.

"Things that go bump in the night, sir. You heard my head arriving at the door before the rest of me."

Towsley shook his head and chuckled. "Are you all, right?"

She, still rubbing her forehead, said, "I'm fine."

"I do believe winter is here." Changing the subject, he said, "I'm sorry to disturb you at this hour, but I have a problem." He removed his overcoat.

Fay took Vern's coat and, after draping it carefully over the back of a nearby chair, walked to her kitchen. She, of course, wondered what urgent occurrence had brought him to her home at two-forty-five in the morning. He could not be that anxious for her briefing on the Charma investigation? But hospitality was always her first and foremost concern—Southern hospitality was an ingrained habit. "Please, Vern. Make yourself at home. I will put on a pot of my favorite brand of coffee."

Towsley laughed. "Do you own any stock in that coffee company yet?"

"I should!" she called from the kitchen. "I cannot function without a cup of this stuff. There is no doubt in my mind I am a caffeine addict. According to you, anyway. I am going to open an espresso store someday," she added. "Coffee is considered breakfast to some people."

He again laughed. "Faydra Green included. Although, in your case, I'd suspect coffee drinking to be a religious belief." His comment drew a giggle from the kitchen.

"Make yourself comfortable, boss. I will be with you pronto."

Captain Towsley responded to his subordinate's direct order by sitting down on her living room sofa. Barnacle Bill's feline curiosity must have finally prodded him from his resting place at the foot of Fay's bed to join in the conversation. She watched from the kitchen as the cat made himself busy by sniffing Vern's fingers, rubbing his head on Vern's arm, and generally making a pest of himself. Vern tried to discreetly shoo the animal away, to no avail.

Fay returned with two steaming mugs of coffee. Placing one of the cups on the coffee table in front of the captain, she sat next to him. "Billy!" she barked as she swatted at the cat, "leave Vern alone; that is an order, Mister!" With an indignant swish of his tail, Billy scurried away. She smiled, "Sorry, sir." She settled in, tucking her cold and bare feet up under her legs. "Okay, I'm ready to listen."

"Fay, we were going to meet later this morning regarding your investigation. Something has come up, and I need to know your finding." She started to get up off the sofa, but he stopped her. "We can go over your report later. Tell me verbally your recommendations."

"In a nutshell, I recommend additional investigation in the matter of Paul Charma's death. Regarding Marine Master Sergeant Simon Linn, I recommend no further investigation. My reasons for both recommendations are detailed in my report."

"Thank you, Lieutenant Commander. I look forward to reviewing your report."

"I would like your permission, sir, to conduct the investigation into the death of Petty Officer Charma."

"That's what I wanted to talk to you about. I'm going to assign Rollie to the investigation."

Her face reflected the instant shock and anger she felt. "Rollie? But, sir, I—"

"Stand down, Lieutenant Commander," he said firmly.

Fay submissively directed her gaze down toward the floor and softly said, "Aye, aye, sir." There was an uncomfortable silence for a moment. She lifted her gaze to meet Vern's. "With all due respect, sir…" she began forcefully.

Her captain remained silent. Fay continued. "I do respect and support the concepts of the need-to-know doctrine, and I do understand I was assigned to conduct a preliminary investigation into the death of Paul Charma. But sir, I can't help feel I'm getting jacked around, and sir, I'm madder than a wet hen right now.

Excuse me. That, sir, was an unfortunate choice of words. I meant to say, I am damned pissed off… sir." She knew he would understand. He would know full well how she must feel.

Vern said, "Admiral Wallace called me at home this evening to tell me his wife has suffered a heart attack."

"Vern! Amy's not—"

"Amy's fine," he said. "This does present a problem, however."

Fay dropped her hands into her lap and flashed a sheepish grin. "A problem?"

Vern seemed stern. "Several weeks ago, a North Korean vessel sank the frigate, *Jonathan Carr*. The *Carr* was in North Korean territorial waters. Fortunately—or unfortunately—one life was lost." He sipped on his coffee. "I don't have a lot of details, but I do know I need your help."

She frowned. "I will do whatever I can. It's strange I did not hear about this, though."

"The governments of North Korea and the United States have managed to keep a lid on this, so far."

"So, we do not have an incident then?"

"Not yet."

She could feel the apprehension in Captain Towsley's voice. He was stalling.

Vern finished his coffee and then said, "I was given express permission by Admiral Wallace to brief you on this."

"More coffee, sir?"

"No. I'm fine. Thanks."

"Well then, I'm confused. How are we involved?" Fay asked.

"Let me start at the beginning." Vern paused to

loosen his necktie.

"Please, sir, make yourself comfortable. Where is your pipe?"

"In my car. Why?"

Fay held out her right hand, palm up. "Give me your car keys. I'll get it for you."

"Thank you," he said, "but I don't plan on staying long." Vern continued speaking. "The *Carr* was indeed in North Korea's territorial waters."

"Was she off course?"

"She had permission to be there."

"How odd. Then why did the North Koreans sink her?"

He shrugged his shoulders. "I suppose the captain of the *Carr* knows why, as do President Ross and the North Korean government. What I do know is I need your help." He frowned. "President Ross has sent the *Nalon Vet* to Chinhae, South Korea."

So that's where the Vet and Egan Fletcher were off to, she thought. Fay sat for a moment, looking at Vern.

He sighed.

Time to quit beating around the bush. "Captain, you have a specific reason for being here this morning," Fay prompted.

Vern took a deep breath, paused, and then said, "Admiral Wallace was scheduled to attend an inquiry in Chinhae related to the sinking of the *Carr*. For some reason, the inquiry was postponed until next week. With Amy in the hospital, Wallace is unable to attend the inquiry. He'd like you to attend in his place."

Beyond the look of doubt and disbelief evident in her expression, it was Fay's turn to remain silent.

"I can understand your concern, Fay, but you are a

natural for this assignment," Vern insisted. "You have a degree in international law. Your father was highly respected by all the Asian governments. I'm sure Wallace realizes there are sound diplomatic reasons to have you there in his place."

"I'm sure he does. When do I leave?"

"The day after tomorrow. You'll fly commercial air to Seoul, stay overnight in Seoul, and then fly military air to Chinhae."

"And Miss Pearce?"

Vern nodded. "She and Petty Officer Winslow will accompany you."

This was the first good news Fay had heard. A smile came to her face.

"Now, Lieutenant Commander Green," he said in a different tone of voice. "We have one piece of unfinished business to discuss. We are putting the Charma investigation to rest, here and now."

She gazed intently at Vern.

"I've been as upfront with you as I am allowed to be. You have done your job, and now it's time to let it go. Rollie will investigate. The Cold Case Squad is on its way to Bremerton from NCIS HQ. You and I will pray— from the sidelines—that those two entities will somehow manage to do what's right for Paul Charma."

Fay said, "Will you excuse me for a minute? The coffee is taking its toll on my kidneys. Be right back." When she returned, she said, "You know, I was thinking…" She stopped when she realized the tired captain had fallen asleep.

She shrugged her shoulders and retreated to her bedroom to retrieve a pillow and blanket. Gently, she eased her captain's head onto the pillow and covered him with the blanket. She snapped off the living room light as she passed by the switch.

Fay curled her lanky frame back under the chilled sheets. Soon, her thoughts turned to the *Jonathan Carr.* Her inquisitive mind would not let her sleep. *What was the Carr doing in North Korean waters? Why did the Koreans sink her? And why, if the crew was given time to abandon ship, was even a single life lost?* Finally, she fell asleep, long before she had an answer to any of her many questions.

It was still early the same morning when Fay silently pulled the entry door of her condominium shut. A chilly Pacific Northwest morning greeted her with a light dusting of snow. She had left Captain Towsley sleeping peacefully, and she could not help but chuckle when she had noticed Mr. Bill snuggled under the captain's protective arm. She had thought to place an alarm near him, set for 08:15. It would give him plenty of time to wake, eat the breakfast she had left in the microwave for him, and still allow him time to get to the office by a respectable 09:00.

One mile from the Navy Yard's main gate, Fay noticed the glare of flashing red-and-blue lights in her rearview mirror. "Geez," she sighed and lightly pounded on the steering wheel with her fist as she slowed her car and guided it to the side of the road. A Washington State Patrol trooper approached. She lowered the window while searching for her driver's license, insurance, and car registration.

"Good morning, Miss." The trooper brought his right hand to the brim of his hat. "How are you this morning." His greeting sounding more like a comment than a question.

"Fine, officer, thank you." She handed him the three certificates.

"I stopped you this morning," he said, not taking his gaze from her, "because you were traveling in a thirty-five-mile-per-hour speed zone more than fifty miles per hour."

"I have to confess," she said, slightly embarrassed, "I was not paying attention, officer. I guess I have a lot on my mind this morning." This Navy lawyer knew a polite and courteous confession often brought leniency in this roadside court of law.

The trooper, who had not lost his courteous smile throughout the exchange, glanced at her license and said, "I'm going back to my car, Miss Green, to run a check. I'll be back in a moment." The trooper wheeled around and returned to his car.

Five minutes later, he was back with her documents in hand. "I ran a check; your driving record is clean." He handed the documents back to her. "If I asked you nicely to be cautious, can I let you go this time? I'm not going to issue a citation."

Fay nodded. "I will be cautious."

The trooper smiled and said, "Have a nice day, Lieutenant Commander Green."

Fay returned the smile. The trooper returned to this car. She restarted her car and wondered (every incident and occurrence made her wonder): *Why is this my lucky day? What did I do to deserve this? Is it because I'm a woman? Or an officer in the U.S. Navy? Or? ...* She shut off the roadster's engine.

After checking the rearview mirror for oncoming cars, she opened the car's door and got out. She purposely walked back to the State Patrol car. She only stumbled once - heels had never been her strong suit - and stood next to the driver's window.

The trooper, who had been jotting down a note, looked up and lowered the window. "Can I help you?" the state trooper asked.

Fay held out her right hand. "I want my citation," she said politely and wiggled her fingers in a demanding manner.

"I beg your pardon?" the astonished trooper replied.

"My citation, sir. I want my citation." She then added, "Please." She thought she could read the look on his face; it seemed to convey, *Are you nuts, lady?* She was nuts; she would attest to it—his assessment was fair.

"Please return to your car, ma'am."

Fay returned to her car, slipping on a patch of ice en route, and waited. The trooper returned to her car and handed the ticket to her. "Please sign here, Miss Green," he said and pointed to the spot for her to sign.

She signed the citation, then handed it and the trooper's pen back to him. "Thank you, sir."

"Have a good day, ma'am. And please drive safely," he added. "The roads are slick this morning." He brought his right hand to the brim of his hat, nodded, and returned to his car.

****

Later that morning in Captain Towsley's office, Fay was peering through the window behind the captain's desk. "Looks like a great day. Clear, crisp," she said.

Vern turned slightly to confirm her observation, turned back, and reflected, "It's been a while since you and I spent a day on the golf course."

"Last time was when we caddied for the enlisted people at the enlisted people's golf tournament."

"I recall the Admiral's player won the tournament. I still think there was some sloppy scorekeeping going on there," Vern said.

"Well, sir, he is the Admiral." She cleared her throat. "Sir, I stopped by for a specific reason."

"Of course, you did." Vern knew Faydra Green always had a specific reason for whatever she said or did. "What can I do for you?"

"I plan on taking leave after this business is done in Korea. Do you recall the beach house on the Hood Canal I purchased last summer?"

"The one that occupied every one of your weekends?"

"Yes, sir," she laughed. "I did bust my butt getting the place whipped into shape, I must admit. I was looking forward to spending some time there. It is so peaceful. I discovered your favorite writer wrote some of his mysteries just up the beach from my place."

"My favorite writer?" Towsley listened patiently while his irrepressible charge beat her way around the proverbial bush. This was not about leaves of absence or vacation spots at all.

"Erle Stanley Gardner."

His eyes lit up. "That favorite writer: my old friend, Perry Mason." He chuckled. "Of course."

"I did enjoy the Labor Day weekend there," Fay said, with a fond look in her eyes. "I had a picnic of clams and oysters. I think the highlight for me was the scuba dive I took. Huge octopus, sir." She demonstrated the creature's estimated size by stretching her arms wide. "The largest in the world, I understand, live in the waters of the Hood Canal and the neighboring waters of Puget Sound."

Vern surveyed the distance between her two outstretched arms. "I recall Jacques Cousteau telling me that via an animal-related TV program a while back," he said. "I've also heard them referred to as devilfish," he added.

"*Capitaine Cousteau était un grand homme, monsieur.*" Fay dropped her arms—*time to get to the point.* With a hopeful look on her face, she said, "Sir, I am concerned about Mr. Bill. No telling how long we will be in Korea."

"I'd be happy to have your cat as a houseguest while you're in Korea."

"Thank you, sir." She beamed. "I will send you an e-card. I know the two of you will get along just fine." She knew he hated the cat, but he was the only one she trusted with her kitty. The cat seemed to like Vern. At least she hoped so. And, if the truth were to be known, she secretly hoped he would become so attached he would take ownership of the little pest.

"I think your cat and I have come to terms," he said. "I'll be glad to care for the little fellow while you're gone."

Towsley had repeated himself. *He must be trying to convince himself he wouldn't mind having the cat for a guest.* "Sir, not to change the subject, and if you do not mind me asking, you do not seem like your old self today. Are you feeling okay?" Fay asked.

"No, but thanks for asking. I've felt a little off the mark all morning." He furled his eyebrows momentarily as if to take a quick internal assessment. "I don't know what it is, though."

Recalling Admiral Wallace's wife Amy's recent heart attack, Fay cautiously asked, "Sir, have you been taking care of your heart—you know—exercising?"

"Yes, I have," he assured her. "You know, my mother worries a lot about me. Don't you start on me, too."

Fay chuckled. She could visualize a little old woman shaking her finger at the tall silver-haired captain, then leading him by the ear to the medicine cabinet for a dose of cod liver oil. Fay smiled. "Take care of yourself, Vern. There is a virus going around."

Chapter 19

Fay peered through the jet's small rectangular window. "Thank goodness they are on time," she said.

"Calm down, Fayzie," Pearce said. "Everything will go just fine!"

Not until the sleek red, white and blue jet began its takeoff run did Fay relax. "I don't know what to think. One moment I feel excited about this trip. The next moment, I feel deep trepidation."

"You act like you've never flown before," Pearce said. "Everything will be peachy. Want me to see if the flight attendant will fetch y'all a relaxing drug?"

Fay answered, "It's not the flying that's bothering me. It's everything else that's happened." She smiled. "I will be fine. Hope I haven't forgotten anything. I feel like I have forgotten something."

"Ma'am, I have a question."

"Fire away."

"Excuse me for being noisy. What is the story behind the bump on your forehead?"

Fay laughed. "I ran into a door."

"I can see there's no hope for y'all. I just hope I don't have to listen to this for the next eleven hours and thirty-five minutes."

"You've got it down to the minutes?" Fay asked.

"That's what Winslow said."

Fay settled back into the spacious business-class

seat.

Pearce turned to Winslow. "She ran into a door," Pearce reported. Then she turned back to Fay and asked, "Every time I fly, I think of Bart Hay. Y'all remember him?"

"That arrogant and egotistical good ol' boy Texan Secret Service pilot?"

"Yes."

"I can't say I do recall him."

Pearce snickered. "Kind of liked him, huh?"

"He was handsome; I'll give him that," Fay said, pretending to sound disinterested.

"I see. Excuse me. I'm dyin' to hear how your dinner with Ford went the other night. Did y'all end it?" Pearce asked.

"Yes and no." Fay sighed. "My plan was to end it, but you know as well as I do Ford is a brilliant man. He must have sensed what I was up to."

"What happened?"

"He is such a gentleman." Fay snatched a handkerchief from the pocket of her blouse and dabbed at the corner of her left eye, then softly blew her nose. She chuckled and sighed. "He dumped me before I had a chance to tell him."

"So, he took ya off the hook, and now it's over. Are ya feelin' pretty rotten about it?"

"Yeah. And I feel pretty good about it, too," Fay replied.

It was well into the evening when Flight 199 touched down at Incheon International Airport, five minutes ahead of schedule. The trio had traveled for fifteen weary hours. Fay watched the runway lights flash past her window. The jetliner slowed to its usual taxi speed and made its way from the runway to the passenger terminal. Fay thought of nothing of consequence as she sat, mesmerized by the evenly spaced, uniform lights parading by the window, one after another, seemingly never-ending.

The jet came to a halt. Passengers rose from their seats and scrambled for their carry-on luggage stowed in the overhead bins. Fay stood and retrieved her carry-on bag and sat again while she waited until the last passenger had trickled through the cabin door. Pearce and Winslow followed suit.

When they reached the exit, a cheerful flight attendant stationed there said, "Good evening! Thank you for flying our airline!" He continued, "It was an honor to have two celebrities aboard today. Your father has always been sort of a hero of mine. Please give your father my regards."

Fay did not realize she and Pearce had even been recognized. It was not particularly a hard thing to do. They looked much the same now as they did when President Green served in office. "I will do that! We very much enjoyed the service!" Fay replied as she began her exit through the jetway and into the terminal building.

Not wanting to take time to search for her eyeglasses, Fay opted to instead to squint. Looking for a big sign that would direct them to the customs and baggage claim areas, she declared, "I should put my eyeglasses on. Perhaps it would help."

"I suspect," Pearce commented, pointing toward what appeared to Fay as a green blur, "the man in the Army camos may know. He's holdin' up a little sign that says, 'Lieutenant Commander Green' on it." She then added, "You should get corrective eye surgery."

"A good indication he may know. Good work." With that said, Fay picked up her carry-on and marched toward the green blur.

The man dressed in a South Korean Army uniform smiled at the approaching trio and asked, "Lieutenant Commander Green? Petty Officers Pearce and Winslow?"

Fay returned the smile. "It's us." Once again, she set her carry-on down.

"Thank you! I thought I had missed you," he said. "I'm Major Jangho Kim. I represent the Republic of Korea Armed Forces. Welcome!" Kim extended his hand.

Fay firmly shook his hand and then introduced herself, Winslow and Pearce.

"I'm here to escort you to your hotel, Lieutenant Commander. Please, come with me," Kim stated.

"Thanks," Fay replied.

"We'll process you through customs. I have a car waiting."

"What service, Mr. Kim," Fay said. "I did not know we would have someone to greet us."

Kim offered to carry a few pieces of their luggage. "Please, Lieutenant Commander, call me Jangho."

Shortly after, they arrived at customs. The area was teeming with hundreds of passengers from numerous flights; most of the travelers were pushing, shoving, and maneuvering their travel-weary bodies through the mass of humanity. There were swarms of people, each impatiently waiting for a turn to be processed through South Korean customs.

The trio retrieved their suitcases from the baggage carousel. Major Kim pointed to a door at the right side of the massive customs area. "This way." Standing near the door was a military policeman, who saluted as the four people approached. Kim returned the salute, and the MP opened the door.

"This is a special customs area set up to process armed forces personnel," Kim explained. "This will be much quicker than waiting in the other lines."

Major Kim was correct. Fay saw several customs agents milling around and not one soul in line. The customs agents stopped chatting with one another and crewed their stations as the four approached them.

"Good evening, welcome to the Republic of Korea," an agent greeted Fay when she arrived at her station. "May I have your ticket and passport, please?" The agent smiled and extended her a hand.

Fay released her grip on the handle of her suitcase. The suitcase struck the floor with a loud thump. She pulled the strap of her pocketbook off her shoulder, opened it, removed her passport and concealed weapon permit, and then handed the documents to the customs agent. Although the unloaded weapon was packed in her checked suitcase, she knew airport people tended to get twitchy when they spotted a gun on airport property.

Fay pointed at her suitcase. "I have an unloaded weapon in my suitcase."

The customs agent, giving no indication her declaration concerned her, took Fay's permit and passport. She might have looked at Fay's documents, but it did not seem like it to Fay. The agent returned Fay's documents. The agent did not acknowledge the concealed weapon permit. "Miss Green, are your anthrax inoculations current?"

"I had my last booster three months ago," Fay

said. *Anthrax?* she thought.

"Thank you, Lieutenant Commander Green." The agent glanced at Fay's suitcase. "Your luggage, please."

Fay returned her pocketbook to its place on her left shoulder, then wrestled her suitcase onto the low counter that ran between her and the agent.

"No. I meant for you not to forget your luggage, ma'am." The agent smiled and turned her attention toward a group of Air Force personnel who entered the customs area. "Good evening, welcome to the Republic of Korea," she said, once again.

Fay retrieved her suitcase and rejoined Jangho near the room's exit. "That's it? I'm done?" She truly believed her possessing the derringer would have invited at least a search.

"You come here with high recommendations, Fay. No need for the formalities."

While Fay cleared customs unscathed, Winslow ran afoul of the process. It was discovered his anthrax boosters were not current. He was led through a side door for a date with the public health officer. Several minutes later, he reemerged through the door with a smile on his face and an up-to-date shot record in his hand. "My anthrax booster lapsed," he informed Fay.

"Anthrax?" Pierce whispered as she passed by Fay on her way to the waiting car.

During the drive from the airport to the Park Hyatt Seoul, Fay learned Major Kim was a South Korean Army interpreter. *This, more than likely,* she privately speculated, *means he is firmly connected with a South Korean Army intelligence unit. Or with the South Korean equivalent of the CIA, known worldwide as the KCIA.* Major Kim, a Korean, possessed a warm and infectious smile. She sensed Kim was a kind and generous man - much like a happy and contented great white shark.

A light rain was falling when the army staff car arrived at the hotel. A valet promptly opened the rear passenger door. All four passengers emerged from the car into the cold night air and scurried into the hotel lobby. At the same time, the bell captain retrieved their luggage.

The Park Hyatt Seoul was grand indeed. "How elegant," Pearce remarked, her mouth agape. She almost fell over backward as her head lifted to view the top of the lobby's ornate four-story high ceiling.

Fay went to the front desk to register. The desk clerk retrieved her room key card and a message. She accepted both, thanking the gentleman for his hospitality, and turned to Jangho. "Well, Jangho, we are off to our rooms. Will we see you later on?"

"I'm staying at the hotel for a few days—room nineteen-forty-six. Please call me if you need anything. I am at your disposal."

"I will, Major. Will you join us for breakfast? Say, nine?"

"That would be enjoyable. Nine is fine."

The trio's eighteenth-floor adjoining rooms were spacious and modern. After tipping each of the four bellmen who had comprised their entourage to the room, Fay quickly settled in. First kicking off her shoes and unpacking, she reclined on her bed and opened the envelope she was been given at the front desk. "It's from Captain Towsley," she called to Pearce through the open door separating the two rooms. "He wants me to call him ASAP."

Pearce entered through the door, smiled, and then sat down at a desk near the window. As she perused the various pamphlets adorning the desk, she remarked, "Says here room service is available twenty-four hours a day. Gosh, I'm hungry." She rubbed her stomach. "Oh! Oh! There are eight restaurants in the hotel. Do ya want to hear about them?" She looked at Fay, then declared, "Of course you do."

"Of course, I do," Fay said in unison.

"There's the 'Akasaka,' noted for its sushi," she wrinkled her nose. "Yuck. And teppanyaki, whatever that is. Freeze-dried monkfish, I bet. Anyway, 'The Chinese' for Cantonese, Szechuan, and dim sum. 'The Paris' for European dishes. 'The Terrace' for international cuisine. I thought European and international was the same thing? And there is the 'Gut Bomb' for twenty-four-hour room service. How many nights are we gonna be here, anyway?"

Fay laughed. "There's one called the 'Gut Bomb?' What the hell!?"

Pearce flipped the pamphlet back onto the desk and sprawled back into the chair. "This is going to be great! And I was just kidding about the 'Gut Bomb' place. Anyway, all's I know is we are livin' in high cotton this week!"

"Before y'all and your cotton start eating your way across the world, let me give Towsley a call. Let's see." Fay put her finger to her cheek and frowned. "I'd say it's about six in the morning in Bremerton." A smirk crossed her face. She had not forgotten her early morning awakening from Captain Towsley several days prior.

It only took a few moments for the connection to go through to Towsley's home. "Hello," the barely audible voice said.

"Captain Towsley? Is that you?"

"Uh-huh."

"Good morning, sir. I am in Seoul," Fay said. "I got your message. You asked me to call you ASAP."

"No! No! it's fine, but thanks for calling, Faydra." He coughed.

"Are you not feeling well, sir?"

"I have the virus hex you put on me." He sounded like he was clamping his nose shut with his fingers while at the same time lying on a bed of nails. He continued, "Admiral Wallace asked me to tell you how grateful he is you volunteered to fill in for him at the inquiry." Again, Vern coughed.

"Not a problem, sir. And Amy? How is she?"

"Amy is resting at home and doing fine. You must be exhausted. I'll let you get to bed. Goodnight, Fay. And stay in touch."

She wished him the same and then returned the phone receiver to its cradle.

Chapter 20

Heavy traffic delayed the trio's arrival at Gimpo International Airport for a 17:00 hours flight to Chinhae. The South Korean Army staff car drove up to the waiting, unmarked *C-40A Clipper* U.S. military personnel jet. The sonic whir emitting from the jet's twin turbine engines, the flashing red lights atop and beneath the jet's fuselage, and the smell of kerosene made Fay realize had she been one minute later, they might have left without her and her companions.

The trio boarded through the forward passenger door, noting three other passengers—two admirals and a captain - seated near the aircraft's rear. Fay offered an apologetic grin in their direction. She heard the passenger door thump shut as she hastily made her way to a nearby seat and sat down.

Within moments, the jet rolled forward. Fay watched through the small window while they taxied to a nearby runway, then paused as an Aeroflot crossed in front of them. Shortly after, the jet moved forward again and quickly turned onto the runway. The jet's twin engines roared to life. The plane's rapid acceleration pressed her back into her seat. The plane lifted from the ground and screamed into the evening twilight at a steep angle. Not long after, it banked sharply to the right. She found herself looking through the window, straight down at the ground.

The twisting and turning motion, combined with her not having a reference point, left her disoriented. It felt as if they were slipping back toward the ground. Fay clamped her hands around the armrests. "Mercy!" she whispered to Winslow, sitting next to her, who appeared to be asleep. "You prayin' or sleeping, Mister Winslow?"

A slight smile formed on his lips. "I'm savoring the moment, ma'am?"

The jet continued to bank for what seemed to be a three hundred sixty-degree turn on its wingtip before the pilot snapped the plane back to level flight.

Once the plane regained its stability, Fay felt compelled to introduce herself to the other passengers and apologize for her late arrival. She took a deep breath, pried her fingers from the armrests, muttered, "Well, here goes nothing," unbuckled her seat belt, and emerged from her seat with a gracious smile on her face. She assertively made her way to the back of the plane to greet her fellow passengers.

The two admirals were seated next to one another, chatting. "Good evening, sirs," Fay said, crisply extending her hand toward the admiral nearest her. "I'm Faydra Green." A genuine smile and a beautiful set of white teeth worked wonders in awkward situations such as these. "I wish to apologize to you for our late arrival. The traffic was terrible. We—"

"No need to apologize, Lieutenant Commander," one of the men assured her. "I'm Quentin Morton, and this is Brandon May." Morton smiled and extended his hand. May did likewise. Fay shook each man's hand, and then Admiral Morton spoke, "I think we can forgive a late arrival here and there, Lieutenant Commander.

We're all busy people who run late from time to time."

"Enjoy the flight, Miss Green," May said. "Glad to have you aboard."

"Why, thank you, kind sir. It has been a pleasure meeting you." She smiled then proceeded along the aisle to greet the captain. Once again, she extended her hand. "Good evenin', Captain," she said. "I'm Faydra Green, JAG Corps."

He smiled. As he shook her hand, he said, "I'm Matt Nevada."

Surprise number two! First the mysterious Admiral May, now the Jonathan Carr's captain, Matt Nevada.

Following a brief but lively chat with Captain Nevada, Fay returned to her seat. "The handsome four-striper is Matthew Nevada," she whispered to Pearce. "The admiral near the window is Admiral May."

"You're kiddin' me?" Pearce turned to peek over the top of her seat. "Goodness, Nevada is yummy."

This talk attracted Winslow's attention. He, too, peered over his seat back and said, "I recall seeing the flag in Admiral Wallace's office the other day."

"Which one?"

"The one on the right," Pearce confirmed. "I saw him too."

"May?" Fay asked.

"Yeah," Pearce replied.

Fay lightly jabbed Pearce in her ribs with her elbow. "And you guys didn't tell me?"

Pearce whispered, "To see a flag officer in a flag officer's office is commonplace." Pearce paused for a moment. "Did what I just say make sense?" She shrugged her shoulders and continued, "I didn't know who it was until just now."

"You're right. I'm sorry. I'm just surprised, that's all." Fay glanced back at the admirals. "May looks awfully young to be an admiral."

Forty minutes later, the jet touched down on a tiny airstrip at Chinhae and quickly taxied to a tarmac near several gray hangers. Fay could see two white Navy sedans waiting. Their engines were running, evident by the wisps of exhaust wafting up from the vehicles' tailpipes.

The trio respectfully waited while the senior officers deplaned. As each man passed by Fay and her team, each officer wished them goodnight. May added, "We'll see you tomorrow at the inquiry."

The three officers entered the first of the two cars and sped off into the night. Fay, Winslow, and Pearce deplaned and walked to the remaining vehicle. A driver was standing by the car's open rear door and saluted as the three approached.

"Evenin', ma'am," she said.

Fay returned the salute, and all got into the car. The driver held the door open until they were seated and then closed it and took her place behind the steering wheel.

"Excuse me, Miss," Fay said to the driver. "What are we waiting for?"

"I'm sorry, ma'am," the driver said, turning slightly toward Fay. "We're waitin' for the pilots."

Fay glanced through the window toward the jet. "Seems like we needed another car."

"Yes, ma'am. This car is more like a hotel limo, ma'am. But we can get cozy, ma'am," the driver replied.

"I was just curious, that's all." Fay wondered what Admiral May was doing on their jet and in Korea. Might the U.S.S. *Jonathan Carr* and Paul Charma have an affinity?

"What are they doin' here?" Pearce whispered and pointed past Fay toward a nearby hanger.

Fay's line of sight followed Pearce's pointing finger, and her gaze settled on what appeared to be a black twin-engine jet just disappearing into a darkened hangar. "What was that?"

"Looked like an *AN-Seventy-Two*, ma'am," Winslow offered.

"An AN what?" Fay asked.

"A Russian military passenger jet, ma'am."

"A Russian? Here? On an American military base?"

"Obviously somethin' we didn't see, ma'am."

"See what?"

Fay's train of thought was interrupted when the rear two passenger doors opened simultaneously. Pearce slid to the middle of her seat to make room, and the two pilots got into the sedan. Fay immediately recognized the man who sat at Pearce's left. "Speak of the devil. Bart Hay!" Fay said.

"Howdy, Lieutenant Commander. Miss Pearce." Hay smiled as he nodded in both women's directions. "This is Ace Tag, our copilot. Ace, this is Commander Faydra Green and Miss Pearce. And a gentleman I do not know."

"Petty Officer Winslow," Fay said.

Ace smiled. "Pleased to meet you all."

"Likewise, Mr. Tag," Fay replied. "That was an exciting takeoff back there at Gimpo, Bart."

"The air traffic control had us on a leash tonight." Hay spoke with a Texas twang.

As the car moved away, Fay glanced back at the plane. "A jet from the Secret Service fleet, Bart?"

"Yup. We've been drivin' Admiral May around for over a month now."

"You were in Bremerton, and y'all didn't call lil ol' me, Mr. Hay?" Fay teased. "I'm disappointed."

"Sorry, ma'am. I didn't know."

Bart Hay seemed the same jet-jockey she had remembered: cocky, arrogant, egotistical, and good-looking, in a cowboy sort of way. Everything she did not care for in a man. Yet, Fay found him charming. Because the Texan's attire usually included a black cowboy hat with matching western boots, Pearce, at their last meeting, had dubbed him "Black Bart" in honor of a TV cowboy badman she recalled from her childhood.

For a good portion of the ride, Bart conversed with Pearce, who was obviously smitten.

The car came to a stop at a hotel near the navy base. Bart and Ace got out, said goodnight, and disappeared into the hotel.

Fay jabbed Pearce. "Y'all and Mr. Hay seem to have somethin' to talk about," she teased.

"Naw. Nothin'. Mr. Hay is aware of my Native American ancestry, so we have many inside jokes to catch up on. Nothing more."

Ten minutes later, the trio arrived at their own hotel. After checking in and having a quiet dinner, they retired for the night.

****

07:55 hours, Chinhae, the next morning

Fay, Pearce, and Winslow marched into the inquiry conference room with purpose. All eyes were on the tall, well-tanned, blonde officer. Fay took little notice that she was the only junior officer in a room full of senior officers.

The inquiry, conducted by Admiral May, was routine and primarily dull, as the details of the sinking were tediously reviewed. Nothing unusual was discovered or uncovered. Captain Nevada had followed proper procedures. That was their conclusion. Fay's was different. Perhaps it was her inquisitive mind nagging at her investigative soul, telling her there was more to the sinking than was revealed at the inquiry.

After the inquiry, Fay and her crew returned to their hotel rooms. They would spend the night in Chinhae and return to Seoul the following day. The quiet evening time gave her a chance to compile Admiral Wallace's report.

****

The white jet glistened in the early morning sun while it stood waiting for Fay and her team. This time, Admirals Morton and May were the ones late in arriving. As she boarded the plane, the cockpit door stood open. "Mornin', ma'am," Bart Hay called from the cockpit.

"Mornin', Mr. Hay," Fay responded.

"I was feelin' bad about not callin' y'all when we were in Bremerton. Would ya like to join us in the cockpit this mornin'? There's room in here for two more."

She thought for a moment. "Tell you what, Mr. Hay. How about my Legalman sit in for me?" Winslow seemed elated to have the opportunity.

"Ma'am, this will be fun for you," Pearce said. "You and Don go."

The flight to Seoul gave Fay a chance to chat with Bart. "He wasn't so bad once you got to know him," she would later tell Pearce. The visit did allow her to get better acquainted with the Secret Service Casanova.

She learned Bart had been an Air Force major before

taking his assignment as a pilot with the Treasury Department and Secret Service. His last duty assignment with the Air Force had been as pilot of the *SR-71*, a spy plane known as the *Blackbird*.

Major Kim was waiting at Gimpo to retrieve Fay and her team. He was not very talkative. *Kim seems to have a lot on his mind, and well, Major Kim should*, Fay reasoned. But he did ask if she would join him for coffee at the hotel. She felt tired and thought she should decline the offer, but it sounded important. On behalf of Winslow and Pearce, she agreed to join him.

After making themselves comfortable in the hotel coffee shop, Kim began, "Fay, I think you know this is not a social visit."

"I knew that."

Kim responded with a nervous chuckle. His voice turned somber. "We do have a problem. We need your help."

"Another crisis, Mr. Kim? I'm sorry. My schedule is plum full."

The waiter arrived ready to take their orders. Each person ordered, and Fay waited until the waiter left the table, then said, "Problem? I am getting used to the word. What is going on, Jangho? It has something to do with the *Carr*."

"Something we learned at the inquiry."

She was not aware Major Kim was connected to the *Carr* inquiry. "The inquiry was routine; Nevada followed procedure. One life was lost." Fay picked up a spoon from off the table; unconsciously, she tapped it lightly on the table. "Unfortunate and tragic as it is, Mr. Kim, one life was lost."

"That's the problem. For a moment, recall Captain

Nevada's statement about the death."

"Nevada said he was the last to leave the ship. He asked for a sweep of the ship and all hands were accounted for." Fay paused for a moment as she recalled Nevada's testimony. "And Nevada said he returned to his stateroom to retrieve sensitive documents from his safe. Once he was satisfied all hands had abandoned the ship, he left the ship."

"Exactly," Jangho said. "Last night, *Nalon Vet* returned to Chinhae from the wreck of the *Carr.*" He paused when the waiter returned to the table to refresh their glasses of iced tea. After the waiter left, he continued, "They returned with the missing man's body."

"I presume the body was found on the *Carr*?"

"Divers recovered the body from the passageway near Nevada's stateroom."

Fay played the scenario out in her mind. "If Nevada returned to his stateroom, as he claims, he would have to pass through the passageway on his way topside."

"You're on track," Kim said.

"Nevada wouldn't have missed seeing the sailor in the passageway." The look on Kim's face suggested to her she was right. "The Navy would like for me to investigate this death, which they believe to be accidental."

He responded with a sarcastic grin.

"Mr. Kim, you believe otherwise, don't you?" Fay asked.

He did not answer.

"The *Carr* inquiry determined," she said, "a JAGMAN investigation was not required in the death of the sailor. The decision is consistent with JAGMAN directives regarding shipboard deaths resulting from enemy actions."

"We've spoken to the JAG," Jangho said. "He's given his permission to have you and your team remain in Seoul to conduct a preliminary investigation. Three days maximum. If you agree, of course."

"I agree," Fay said hesitantly. "Mr. Kim, would you be available to us, should we need help?"

"I'm at your disposal. I'm sure you would find me to be invaluable."

"That's reassuring. I would be deeply honored to have your assistance. We look forward to working with you."

Kim smiled. "And I with you, Fay. I was on the *Carr*. I'll be able to provide any details necessary to your investigation."

"Very well," she said. "I will meet with you tomorrow morning. Will that be convenient for you?"

Kim nodded.

Nothing about his request sounded encouraging to her—except that Major Kim would be assisting her. Fay knew she had stepped from the Charma frying pan into the *Carr* fire, although a bit of help from the Korean CIA could prove advantageous.

The trio wished Major Kim goodnight and departed for their rooms. They not only had a new mystery to solve, but a report to finish for Admiral Wallace. Fay wondered when she would next sleep; she dialed room service to order an entire pot of coffee—strong and black.

Chapter 21

The shadows of dawn crept across the city as Fay watched from her hotel room window, surveying the scene below her. Wisps of steam rose from the exhaust stacks atop the lower office buildings, indicating the temperature outside was cold. Seoul was beginning to wake. It was a peaceful time: dawn, that delicate balance between night and day. As soft as it seemed, she sensed the world was trembling.

Her report was complete. Pearce had crashed hard, sleeping on the floor next to the bed. JP had not bothered to remove her uniform. The coffee had long grown cold; Fay poured the last few drops from the insulated container into her cup. She would drink it anyway.

In a few hours, Fay would meet Major Kim, and she had remained awake for twenty-four hours. Her brain felt numb. Nothing made sense to her this morning. Nor did she particularly care if anything did make sense. She removed her uniform and crawled into bed for a short two-hour nap. She had expended herself and immediately fell asleep.

Two hours seemed but a second when one was soundly sleeping. It was 08:30. Fay peered over the side of the bed. Pearce had vanished. She surveyed the room through reddened eyes. *God...where am I? I could use a cigarette. Why didn't I ever take up smoking?*

Crumpled papers, partially full coffee cups, and plates with half-eaten sandwiches on them littered the room. Fay's eyes protested the morning's intrusion; they felt painfully sore. Worse was the headache pounding at the right side of her head.

She fumbled for the phone at the left of her bed. "Room service?" she asked in a hoarse voice. "Room eighteen-fifty-six, I think? Bring coffee. Hurry."

Fay next called Major Kim's room; they agreed to meet at 10:00 hours. She rolled from her bed and flopped down into the chair at the desk located near the window. Massaging her throbbing left temple with one hand, she began scratching out her investigation game plan with the other.

The team met in the hotel lobby. After finding a secluded spot, they sat down. Pearce produced a notepad and pen, ready to take notes as needed.

"Major Kim, where do we begin?" Fay asked.

"Let me bring you up to speed, Fay."

She nodded but remained silent.

"In response to the sinking of the *Carr,* President Ross ordered U.S.S. *Nalon Vet* to enter North Korean provincial waters," Kim began.

Fay nodded. She was aware of the *Vet's* existence and capabilities. "The *Vet* is a ghost-ship, Mr. Kim. Can you tell me why she was sent to North Korea? President Ross knew he risked retaliation from the North Koreans had the *Vet* been detected."

"The discovery of any U.S. Navy vessel would be deemed an act of aggression by the North Koreans. That's why the mission needed to be performed by the *Vet*."

"Mission, sir?"

"Sensitive data was left on *Jonathan Carr*," Kim explained. "A team was sent to recover the data. Only *Nalon Vet* could slip the recovery team in and out of North Korea undetected."

"I see," Fay said thoughtfully. "Major Kim, why was the *Carr* in North Korean waters?"

"I'm sorry, Lieutenant Commander, I am not at liberty to tell you."

Although Fay was surprised by his response, she understood she did not need to know. "The information is not relevant to my investigation, then?"

"No, it's not."

Fay looked away from Kim, fixing her gaze on an object across the room. "Mercy," she quietly declared. She collected her thoughts, then said, "Let's try this. The recovery team dove on *Jonathan Carr* to recover sensitive data. They found the dead sailor." She glanced at the file she had started on the investigation. "Remains were recovered," she said, peeking again. "Mr. Rodman, along with the data, was returned to Chinhae, and an autopsy was performed."

Kim took a quick sip of coffee. "Some data was recovered; the *Vet* will make a second trip to the site. The autopsy revealed Mr. Rodman drowned."

"Hence, an accident."

"That's the current thinking."

She took a breath and looked Jangho squarely in the eyes. Speaking without emotion, Fay remarked, "I get it. Captain Nevada said he left his stateroom, passed through the passageway, and saw no one. It would have been difficult for Rodman to drown; the crew was given thirty minutes notice before the *Carr* was sunk."

Jangho once again nodded.

"But he did. How does that happen?" Fay continued.

Jangho shrugged his shoulders. "All hands were accounted for."

"Maybe Mr. Rodman was asleep," Pearce offered, "didn't hear the alert, and then woke up only to find himself trapped in the sinkin' ship."

"Only you, darlin'," Fay said with a slight chuckle, "could sleep through a calamity like that. But thanks for your input." She then said to Major Kim, "Tell me about the autopsy." She took a sip of coffee. "The autopsy report concluded Rodman drowned?"

"He drowned," Kim confirmed.

"Nothing else?"

Kim thought for a moment. "The doctor found a contusion under his left eye."

"Blood system clear, nothing unusual in the digestive system?"

"I don't know."

Fay drummed her fingers on the surface of the table. "Huh," she murmured. "Jangho, I want to view the body and review the autopsy report. ASAP."

"Not a problem. The Navy has shipped Rodman's remains from Chinhae to Yongsan Army Post near Seoul. I'll make arrangements for us to view the remains and report today if you like, Lieutenant Commander."

She nodded. "I would like, Major."

It was silent as each person reflected for a moment.

Fay broke the silence. "Tell me about the recovery team who dove on the wreck."

"I don't know much about them. I do understand they were Treasury Department personnel," Jangho offered.

"The Secret Service? I am surprised." *Could he have*

been mistaken? Fay would have thought it would have been a military operation, but it would explain why Bart Hay was chauffeuring her around. *Jangho knows who the operators are. He knew all about them. Hell, he was probably one of them. He's just getting tired of saying, "I can't tell you." I am getting sick of this.*

"I do know they report directly to the President of the United States," Jangho said.

Fay's eyebrows arched. "The President! Mercy, again," she said, following up her remark with a low whistle. She yawned and looked at her watch. "Mr. Kim, I've had about two hours of sleep in the past thirty. And as you can tell," she tugged at the lower eyelid of her left eye with her fingertip, "my eyes are shot. How about I get a nap, and we meet at, say, fourteen hundred hours?"

Jangho said, "Fourteen hundred will be fine."

Fay gave him a confirming nod. "I would like to set up a temporary office in my room. A modem, and a printer, for word processing and computer. Oh, and see if we can get a secure phone line."

He agreed to have the equipment delivered and installed in the afternoon.

Fay knew if she did not rest, she would get sick— it was a certainty. It seemed she had been ill a lot lately, and she was sick and tired of being sick and tired. On the other hand, Pearce and Winslow were as alive as chipmunks in a box of peanut brittle. She would rest; they would explore the neighborhood surrounding the hotel.

****

Later the same day, the foursome found themselves standing next to a stainless-steel table bearing Seaman Gregory Rodman's remains. Nothing about his appearance looked unusual to Fay, other than he was chalk white and dead.

"He drowned," Army Doctor Major Henry said flatly. "Other than a laceration under the left eye," he pointed to a wound near the deceased's eye, "nothing unusual was found."

"What would cause the cut, Doctor?" Fay asked.

"I don't know, Lieutenant Commander. Perhaps the man ran into a bulkhead in his haste to flee the ship."

"I suppose so." Thoughtfully, Fay studied Rodman's lifeless body. "The dead look so dead when they're dead," she remarked to no one in particular.

"Looks like someone punched him," Pearce commented.

Fay leaned forward, bringing her nose to within inches of Rodman's head. She sniffed the corpse's ear as if she were sniffing a rose. She glanced up and caught an odd look in Doctor Henry's eyes. Jangho, Winslow, and Pearce looked as if they were holding their breath.

"You have a question, Miss Green?" Henry asked.

"*L'Observe.*" Fay stood erect. "I thought I smelled aftershave." She looked at Pearce, seeking support. "I guess I was wrong."

The look of doubt, evident on Doctor Henry's face, confirmed it. "You might be smelling humectants or formaldehyde. Those chemicals have a sweet odor to them."

"You're preparing the body for shipping?" Pearce asked.

"He's going home."

"Where's home?" Winslow asked.

"Olympia, Washington."

"Not too far from us, in Bremerton." Fay thought for

a moment. She turned to Pearce and asked, "Do you recall Paul Charma's hometown, Miss Pearce?"

"His service records listed Olympia as his hometown, ma'am."

"Mercy." Turning back to Dr. Henry, Fay said, "Hold up on shipping Mr. Rodman's remains, Doctor, until you receive my report."

"As you wish," Doctor Henry replied.

"Has the next of kin been notified?" Fay asked.

"He had a mother and a sister. They've been notified."

She surveyed the cadaver from head to toe. "He looked to be very athletic."

"If you asked me to show you an example of the perfect human, if there was such a thing," Doctor Henry offered, "I'd show you Greg Rodman. Internally and externally, the man had the attributes of an Olympic athlete at his vertex."

"He would have been able to hold his breath for a long time," Winslow observed.

"I would think longer than an average person, Petty Officer," Doctor Henry replied.

"Doctor, were any personal items found with the body?" Fay asked.

"A wallet, a set of keys, a pack of cigarettes. This is the extent of it."

"May I see those items?"

"Of course." The Doctor motioned for his guests to follow him. "Let's go to my office."

The group proceeded to Doctor Henry's office. After offering his guests a seat, Henry produced a large plastic freezer bag containing Seaman Rodman's personal effects.

"Doctor, I would like to take these items as evidence," Fay said. "Will you prepare a release form?"

"As you wish; will there be anything else?"

"It will do it for now. Your hospitality has been greatly appreciated," Fay said with a grateful smile.

The women returned to the Park Hyatt Seoul to discover two strange men in Fay's room. Seamen Takahashi and Seaman Horner had just finished installing the team's computers. Fay asked Pearce to set up an e-mail address and then send the address to Captain Towsley.

"Sure thing," Pearce said.

"I'm beat," Fay replied as she flopped back onto her bed, kicking her shoes off in the same motion. She was asleep before her head touched the pillow.

****

22:00 hours, Chinhae, South Korea

The articulate man in the navy-blue European suit wore a neatly trimmed gray beard and spoke with compassion as he addressed Egan Fletcher and the E-Team. "I am Viktor Pavlodar," he said, "I represent the *Glavnoe Razvedyvatel'noe Upravlenie*, Russian Military Intelligence, or G.R.U."

Fletcher thought it curious how the world had changed over the past several years. There was a time when the two adversaries' ideologies would not tolerate a Russian agent in attendance at a VFW club meeting, much less a highly classified U.S. military facility.

The woman seated next to Pavlodar then introduced herself. She was Irina Sergeevna, of the Intelligence Directorate of the Main Staff of the Russian Navy.

Following the introductions, Admiral May took his customary position at the head of the conference table.

He turned and pointed to an image of a ship that was projected onto a screen behind him. "This is the Russian guided-missile cruiser *Admiral Moskva*."

The image changed. "Next is the Russian guided-missile destroyer *Nastoychivy*." Admiral May paused for a moment. A third image was flashed on the screen. "This is the American Landing Helicopter Dock U.S.S. *Bon Homme Richard*."

A final image flashed onto the screen. Egan knew this one. "This is the American Burke-class guided-missile destroyer U.S.S. *Nalon Vet*. The *Vet* is our latest and, I'm happy to say, our most successful attempt at radar evasion technology," the Admiral said. "The *Vet* boasts new radar-deflecting paint and some sophisticated electronic radar-jamming gear. The paint, ironically developed by our Russian friends in nineteen ninety-three, renders *Nalon Vet* almost invisible to any radar."

The lights were restored to the room. "Ladies and gentlemen, we have a severe problem—a problem we know you will help us resolve. Each of you has been preparing for an operation we have code-named Operation Caspar the Friendly Ghost," the Admiral continued.

May paused, then said, "For the purpose of Operation Caspar, we have code-named the various ships. You will need to memorize these names. Reference notes are prohibited this evening. Each of you will be searched when you leave this room, and all items found in your possession will be destroyed." Admiral May glanced around the room. "If you have a favorite pen, briefcase, any jewelry, surrender it now," he pointed to two SP's stationed at the door, "to security. Those items will be returned to you following our meeting." May waited while those in the room removed and surrendered any items they did not wish to have destroyed.

When those in the room settled back into their chairs, and the security people had left the room, Admiral May continued. "*Admiral Moskva* has been code-named Rapunzel. *Nastoychivy* will be referred to as Sister Golden Hair, *Bon Homme Richard* as Hotel California and *Nalon Vet* as Caspar."

A sectional map depicting the western half of Russia, the Black Sea, the Mediterranean, the Indian Ocean, the South China Sea, and the East China Sea was shown on the screen. "This week, Sister Golden Hair and Rapunzel departed from the Russian Black Sea Fleet in Sevastopol." May traced the route with a laser pointer as he spoke. "They will travel through the Black Sea, headed south to Suez. Once they reach the Indian Ocean, they will travel east, past the Malaysian Peninsula, then north to this approximate location." He pointed to a spot in the East China Sea near the thirtieth parallel. May paused, allowing the group time to absorb the information.

"Rapunzel carries a cargo of long-range ballistic missiles," he continued. "She will be escorted by Sister Golden Hair. The missiles are to be exchanged with the government of North Korea for perfectly counterfeited U.S. greenbacks." The image of Sister Golden Hair reappeared on the screen.

"It appears the Russian government has established an arms trade with North Korea. Not so," May said. "More specifically, a powerful political faction within the Russian government—with ties to the Russian Navy and the Russian Mafia—has arranged this transaction."

A man then stood to address the group. "As you know, my country has been in political chaos since nineteen ninety-nine. The Commonwealth of Independent States has experienced many growing pains as we struggle to wrestle ourselves from the grip of Communism. Our biggest problems are the unsettling continuation of ethnic violence and increased violent crimes. The crumbling economic and social systems fostered these increases." He paused for a moment, surveying the room. "Good morning. I am Admiral Streika of the *Rossiyskaya Federatsiya* and commander of the Russian Joint Armed Forces."

Streika continued, "It is common knowledge our reforms have left our various military branches in decay. We were unable to pay our officers and enlisted men for several years. As a result, over one hundred thousand of our career officers and their families went without housing during this time. With this in mind," he said, "it is not hard to understand that a group of rogue naval officers—backed by several overzealous politicians - decided to profit off of this turmoil. The concept of trading Russian ballistic missiles for U.S. greenbacks appeared highly lucrative to them."

Admiral Streika paused to take a sip of water. Egan could tell the event, and its ramifications, had ardently shaken this proud Russian sailor. He felt sorry for the Russian.

Streika explained, "The Russian Mafia now controls almost fifty percent of all Russian business enterprises. The Russian Mafia will sell the counterfeit currency on the streets of Rossiya. Large amounts of heroin and opium are presently entering the C.I.S. through

Turkmenistan and Tajikistan's borders. As you are aware, those countries share a border with Afghanistan—we will not allow this shipment of money to add to our problems as we work to unify the Motherland." Again, he surveyed the group. "Thank you," he said simply, stepping away from the podium.

"The Russian good guys have asked for our help," May said. "They want the missiles returned, along with the ships and their mostly innocent crews. They also want the perpetrators brought to justice in a Russian court of law. The President of the United States wishes to prevent the missiles from falling into North Korea's hands. The possibility of North Korea obtaining missiles carrying nuclear or biological warheads capable of reaching Alaska and the west coast of the United States has become a genuine threat."

Russian good guys. The irony of the words echoed in Fletcher's mind. *Aren't these the same Russians who, to this day, have stockpiled more than twenty thousand nuclear missiles? And are currently deepening their missile silos, for whatever reason?*

Admiral May explained that the Drug Enforcement Agency had apprehended a U.S. businessman in Russia. The man had attempted to purchase a decommissioned Russian attack submarine on behalf of a Colombian drug cartel. The asking price was a mere five million U.S. dollars, a tempting offer for a cash-starved government. Fortunately, the DEA had been able to arrest the businessman before the transaction could occur.

"One can only imagine how the cartel would utilize a Russian attack submarine," May said. "But it's indicative of the extremes these people are willing to go to for cash."

Streika explained his government was unable to trust its own military leaders. With this in mind, they had called on their old friends, the United States. Under the circumstances, the Americans were eager to help. E-Team's role was to seize the Russian vessels and return the ships and crew to the Russians.

Admiral Streika nodded and sat down.

Chapter 22

Fay awoke to the sound of a clicking keyboard. Pearce was already busy at work.

"What time is it, honey?" Fay moaned.

"Seven-thirty. Mornin'," Pearce said. "I just sent an e-mail to Captain Towsley. He replied and has given us his home e-mail address. He was happy to hear we have a computer set up here." She continued to type.

"How about we get breakfast," Fay said, "and then we'll meet with Major Kim?" With a puzzled look, she added, "I wonder why they don't have hoecakes here?"

****

"How is your communication system working?" Kim asked.

"Fine, thanks," Pearce responded. "We're up and runnin'."

"Fay," Kim said, "I have another request."

"Bring it on, Major."

"NCC has been nosing around," he said, with a confidential tone in his voice. "Media attention regarding the *Carr* isn't something we want to attract right now."

"What do you want me to do?"

"Leak a story to the NCC foreign correspondents here in Seoul. Something to satisfy them yet hold them at bay for a while longer." He handed her an envelope. "This should suffice."

Fay took the envelope from him and slipped it into

her pocketbook. "How do I find these correspondents?"

"They will find you."

"Fair enough. You can count on me."

Fay returned to her room. With the intrigue of the Rodman investigation foremost on her mind, she sat down with the bag Dr. Henry had given her containing Rodman's personal belongings. As she spread Rodman's personal effects out onto the table near the window, she wished she had thought to pack a pair of latex gloves. Her wardrobe gloves would have to do.

Gingerly, she opened the damp wallet. There was nothing outwardly unusual about its appearance. She noted the wallet's contents: a twenty-dollar bill, a Washington State driver's license, a credit card, and a photo of a young woman. She closed the wallet and placed it back on the table, then picked up the keyring, counting six keys in all. Next, she examined the pack of cigarettes. The box had been opened; several cigarettes were missing. She flipped the box over; she noticed a book of matches wedged behind the box's cellophane wrapper. She carefully removed the matchbook; the side facing her was blank. She flipped the book over and gasped. The word *Trance* was embossed on the cover. The matchbook was identical to the one she had found with Paul Charma's personal effects.

Her phone rang. "Fay Green," she answered.

"Good afternoon, Miss Green," a cheerful voice announced, "this is Gifford Champion. I'm with NCC." Without giving her a chance to respond, Champion continued. "I'm sorry to bother you, but I'm here, in the hotel lobby, and I was hoping you and I could meet. I'd like a few moments of your time."

"Forgive me, ah…Mr. Champion, is it? But I do declare I do not have anything of interest to say to the likes of NCC. Good day, sir," Fay said politely. She had learned how to handle the press diplomatically by observing how her father handled journalists.

"Please, Lieutenant Commander, I'd like to talk with you for just a few minutes."

"Once again, Mr. Champion, I have nothin' to say to y'all. Good day." As she hung up the phone, a slight smile came to her lips. She glanced at her watch. *I'll give him thirty minutes, and I bet he calls back.*

Fifteen minutes passed. Fay heard a knock at the door. "Yes," Fay called.

"Room service!"

"I didn't order from room service. I'm sorry," she called and peeked through the peephole in the door. In the hallway stood a hotel staff member holding a large fruit basket. She smiled and opened the door. "For me?"

"Yes, Miss Green," the staff member replied.

She accepted the basket, tipped the delivery person, and said, "It's Fay," as she closed the door. A card was attached to the handle. Fay knew who had sent the basket. Champion would dangle in the wind for fifteen more minutes, and then she would call him. *Mr. Champion was going to have to work for his hot tip. Perhaps it would cost NCC a dinner?*

Fifteen minutes later, Fay phoned the front desk. "Excuse me, this is Faydra Green in room eighteen fifty-six. Is there a Gifford Champion in the lobby, by chance?"

"One moment, Miss Green," the courteous voice replied.

Five minutes passed. "Hello, this is Gifford

Champion. Thank you for calling me back." He sounded out of breath.

"Mr. Champion. I want to thank y'all for the exquisite fruit basket."

"Our pleasure, Miss Green. I was hoping you and I could meet. For just a few moments."

"I don't know, sir," she said, with hesitation evident in her voice. "I am very reluctant to speak to the media. And yet I cannot help but wonder what it is y'all seem to think I know—about any lil' ole thing."

"Please, Miss Green, five minutes of your time," the reporter pleaded.

"Why, Mr. Champion, I must say, you are the persistent one. All right, but only five minutes, and only if you promise to call me Fay from now on. I'll meet y'all in the coffee shop." She smiled and hung up the phone.

It did not take her long to find Champion. As she had imagined him to be, he was distinguished, neatly groomed, and middle-aged. His short silver hair and well-tailored dark blue suit conveyed a CEO or a diplomat's aura. Champion was a charming gentleman— not the stereotypical reporter she had accumulated a distaste for over the years. She liked him immediately.

"Commander Green!" he chirped as he extended his hand to greet her, "it's an honor to finally meet you."

She returned the pleasantry and joined him at his table. "Mr. Champion, I dearly wonder what has NCC in such a hissy. Please enlighten me."

"Fay, we've heard rumors a U.S. naval vessel may have sunk. We, of course, want to confirm it."

She looked him squarely in the eyes. "Mr. Champion, I have two questions: why do y'all presume I have knowledge of such things, and if I did, why would

I divulge it to the news media?"

Champion held up his hands, just slightly above the table. "Two fair questions. Let me begin by saying my sources inform me that you recently attended an inquiry in Chinhae. An inquiry related to the sinking of a U.S. warship, somewhere in the Yellow Sea."

"If any information is to be released concerning the operation of the United States Navy, surely, sir, y'all must know I would not be their spokesperson."

"I realize that. Reliable sources gave us your name. I'm just doing my job by following up. You understand, don't you?"

"I do understand. I am afraid, sir, I have nothing to say on the subject." Fay would play this out a while longer before she caved.

"May I ask you this? Can you confirm you were in Chinhae two days ago?"

"I was," she replied.

"To meet with a group of senior Navy officers regarding a U.S. Navy vessel?"

"No comment."

"Is there anything else you can tell me, Fay?"

"No." She paused for a moment as if she were pondering a thought. "Let's approach this from another angle. Tell me what y'all know." A shrewd question to ask. Perhaps she could learn something from Champion that she did not know.

He sighed. "We understand a U.S. Navy ship was sunk in the Yellow Sea. We don't know where, we don't know how, and we don't know why. The tension between the U.S. government and North Korea's government is obvious. We believe it may have something to do with the sinking of the ship."

"Your suspicions have merit. I would hope NCC would not release a story of this magnitude based on anything other than fact?"

"We've been sitting on this story for several days now. It's only a matter of time before something breaks, be it accurate or inaccurate."

Fay leaned toward Champion, lowering her voice to a whisper. "Look, Champion, off the record and speaking with anonymity - we can do that, can't we?"

"I assure you."

Fay continued. "I have been given the latitude to release a certain amount of information. Strictly confidential and completely anonymous."

"Much of our information is gathered that way, I assure you."

"To add to what you already know, the frigate U.S.S. *Jonathan Carr* did indeed sink in the Yellow Sea several weeks ago," Fay confirmed.

Champion snatched a small notepad from the table. "How did it happen?"

"It seems the *Carr* was near North Korean provincial waters when it struck a mine."

"Near but not in?" he clarified.

"Not in, Mr. Champion, near. We believe the *Carr* struck a creeping mine and sank. One life was lost."

"Is there anything else you can tell me? May I have the deceased's name?"

"To say less would be unwise. To say more would be injudicious," Fay replied. "Nothing else to tell, and the name of the deceased is classified. The inquiry found the incident to be nothing more than an unfortunate accident. The North Korean government has informally apologized to the United States."

"Thank you." Champion was genuine and sincere. "My employer and I appreciate your cooperation." He paused for a moment, then said, "By the way. Where was the dead sailor from?"

"Olympia, Washington."

He placed his notepad and pen on the table, gazed at her, and said, "Once again, it's an honor to meet you. I covered many of your father's visits to the Far East."

She smiled. "Thank you."

Champion had bought her story, hook, line, and sinker. Fay detested having to tell an outright lie to anyone, much less a dedicated professional like Gifford Champion, but it was her job, and who was she to question orders? From a logical viewpoint, whatever the real reason was for the *Carr's* misfortune, the Navy did not want sensitive information to become public knowledge. The newshounds had effectively been sent on a false trail for the time being.

Fay returned to her room feeling relieved. It was 17:00. It occurred to her she had not seen Pearce or Winslow since the morning. She briefly wondered where they might be.

She was done leaking information. Her thoughts of the *Carr* turned to Seaman Rodman. Nagging questions, things, and events did not make any sense, such as the matchbook she had found with Greg Rodman's effects that seemed to be a direct link to Paul Charma. Yet, she was tired and in need of rest.

When she awoke an hour later, Fay was hungry. Forty-five minutes later, her room service order arrived.

She had been monitoring NCC on her television throughout the evening. Around 20:00 hours, the news was broadcast to the world: "Reliable sources, high within the U.S. Navy, confirm that frigate *Jonathan Carr* struck a mine in the Yellow Sea and sank. One life was lost." A few action video clips of the *Carr*, likely taken when she had first been launched, accompanied the report. A picture of Captain Matt Nevada standing, handsome in his white dress uniform, was shown.

The report was comprehensive but short. A complete disaster leading five nations to the brink of war was dealt with in a few incidental minutes. Fay wondered why the NCC coverage was not more extensive. Still, she reasoned the Navy probably had a hand in dictating just how much information NCC was allowed to present.

"I'm dangerous," Fay chuckled. And yet, she did appreciate Gifford Champion and NCC for the professional and responsible manner in which they had handled and reported her misinformation.

****

10:00 Hours, Park Hyatt, Seoul

Pearce studied Greg Rodman's personal effects. "I'm gonna see what Winslow's doin'," she said to Fay as she flicked on the computer, logged on, and accessed an online visual meeting platform. She quickly found him. "Where are you?"

"I am at the park across the street feeding the squirrels. I left you a message."

"I did not get it! Oh…maybe I did?" Pearce said. "Anyway, I have a question for you."

"Go for it."

"I have four clues. A wallet, a pack of cigarettes, a set of keys, and a book of matches."

"Rodman," he noted. "Hold on. I am almost there. Which room are you in?"

"I will be in my room." Shortly after, Pearce heard a soft knock at her door.

Winslow entered. After removing his jacket, he said, "Do you have your clues here?"

"I do. The wallet, cigarettes, keys, and the matchbook." Pearce handed him the wallet.

He sat at the table near the window and removed the wallet's contents. "Money, ID, and a photograph of a woman." He showed the photo to Pearce. "Who does this look like?"

"Julia Roberts? Kyra Sedgwick?" Pearce replied.

Winslow looked again at the photo. "Huh! But for now, let's assume it's Rodman's sister."

Pearce next handed him the matchbook.

Winslow examined the matchbook. "*Trance*," Winslow said. "Let's google it with Seoul included in the search."

Winslow and Peace joined Fay in her room and moved to the computer. A quick search revealed *Trance* was a Seoul nightclub. "You are brilliant, Winslow," Fay said.

Pearce replied, "Charma and Rodman both had the same matches from the same club. What are the odds? They knew one another and had met at the club for a specific reason. And now they're both dead."

"Died on opposite sides of the world at around the same time," Winslow added.

Fay said thoughtfully, "I need to get myself aboard the *Jonathan Carr*."

Chapter 23

17:35 hours, U.S. Navy Guided-Missile destroyer Nalon Vet, the Yellow Sea, Pacific Ocean

"It took a bit of finagling to get me aboard," Fay explained to Captain Fletcher. "But I pulled it off! And thanks for your support, Egan."

"I can't say I am in favor of this. But I know you well enough that a 'no' was not going to cut it," Fletcher said with a chuckle. "Let's go below. I want to introduce you to our team members."

Fay and Egan made themselves comfortable in the captain's stateroom.

A knock came at the door. "Enter," Egan called in a commanding voice. The door swung open, and six men entered.

The word "surprised" would not capture the feeling that gripped Fay at that moment. This was well beyond it. "Sergeant Linn!" She exclaimed as she sprang to her feet. "Mr. Rayzon. Mr. Wu. Mr. Lawrence. Mr. De Vinsone. Hello all!"

"Ma'am," each man responded, along with a nod.

"Lieutenant Commander," Linn said. "I would like for you to meet Luke Valentine. He's our number six."

Fay smiled. "Good to meet you, Mr. Valentine."

"Captain Rayzon, Delta Force," Linn said, "will brief us on your mission."

Captain Rayzon, Fay noted. One more item

203

regarding Mr. Rayzon, aka Major Irvin, had been struck from her James Rayzon list of mysteries.

"Thank you," Rayzon replied. "Faydra, we are here to conduct a double op. Yours is not related. Lawrence will team with you for your dive on the *Carr*. Your mission is to search for clues that may shed light on the matter of the death of Mr. Rodman. And, time permitting, to review Captain Nevada's stateroom for top-secret data that Captain Nevada inadvertently left."

"So noted and clear," Fay replied.

"Not including your descent and return, you will have thirty minutes to conduct your search. Lawrence is your team leader, and considering this op's dangerous nature, you are to follow precisely his every direction," Rayzon instructed.

Fay responded, "Mr. Lawrence, I wish I could say this pairing is a pleasure. Instead, I will thank you for accepting the responsibility to protect my life."

"Ma'am, it is my honor. I could ask for no better partner."

"There will be two other teams diving as well, Fay," Rayzon informed her. "A team led by myself, and another team who you have not yet met. If you come with me, you will meet them now."

Faydra and James, accompanied by Egan, left Fletcher's stateroom. After traveling through a series of passageways, they arrived at the ship's stern storage area. Centered in the dimly lit room were two water-filled structures resembling large aquariums. The entire scene was reminiscent of something from a science fiction film.

Fay counted three dark forms moving around the structures. She could tell they were sailors, but she could not see their faces in the dim light.

"Are they sleeping?" James asked a sailor standing near one of the structures.

"They're resting, sir. But it's time they got busy, so we'll roust them for you," the sailor replied.

The sailor drifted back into the shadows. Soon, the intensity of the light in the room increased. James motioned to Fay to move closer to the structures.

She responded. Peering down into one of the five-foot-high structures, her gaze locked onto something floating. She said, "It's a dolphin!"

"A bottlenose dolphin," James said. "Meet your diving partners. The one on the right is Romeo; the other is Juliet."

Fay was astonished; she instinctively reached down into the tank to pat Romeo on the head. "James, I had no idea."

The two dolphins seem to respond to her voice with a series of soft clicks. "They recognize you as an officer," James said. "They'll expect a return salute."

She straightened and saluted the two dolphins. She could not help but add a generous smile.

"They've been trained to work with Navy divers," Egan said. "These two were responsible for locating the *Carr,* attaching locators to the hull, and guiding our divers in the dark water to the wreck. They've proven invaluable."

Fay stood admiring the magnificent mammals. "I have read about the Navy's use of dolphins. I never dreamed I'd be involved with them."

"They'll be your best friends on this dive," Egan said. "Your life will depend on them."

"They're so sweet," Fay remarked as Romeo and

Juliet chirped back and forth to one another. She momentarily forgot she was going to risk her life. There was something special about the dolphins that gave her an overwhelming sense of confidence.

"Romeo and Juliet seem to like you, ma'am," James observed. "They make good bodyguards."

"Bodyguards?"

"The sharks, Fay," James said. "As you well know, it's so dark down there you could virtually swim right down the throat of a Megalodon and not know it until it closed its mouth on you."

She cringed at the thought. If this was his last and best shot at making her change her mind, he almost succeeded. "I've had it happen in the courtroom, Mr. Rayzon. Plenty of sharks in the attorney ranks."

"Romeo and Juliet will keep the sharks at bay while you transit to and from the wreck. They're very good at it."

"Thanks. I feel much safer knowing that."

"Let's get ready to dive," Egan said. "You have a date with the ship's doctor; you'll get a complete physical before you're allowed near the water."

****

01:15 hours

Fay and Egan watched from the stern of the *Nalon Vet*. Simultaneously, a sailor team lowered Romeo and Juliet's slings into the water. Fay's eyes were transfixed on the water.

Without shifting her gaze, Fay said, "Just have a warm blanket, a pot of coffee, and a bottle of rum ready for me when I return, sir." She turned to face Egan. Ignoring protocol, she threw her arms around his neck and kissed him on the cheek. "Thank you for being here for me." She had grown quite fond of the handsome captain.

"Always," he replied.

Fay turned and descended the ladder to the waiting boat. She dug deep into her soul to gather what courage she now carried with her to the dark and foreboding place known to all seafarers as "Davy Jones' Locker."

The frigid night air slapped her face as the small boat raced across the flat surface of the night water; sea spray soaked her face and hands. She squinted and fixed her gaze on the wall of black now standing before her. *I'm going to need severe beauty salon time when I get back to civilization,* she thought.

Shortly after, the boat arrived at the prescribed dive location. The dive team donned their facemasks and tested their gear—then, one by one, the divers rolled backward from the boat and into the water. Fay was last to leave the safety of the small boat.

The cold salt water stung her skin momentarily, until the thin layer of water between her skin and her wetsuit warmed to a tolerable temperature. She bobbed on the surface for a moment, then flicked on her underwater torch. Fay then slipped beneath the water's surface and began her descent toward the bottom.

The wreck was ninety feet below. The *Carr* came to rest upright on the edge of a reef. The ship had not completely settled and was subject to shifting with each tide change. All good reasons for her to exercise extreme caution.

Nothing could have prepared Fay for the frightening feeling she experienced as she struggled to see and gain some sense of direction. She could tell she was sinking, but only because the luminous dial of her depth gauge so indicated. Following the eerie flickering lights of the three torches preceding her, she suppressed her fear and the feeling of claustrophobia by thinking of those people nearest to her heart.

Occasionally, the glow cast by the divers' torches below her would momentarily disappear. She supposed—prayed—it was perhaps Romeo or Juliet passing between her line of sight and the torches, temporarily interrupting the beams of light, rather than a predator.

Fay grew fascinated by the many air bubbles emitted by the divers, reflected in the light of their torches' eerie glow. Like a surreal field of vapor flowers, they appeared and disappeared as they slowly wobbled toward the surface. Fay reached for a bubble but instead found it to be a jellyfish, not a bubble as she had first thought.

Fay stopped sinking. Although she could not see it, she assumed they had reached the wreck. She brought her wrist to within inches of her face to check the luminous reading on her depth gauge. Eighty-seven feet.

She strained her eyes in a vain attempt to see through the black water. Fay may as well have been swimming in a cup of coffee. All she could see was the light from the torch she held in her hand. She experienced complete disorientation. No up, no down. Someone, Andrew Lawrence perhaps, grasped her wrist. He was dragging her somewhere. She saw a deck rail, then a deck, and finally passed through a hatchway. They were now inside the *Carr*. There was only one light ahead of her—Andrew's.

The two divers swam along a passageway, around a corner, down a ladder. Fay felt confident Andrew knew where he was going. She repeated her diving mantra, *breathe slowly, breathe naturally*, again and again. The two divers reached another hatch; she assumed it was the entrance to Nevada's stateroom.

In the light cast by their torches, Andrew motioned for her to enter. Fay paddled past him and into the room. He stayed outside. She found it much easier to see once she was inside the room. The gray metal walls reflected the light from her torch.

Her habit was to observe—the Lord had blessed her with a photographic memory, a handy tool for a lawyer and a detective. Captain Nevada's quarters were a disaster. A bunk, a desk with a PC, a wooden closet door ripped from its hinges, a gray carpet. The room's porthole was securely closed.

She pushed shut the hatch to Nevada's stateroom, looked behind it, and then swam to the closet. Fay sensed a slight vibration around her; the ship was settling. Sweeping the beam of her torch up overhead, she observed numerous electrical wires had been dislodged and now looped down into the cabin like large black spider webs. She glanced at her dive watch; fifteen minutes remained.

A sharp metallic sound, coming from the hatch's direction, caught her attention. Fay turned the beam of her torch toward the hatch. Someone was tapping on it. *Tink, Tink, Tink.*

Fay swam to the hatch, reached for the handle, and pulled. The hatch would not open. She tugged again; the hatch would not budge. When the ship settled, the bulkhead must have buckled, causing the hatch to jam. The pounding she heard was Andrew trying to free it. She knew in an instant she would be trapped in Nevada's stateroom unless she and Andrew could release the hatch. *Don't panic. Breathe slowly. Breathe naturally. Breathe.*

Their efforts were futile; the hatch was sealed, permanently. The tap was now rhythmic, like Morse code. Andrew was sending her a message; she tried to remember her Morse code, but her brain seemed fogged. She tapped back to let him know she was all right. Then the tapping stopped. Once again, she glanced at her dive watch. Five minutes. *Don't panic. Breathe*, she repeated. *Don't panic. Don't panic.*

****

Eighty-seven feet above, Egan Fletcher paced the *Nalon Vet's* bridge, repeatedly looking at his watch. "Any word from the dive teams?" he said into a hand-held radio.

"Sir," replied the metallic voice, "one team is in the boat, one team is still down."

He knew the answer to his next question but asked it, anyway. "Which team is still down?"

"Lieutenant Commander Green and Petty Officer Lawrence, sir."

Fletcher shut off the radio. "Damn it!" He slammed the palm of his hand hard into a nearby bulkhead. "Damn, I knew it!" Time had run out. "Recall the boat," he announced to the bridge crew. "Prepare to get underway, X-O."

"Aye, aye, Skipper," was the reply.

"X-O, when the two divers are aboard and have been secured, set your course for one-eight-five, ahead one-third," Fletcher instructed.

"Sir?" the X-O questioned.

"Course one-eight-five, X-O," Egan patiently repeated. "Ahead one-third, no deviation, until I return

210

to the bridge. I'm going to my quarters."

The X-O paused momentarily. He looked his captain quizzically in the eyes. A slight grin formed on his lips, and then he turned to the helm and confirmed the order, "Course one-eight-five, ahead one-third."

****

Andrew was gone. Fay didn't blame him. His air was low, and he, too, would miss the *Vet* if he did not return on schedule. She turned the beam of light away from the hatch and back into the room. *The porthole! I can squeeze through the hole. I'm thin.*

Swimming toward the porthole, Fay caught a glimpse of the PC on the desk. She thought of Pearce and recalled something the other woman had said to her, "You can find anything on the Internet." She swam to the PC, rummaged through the desk's drawers, and found what she was looking for, a small box filled with the PC's flash drives. Hastily, Fay tucked them in her wetsuit, then swam for the porthole.

She was swimming, but she was not moving. She was horrified to discover her air tank was fouled on one of the loose overhead wires. She would have to remove the tank to free herself. Her numb fingers fumbled with the clasps holding the tank to her back. Finally, she was free. She tugged on the tank to release it, knowing she had little time to spare. *Keep your head. Don't panic. Breathe normally. Conserve air.* She needed to shed the tank anyway if she hoped to squeeze through the small porthole. It would be nice to pull the tank through the hole with her. But time was against her, and the tank was tangled. She took one last gulp of air, released her weight belt, and swam for the porthole. It opened easily. She wiggled through the opening and floated to the surface.

211

Fay inhaled a massive gulp of air on her arrival at the surface. She searched for the silhouette of either the boat or the *Nalon Vet*. In the darkness, she could see neither. And where was Andrew? She glanced at her dive watch. "No!" she yelled. *Ten minutes late. Good God, of all times to be late!*

The *Vet* was gone, and she was alone—abandoned—somewhere in the Yellow Sea. Her neoprene suit's buoyancy caused her to float on her back, her feet parallel with her head. There was a calm sea, a full moon, and she felt wholly immersed in a womb of silence. She sensed warmth. *What now? The current might carry me to shore. I wonder if I will be dead by the time I wash ashore in the Marquesas Islands?* She talked to herself out loud: "Then again, if I were to wash ashore on a North Korean beach, it would make it easier for the Koreans to find me."

She floated for a while, then felt a bump. Someone who had experienced a shark attack once had told her before a shark attacks its prey, it first bumps its intended victim with its snout. This person was by no means an expert on the subject.

Fay held her breath and waited. *Where is it?* The silence was broken by what sounded like thousands of large raindrops striking the surface of the water. Fay knew the sound: a school of small fish was jumping nearby. *They do it when a larger fish is chasing them. They leap out of the water to escape the predator who is hunting them. I wish I could jump from the water right now.*

Her floating arms spread wide, Fay resembled an ancient religious martyr tied to a cross, looking up at the moon—thinking. "Oh!" she exclaimed. "I know what I forgot to do—the damn traffic ticket. I forgot to pay it before I left Bremerton. By now, they've issued a warrant for my arrest. Now I'm in real trouble." She smiled. *Hey, I can defend myself in court. I will save me money. No problem. Don't panic. I wonder if the shark thinks I look like a seal? I hope not.* Again, the bump. Something significant—yet a gentle bump, almost a nudge. Her mind was not playing fair. A vivid image of a massive *Jaws*-like creature hovering twenty feet below, lining up for his final lunge, came to her. She laughed. *One rump roast, coming up.*

Another bump. Fay slipped the large dive knife from its sheath on her leg. "Come on, you coward! You wanna piece of me?" she yelled. "Eat me, you sorry excuse for a fish! Come on!"

There was a faint sound, but a sound just the same. It was the sound of a boat. *A North Korean patrol boat?* Her situation was improving. *I now have options: shark bait or target practice. They shoot spies, don't they? Do I yell or not?* She bobbed on the black surface of the Yellow Sea, carefully weighing her options.

The sound of the engine was growing louder. *It's decision time.* Suddenly she was moving through the water. Her friend Jaws had grabbed her; she was going for a ride toward the sound. *Of course! Romeo! He's been nudging me in an attempt to comfort me; now he's dragging me toward the sound of the boat!* "Good job, sailor!" she yelled. *I hope he knows what he is doing. Of course, he knows.*

Only several feet from the boat, she realized it was not a Korean patrol boat, but rather the vessel that had delivered her to the wreck of the *Carr.* The two figures aboard were familiar as well. They appeared to be Egan and Andrew. Fay spat a long stream of seawater from her mouth while she treaded water, waiting for the boat to come within reaching distance. Calmly she said, "Hey guys. What took you so long?" She coughed. "I was beginning to think y'all stood me up or something," she sputtered. "I do know I'm in big trouble when I get back home. There's a warrant out for my arrest, you know." She coughed again. "I'm going to have to buy a different car; the one I have is causing me far too much trouble of late." She looked down into the water. "Hey, are you guys going to stand there and listen to me babble all night long? Or are you going to pull my freezing ass out of here before this shark decides I'm the full-meal deal and turns me into a human sushi snack?"

Egan grabbed Fay by her forearm and lifted her limp body into the boat. She did not respond.

"I think she fainted, sir," Andrew said, cradling Fay's head in his lap as the small boat skipped across the flat sea toward the safety of *Nalon Vet*. He began massaging the circulation back into her nearly frozen face.

Andrew then slipped a syringe out of a small pouch attached to his utility belt. He carefully cut a section of wetsuit away from her leg with his knife then gently plunged the needle into her thigh. "She'll be all right, sir."

Fay awoke with a start. She looked up into the face of a man with blonde hair, sky blue eyes, cherub-like rosy cheeks, and a glorious white smile and said, "I'm in heaven, aren't I?"

"No, ma'am," Andrew said, "You're still in hell with the rest of us freaks."

"Thank goodness," she said. "Where am I?"

"You're here with us. You're safe," Egan assured her. "Rest now; everything is all right."

"I don't remember a thing. Did I get to the *Carr*?"

"You did, and now you're here with Captain Fletcher and me."

"Andrew, I don't remember anything. The entire trip down to the *Carr* was totally wasted. I am so sorry to have bothered y'all." Fay struggled to sit upright. "I gotta go back," she said. "I have to remember." Her arms and legs felt like mush. He helped her into a sitting position. "The field of vapor flowers, Egan. I have to go back."

"The vapor flowers are gone," Egan said.

Soon, Fay regained her strength. Andrew and Egan were preoccupied, so they did not notice her slip over the boat's side, back into the icy black water. She knew she needed to get back to the *Carr*. She hoped she could find it again.

Chapter 24

Descending to the *Jonathan Carr*, Fay realized Romeo had come to her aid. He led the way through the hatch, along the passageway, around the corner, down the ladder, and to the entrance to Captain Nevada's stateroom. The hatch was open; she swam in.

Everything was as she had remembered. The broken closet door, the PC on the desk, the gray carpeting; nothing had changed. *I should leave, but the hatch is sealed.* She remembered the porthole. *Don't panic. Conserve air.* The porthole was also locked, and, sadly, she was out of air.

A gentle voice startled her. "Hi Spider, I'm so happy y'all would join us," a woman said.

Fay blinked her eyes; a woman glided toward her from the dark corner of the room. "Hi, Mama," Fay replied. "Am I late?"

"Why no, Darlin', you're right on time!" her mother said, embracing her. "Our tea party has just begun."

She hugged her mother's neck. "I've missed you so much!"

"I know, Spider, but you're here now, it's all that matters." The woman smiled as she led her Spider to a table set for five. A beautiful table with a white lace tablecloth was set with silverware, English teacups, and lavender candles. "Darlin', I'd like to introduce you to our guests. Mr. Park, the defense minister of North

Korea." Park rose from his place at the table and bowed.

"Captain Nevada," her mother said. Nevada rose from his seat and smiled. "And the nice man who flew here, all the way from outer space," her mother said, pointing to another person seated in the shadows at the end of the table.

Although Fay could not see his face, she greeted the man. "I'm so pleased to meet y'all," Fay said.

"Please join us," her mother said. "Your dad will join us soon. I'm so lookin' forward to seein' him." Her mother turned toward the door. "There's somebody knockin' at the door. Will you see who it is?"

"It's my friend, Mama." Fay felt a tear race down her cheek. "And, oh, Mama, he is just the nicest man! It's almost dawn. I'm sorry, but I have to go."

"Honey, I'm sorry you have to go. But I am glad you are so delighted. Please come again." Her mother's gleaming smile warmed the entire room.

"Okay, Mama, it was good to see you!" Fay hugged her mother again. "I've missed you so much. I love you."

"I know you do, Spider, but don't fret now," her mother said while she comforted her daughter in her arms. "I'll see ya again. And give your dad my love. Tell him I miss him. Will you do that?"

"I will. I promise."

"Fay…Fay!"

She could hear her name being called. Slowly, her eyes opened. Fay found herself gazing up at Andrew.

"She's back, Captain."

Fay felt him press the tips of his fingers firmly to the artery in her neck.

"Her pulse is getting stronger. I think she will be fine now."

She struggled to sit but found she had no strength. Andrew eased her up and into a sitting position. "Hi, guys," Fay chirped. "Where am I?"

"Welcome back!" Egan said. "We're in a boat heading toward the *Nalon Vet*."

"Got any coffee, Egan?"

He reached into a canvas bag near his feet. "I have a thermos." He unscrewed the cup, opened the stopper, and poured a small amount of coffee into the cup.

Her hands trembled as she eagerly accepted the cup from him with both hands. "Where's the *Vet*, sir?"

Egan withdrew a small compass from his pea coat. He studied it for a moment. "That way." He pointed out into the darkness. "I've set the *Vet* on a course and speed that will take her beyond North Korea's territorial waters before dawn. We should overtake her in about thirty minutes."

Fay yawned. "Oh, good, I'm sleepy."

Andrew said, "You've had a rough go of it."

"I don't recall much. I do know I made it to the *Carr*. And I saw my mother."

"You were trapped in Nevada's cabin," he said.

"I remember. I escaped through the porthole."

"But you were supposed to wait for me once you did."

"Wait for you?"

"When the hatch jammed," Andrew explained, "you tapped out a message in Morse that you were going through the porthole and you would meet me there. When I got there, you'd gone."

Fay listened intently, trying to recall the events. "That's right," she said with a nod, "we communicated using Morse code. Now I remember. I recall thinking how rusty I was at coding. I hoped I was making sense."

"Your Morse was fine. It's just when you bolted from the porthole, you didn't wait for me."

She struggled to recall the precise sequence of events. "I think I was out of air?"

"All I know is when I finally found the porthole, it looked like it had been ripped off of its hinges." Andrew chuckled. "Did you stop to open it first?"

"I don't know?"

"I found a large chunk of your wetsuit hanging on the jagged metal edges. I knew you were in trouble."

Egan said, "Andrew surfaced, and with the help of Juliet and Romeo, they quickly located you. You were struggling to stay afloat. We think if you had spent a minute more in the frigid water, you would surely have developed hypothermia and slipped back below the surface."

"I recall floating on the surface. And there was a megalodon."

"Andrew was with you all the time. He held you afloat while I searched for you. We hadn't realized until we had you back that you were suffering from the effects of nitrogen narcosis."

"Rapture of the deep? Mercy, I'm afraid I don't recall." Fay smiled at Andrew Lawrence. "Thanks, Timmy. You saved my life."

He smiled but remained silent; he seemed embarrassed by her comment.

Fay closed her eyes; it was time to sleep.

By the time the trio arrived at the *Nalon Vet,* Fay had awoken, had consumed the entire thermos of coffee, and was warmly wrapped in a pile of blankets. She was shivering uncontrollably. Andrew and Egan appeared relieved to see her lifted, via sling, to the *Vet's* deck. She was then whisked on a stretcher to the onboard medical facility.

Fay remembered nothing after being lifted aboard the *Vet* until she found herself awake and hungry later the same day. She felt refreshed, yet she experienced a slight headache, and her legs and feet were cramping. She showered, dressed, and briefly wondered who had undressed her. She conned the cooks in the galley out of a bowl of soup, a sandwich, and a cup of coffee. She ate and then headed for the bridge in search of Egan Fletcher. She found him there, and he seemed happy to see her.

"Hello! Back among the living, I see," he said.

"I feel great!" And she did feel great. She felt more invigorated than she had in years. "I almost died last night, didn't I?" Fay whispered, so the others on the bridge could not hear.

"Andrew couldn't locate your pulse when we brought you aboard. He got you restarted with one mg of epinephrine and a whole lot of massage. He must have rubbed those feet, legs, and hands of yours for at least an hour, non-stop, in an attempt to get your blood to start circulating again," Egan told her.

"So, Timmy Lawrence and I got up close and personal," Fay said with a snicker. "And thank you," she said sincerely, "for not leaving me."

"The ship's doctor believes you developed hypercapnia toward the end of your dive."

"Hypercapnia is CO-two toxicity," Fay said. "My metabolism must have shot up when I was straining to open the hatch or the porthole. I probably started shallow breathing."

"We thought you might have experienced nitrogen narcosis."

"Whatever it was, I must have been completely out of it. I remember dreaming I had tea with my mother. Captain Nevada was there, the North Korean defense minister, and the *Aurora* pilot. How odd, I thought. My mother is dead. I would assume the defense minister's life isn't worth a plugged nickel these days."

"One of the *Aurora* pilots died."

"How, sir?" she asked.

"I heard he was injured in the crash. He must have died from the injuries."

Fay felt a wave of remorse. "I'm sorry to hear that," she said. "Did we recover all of the data from the *Carr*?"

"That part of our mission was a success."

"And we're not at war with North Korea?"

"We're still at *DEFCON-Three*," he replied. "Did your investigation of the crime scene uncover anything?"

She pursed her lips and frowned. "I don't know yet. I have to ponder it for a while longer."

He smiled. "When Timmy opened your wetsuit, he found the flash drives. They turned out to be the data the Navy was searching for."

"I remember, I grabbed them on my way out of Nevada's room. Although I don't know why." Fay gave Egan an appreciative smile. "Thank you."

He looked at his watch. "It's near suppertime. Are you hungry?"

"I have already…ah…yeah, I am starving," she stammered. "Mr. Striplin," she announced, "the Captain is leaving the bridge." She glanced at Egan. He held up first one finger, then two, then five, and smiled. She gave him a confirming nod. "Steer course one-two-five, Mr.," she said, in a firm and authoritative voice. "The X-O has the bridge."

"Steer one-two-five, aye." Striplin crisply repeated her command.

Following a relaxing chat and a glass or two of wine with Egan, Fay retired to her quarters. He had told her they would make port at Chinhae at 04:30. She opted to sleep until 06:00 reveilles, eat breakfast aboard, and then return to Seoul. Egan contacted Major Kim; he would drive her back to Seoul.

She was up at 06:00. Hunger had awoken her. This was unusual, as it was not normal for her to be awakened by the urge to eat. This morning, Fay decided to eat in the enlisted men's galley. She hoped to find one or all of the dive team there. She wanted to thank them, especially Andrew. However, she soon learned the men had left the ship at 04:30. After breakfast, she located Egan in his quarters and chatted with him for a short time.

"I'm still digesting whether or not I can claim it was nice to have you aboard," Egan said. The expression on Fay's face brought a chuckle. "Faydra, I am kidding you. It was a supreme honor and my great pleasure to have you aboard."

"After all of the trouble I have caused everyone, I am relieved to hear you say that! A heartfelt thank you to you, your crew, and E-Team," Fay said. "Sir, what about Romeo and Juliet? I stopped by the galley to find a fish treat for them but was told they were not aboard."

"We try to keep them penned onboard only for short periods. When they are crew members, they run ahead of us, near the bow, while underway. On a base, they are housed in special pens. But they do fly as well. Our Mark

7 Marine Mammal Systems, also known as dolphins, travel with their handlers aboard a C-17 Globemaster III transport."

"Wow!" Fay said. "I knew none of this. And here I thought I knew everything!"

****

Major Kim was waiting for her dockside.

"How is it you are here in Chinhae, South Korea, Jangho?!" Fay asked as she approached the smiling Major.

He laughed. "I was with you on the *Vet!*"

"I didn't see you aboard!" It was understandable he would be on the *Vet*. After all, he was an interpreter and Army Intelligence. Had the *Vet* crossed paths with an irate North Korean sea captain, Kim would have had to communicate with him.

"I was busy; you were busy."

He was right; after all, it was not a social cruise they were on.

On the drive back to Seoul, Major Kim had several interesting things to tell her. For instance, when she inquired about the E-team, he told her they had departed for Pyongyang, North Korea. It was all he knew or was willing to say on the subject. Fay wondered if they had arrived in Pyongyang via limousine or via parachute. Either way, the trip meant extreme danger for the men.

Jangho knew little about the *Aurora*. He assumed the aircraft, or spacecraft, was on its way back to a secret Air Force base in Nevada or Utah or wherever it was they kept the mystery ship. Fay was sad to learn diplomatic sources, which in Jangho's business meant spies, had reported that Park Seung He had been executed.

Fay was hungry; she insisted they stop soon for

lunch. Jangho spoke the local language and could read the restaurant's small menu where they stopped. Fay was quick to point out he could order for her, as long as the order did not include the word—or anything remotely resembling —*kimchee.*

Shortly after ordering, their meal arrived. Fay called it "Korean BBQ." Jangho had another name for it, although she could not spell or pronounce his version.

"So, you don't like *kimchee*?" he asked curiously.

"Not on your life, Mr.," Fay quickly responded. She did not like *kimchee*, nor did she like standing close to anyone who had just eaten it. An elevator full of Koreans, just past lunchtime, would be the worst-case scenario in her estimation.

Jangho seem hesitant, almost ashamed, when he asked, "May I ask a favor of you?"

"Of course," she replied. "Anything."

"This evening, our President of South Korea, Lee Ka Eun, will be speaking at our hotel. President Lee asked me to ask you if it would be possible to meet the daughters of the Great William Green?" Kim asked. "She is an admirer of your father from when she was a young woman. I know you have been through a lot, and by all rights, you should be exhausted."

Fay interrupted, "Jangho, if I were on my deathbed, I would do this for you and President Lee Ka Eun. Count me in!"

Kim was delighted. A broad smile and an honorable bow conveyed his satisfaction.

"Ah, Jangho?"

"Yes?"

"My Don Winslow is included?" Fay asked.

"Of course."

Another surprise. Mr. Kim had a direct connection to South Korea's Blue House, or *Cheongwadae.*

Jangho was curious to hear the details of her adventure—or misadventure as it were. After hearing her rendition of the tale, he looked as exhausted and tired as she felt. Fay was looking forward to seeing her sister; there would be at least one more telling of the story that day.

****

The two officers arrived in Seoul in the early afternoon. The sun was shining, yet it was chilly. Being back at the Park Hyatt felt like being at home.

After thanking Jangho, Fay retired to her room.

Entering, she noticed Pearce sitting on her bed. Her hands were folded in her lap. "Hi, Sissy!" Fay cried out, throwing open her arms and rushing to her sister.

Following a welcoming embrace, Pearce patted a spot on the bed to her left. "Sit," she directed politely. "Tell me everythin', and don't leave out nothin'."

Fay laughed. "Y'all won't believe it. Do you have a day to spare? You know, for some reason, I'm famished." After telling Pearce everything, she said, "Oh! By the way, President Lee Ka-Eun has requested our presence this evening. She will meet us here at the hotel after her speech."

"Zowie! I do know we have met our fair share of diplomats but not President Lee. She is my favorite!"

"Let Winslow know about it. If he is uncomfortable, tell him to smile and bow a lot, and he will be okay! I'm going to get dressed for dinner. I want to talk to y'all about Gregory Rodman." Fay headed toward the bathroom, stopped, and then retraced her steps back to Pearce. "You think I'm nuts, don't you?"

"Y'all have some doubts?" Pearce deadpanned. "Don't worry, Spider. I'd already decided you were a certified nut-case when I saw ya bury your nose into Rodman's dead ear. What was that?" she asked. "Oh yeah, you smelled aftershave."

"I smelled *L'Observe*," Fay said indignantly.

****

The hotel's Paris Café bustled with activity. The hint of war seemed good for business. Many business and military people were guests at the Paris Café that evening.

Fay had dressed for the special occasion. She had chosen a dress Pearce referred to as her "Jennifer Lawrence" dress. Fay did not know why she called it that. Perhaps because Miss Lawrence had worn a similar dress in a movie - the film *Red Sparrow*, according to Pearce?

The dress was simple, silky, short, and sexy—a traditional "four-S" outfit. It was a combination that would even turn the Pope's head. Fay felt pretty good about herself.

No sooner had her team sat down when Pearce said, "A cowpoke with a familiar face is wavin' at us from across the room. And speakin' of faces, y'all forgot to put yours on."

Fay turned in the direction Pearce was pointing. She squinted, but without the aid of her eyeglasses, she could not make out the face. "Who is it?" Her head snapped back, her jaw dropped, and she asked, "I forgot to put makeup on?"

"Did you miss it when I said 'cowpoke'? It's Mr. Hay. And yes."

"I suppose he wants us to join him." Fay closed her

eyes and let her head drop forward. Shaking her head, she muttered, "Forgot to put makeup on…God, I think I'm losing my mind."

"Yes, ma'am. You lost it already," Pearce whispered. "Here he comes."

Bart did not have much time to visit. Yet, the expression on his face suggested he was not sure who Fay was. Bart explained there was a 04:00 flight, so he needed to catch a few hours of sleep. He, like everyone else, wondered what was going on. Bart had noticed aircraft belonging to several commercial U.S. flag carriers parked at Yokota airbase, near Tokyo, and then again at Osan airbase, near Seoul. He said it was not uncommon for the Military Airlift Command, MAC, to use commercial airliners to transport troops. His assumption was that many soldiers were being flown into Korea from Japan and the United States. It would strain MAC resources, hence the various commercial aircrafts' appropriation.

On the other hand, Fay suspected Bart knew much more than he had led her to believe. *The man is a Secret Service pilot, for God's sake*. But she understood his guardedness; after all, this was a mega-crisis.

Fay learned Bart was transporting medical people from Japan to Korea and the families of high-ranking military officers and diplomats from Korea to Japan. The imminent threat of war would explain the military buildup. The teams of medical personnel were, more than likely, being brought in to deal with the biological aspects of the crisis.

As Bart said his farewells, Major Kim appeared in the restaurant's doorway. "I think Mr. Kim is looking for you, ma'am," Winslow said. Don waved, and Kim waved back. He smiled and briskly approached the table.

"Good evening, everyone," he said in a low voice as he reached the table.

"Were you looking for us, Major Kim?" Mr. Hay was departing, and Mr. Kim was arriving. Fay introduced the two men. After an exchange of pleasantries, Bart left.

Fay motioned toward the place at the table left vacant by Bart. "Mr. Kim, please join us."

"Thank you," he said and sat down. "Are you all ready for this evening?"

"We are excited!" Fay said.

With his voice still just above a whisper, Kim said, "I want to chat with you before your meeting with President Lee."

"I'm glad you found us then. What's going on?"

"Our crisis is growing worse by the hour." Jangho leaned toward her. "An Army doctor has set up a small clinic here at the hotel. Tomorrow morning and throughout the day, he will be inoculating all military personnel staying at the hotel."

"Anti-toxins? We're all current on our anthrax inoculations."

"We've learned, thanks to E-Team's excursion into North Korea, that we face a new threat."

"More black biology?"

"I'm afraid so," Kim said. "Something even more threatening than anthrax. The North Koreans have obtained cultures, from the Russians we understand—a deadly cocktail if you will, a blend of smallpox and the Ebola virus."

Fay looked concerned. "Geez," she said. "It's lethal, I assume."

"Over ninety percent fatal. And the North Koreans have enough of it to wipe out the entire population of the continent of Asia."

"Wow! And the hits just keep on comin'."

Kim nodded. "This evening, a jet, with a cargo of anti-toxin, arrived at Osan. It's being distributed to all military personnel and their families, as we speak. I have left a box containing three gas masks for you at the front desk as a further precaution. The masks are discreetly being issued to all military personnel as well."

"My first thought is to get the hell out," Fay responded.

Kim smiled. "I know how you feel. I want to leave myself, but this is my home, my country, my people. Millions will perish. Sadly, there will be much suffering."

"The E-Team. Have they returned from Pyongyang?" Fay inquired.

"They are still in North Korea. They have been communicating regularly." Major Kim slowly shook his head as he spoke. "It has to be a thankless job. They get caught, they get shot, and their very own country will disavow them."

Fay averted her gaze from him. Glancing down at her coffee cup, she said with a respectful tone in her voice, "They live with that reality every day."

"When will you be leaving Seoul, Fay?"

Fay shifted her gaze back to Jangho. "I don't know. I still have an investigation to conduct. I'm going to wrap it up as soon as I can, in light of the recent developments." She smiled and said, "Why? You trying to get rid of me?"

"Not at all," he mildly protested.

She detected a genuine look of concern on his face.

"I'll arrange for your passage out of Korea when you are ready to go," he said.

Fay reached across the table and firmly grasped the back of his hand. "Thank you, Jangho. You have been a true friend to us. Your friendship and concern are very much appreciated."

Major Kim smiled. "Okay, are we ready to meet President Lee? And she is known by her closest friends as Alex. You may call her Alex if you wish. She will like it."

"Alex?" Fay asked Mr. Kim. "How so?"

"President Lee attended university in the United States. As a result, she Americanized to some extent."

After their visit with Lee Ka Eun, the trio retrieved their gas masks from the front desk and retired to their rooms. Fay needed time to reflect. Not only were she and her team about to be crushed by the sheer weight of an impending biological war, but they also had what appeared to be a murder to investigate. She did not yet understand her feelings on this issue.

Chapter 25

A loud resounding rumble startled Fay from her slumber. She bolted upright in her bed. "JP!" She cringed at the force of the second rumble; the window glass rattled in its metal frame. *The war!* Her heart pounded. *No...wait.*

Fay rose from her bed, crossed the room to the window, and cautiously pulled back the curtain. The sky was uncommonly dark for that time of the morning. The sky exploded in a flash of light, followed by another deep rumble. Again, the window rattled in its metal frame. She let the curtain drop back into place. Nothing more than a violent thunderstorm. Her head snapped toward the adjoining room door when she heard the door lock unlatch.

Pearce entered. "Mornin', Fayzie," she chirped. "There's a big old ass storm brewin' out there." Pearce looked at her sister. "Y'all look like ya seen a ghost."

"I just had the scare of my life." Fay looked back toward the window. "I thought a war had erupted."

"War? No war, see?" Pearce said, pointing to the front page of the newspaper she carried in her right hand. "War." She shook her head. "Used to be, when I was small, war was nothin' more than a fun card game. We grow up, and what do we get?" She flipped the newspaper onto a nearby table. "We get paranoia," she pointed at Fay, "and freaked-out people."

"Hey, was there anything in the paper about the *Carr?*"

"Not much. But it did say a Navy Lieutenant Commander yapped her flap to NCC and got herself into a vat of crap stew over it."

"They actually mentioned me?"

"No, I added that part. Well, actually, I added the whole thing. There isn't anythin' about you in the story."

"Anything else?" Fay asked.

Pearce thought for a moment. "Hey! Why not tell me about them dolphins again!"

Fay obliged her sister and appreciated JP's attempt to divert her nervous stress.

Fay next placed a call to Major Henry requesting a complete and thorough forensic examination of Seaman Rodman's remains. "A complete medicolegal. Microscopic, toxicological, the works," she told Dr. Henry.

"I'd be happy to schedule it for you, Lieutenant Commander. Can I get back to you in a couple of days?"

"A couple of days for you to schedule the autopsy or a couple of days for the results?"

"Excuse me for being unclear," Henry apologized. "I'll get right on it. I meant I would have preliminary results for you in two days."

"Thank you, Major Henry. I want this one put under a microscope." She asked,

"You Army guys get overtime pay?"

"No, Fay, we're just like you Navy guys. No OT," Henry said. "Hold on." He placed her on hold. While she waited for him to return, she drummed out her own rendition of a Fleetwood Mac song with her pen on the surface of the desk, as she listened to the music on the radio.

Dr. Henry returned. "I talked to my staff. They've agreed to do whatever it takes to put this one to bed. Will you give us twenty-four hours?"

"Twenty-four hours would be splendid, Doctor. Thank you so much. I'll be waiting to hear from you."

"Understood. I'll call you as soon as I have something."

Fay hung up the phone, and, with a hint of exasperation in her voice, she turned to Pearce and said, "It looks like we—like Mr. Rodman—have been put on ice for a few days."

"In the words of the immortal Chan, 'Waitin' for tomorrow, waste of today,'" Pearce said with a sigh. Then, with an upbeat tone in her voice, she suggested, "Why don't you get dressed, I grab Don, and we'll have breakfast?"

Fay's face brightened. "Good idea. Call Major Kim. See if he can join us. Say, around nine?"

The coffee shop in the Park Hyatt was busy. Yet Fay and her team managed to find a secluded spot.

"Have you made any progress with your investigation, Fay?" Kim inquired.

"Some progress. I have requested a thorough forensic examination of Rodman's remains. It is my feeling the Army doctor may have performed a hasty autopsy biased by his assumption the death was accidental." Changing the subject, Fay asked, "What news do you have regarding our crisis?"

Jangho lowered his voice to a whisper. "We're receiving new developments on the issue hourly. President Ross will appear on American national television at twenty-two hundred hours Eastern Time to inform the American public."

Fay also lowered her voice. "What happens to the people of South Korea?"

"The Korean population will be informed simultaneously by President Lee Ka Eun." Major Kim's gaze shifted down to the surface of the table. With passion in his voice, he continued, "The people of South Korea have lived in crisis since the Korean War. We don't anticipate a panic on their part. Although our country has never been closer to war than at this moment."

Fay remained silent for a moment and then asked, "Have you any news of E-Team?"

"I'm sorry, I don't. I want to advise you all military and civilians deemed nonessential to this crisis are being evacuated from South Korea. If you feel your investigation is complete, I encourage you to leave ASAP."

"I'll keep it in mind. Thank you for your concern."

Later that afternoon, Fay received a phone call from the secretary to the Honorable Lois de la Croix, the Democratic senator from Louisiana. Senator de la Croix requested a meeting with Fay at 13:30 the following day at The Westin Josun Hotel. The secretary was not specific about the nature of the meeting. Fay reluctantly agreed to meet Senator de la Croix. She did not feel she was given a choice.

****

Yongsan, Seoul, the same day

Admiral May said, "Operation Caspar will take on the element of a sting operation. Once we seize Rapunzel, the Russian ship will sail on to the rendezvous with the North Koreans under the command of an American crew."

Operation Caspar's planners had factored in the odds of probability and outcome in missions of this nature. It was highly probable Fletcher's team would not make it to the rendezvous point. The result was predictable; the commandos would be captured or killed.

Admiral May explained that as the mission unfolded, they would receive more details. Egan surmised it meant the mission's planners were making the plan up as they went along. This entire operation had been made possible by Faydra Green's discovery of the data on the *Carr*. The flash drive had recorded the rendezvous's encrypted coordinates between the Russians and the North Koreans—courtesy of Park He, the North Korean defense minister. Egan thought how proud Fay Green would be to know how important her discovery was to the mission. And if the op were a success, how vital a part she had played in stemming the tide of war. *Sad, these were things she would never know.*

****

09:10 hours, Park Hyatt, the next day

Major Henry called Fay with preliminary results from his forensic tests. "We've found two areas of interest, Fay. The first relating to Rodman's hands, primarily the knuckles and the fingernails on his right hand. We found wood fibers, slivers, embedded in the skin and under the fingernails," he reported.

"Could you determine the type of wood?" Fay asked.

"Mahogany, most likely."

They're mahogany wood slivers from the door in Nevada's room, she thought. "And the other?" she asked.

"When we examined the deceased's clothing, we found fabric fibers snagged on his belt buckle. Our analysis determined them to be gray."

"Like a carpet fiber?"

"Yes, like a fiber from a carpet."

"Anything else?"

"No, but we're still working on it. These two things were what we've found so far. I'll let you know when we have more."

After thanking Dr. Henry, Fay hung up the phone. Pearce again had hit the mark. Someone must have surprised Rodman in Nevada's stateroom. They had fought, as evidenced by the cut under his eye. Rodman had been knocked to the deck, as evidenced by the carpet fiber found on his belt. He must have been unconscious; maybe he was locked in the closet. As the ship had filled with water, Rodman had come to, probably revived by the cold water as it had flooded the room. He must have broken open the mahogany closet door, evidenced by the wood slivers embedded in his right hand. But he had been too late. He had drowned as he had tried to find his way out of what was by then a pitch-black ship.

"Well, gang, based on what I just heard from Dr. Henry and what I observed on the *Carr,* I believe I have a scenario. I may have the evidence I need to link Captain Nevada to the death of Seaman Rodman." Fay ran the scenario by Winslow and Pearce then asked, "What do you think?"

"'Theory like water, easy to make hole,'" Pearce quoted. "Y'all know as well as I, all sailors are drilled on movin' about their ship in total darkness. Rodman could've been blind and still gotten off of the ship."

Winslow continued, "Dr. Henry told us Rodman's

lungs were huge. The man was part amphibian. He could've held his breath long enough to get to the surface and back."

Pearce said, "You was able to hold your breath long enough to swim from Nevada's cabin to the surface. And y'all seen how buff Rodman was. Think about it for a minute, Fayzie. They found Rodman in the opposite direction of his nearest exit. He was headin' the wrong way!"

They were right. Yet, no one could come up with a logical reason to explain Rodman's illogical action.

Fay gave up trying to explain it and picked up the phone to dial the home phone number of Vern Towsley. "Hi Captain, this is Faydra. You're talking on a secure line. I am sorry to disturb you at this late hour," she said. "Sir, I may have evidence Matt Nevada is responsible for Rodman's death." She then recapped her clues and observations. She finished by requesting, "I would like permission to interview Captain Nevada."

"Based on what I've heard, permission granted. Plan on interviewing Nevada. I'll make the necessary arrangements for you. Go easy," Vern cautioned. "Nevada is a respected officer. There won't be any room for error. Know your facts and tread softly."

****

13:30 hours, the Westin Josun Seoul, Seoul, South Korea

Fay left her name at the front desk and sat in the lobby to wait for Senator Lois de la Croix. She wondered what de le Croix had on her mind. It was the time of the day when Fay became drowsy if something was not stimulating her mind. She fought the urge to nod off, thinking any minute the Cajun Queen would appear.

It was 13:55 hours when Queen Lois entered the lobby. She briskly walked toward Fay. Although appearing stern, Fay detected a slight smile on Senator de la Croix's lips. She knew the look. It was the look of someone who was going duck hunting. But that was how she remembered de la Croix. Lois had looked old, even when Fay's dad was in office. *Lois de la Croix always seems as if she is constipated. An absolute classic, a timeless woman,* Fay thought. Fay looked at her watch. *This woman is worse than I am when it comes to being on time.*

She rose to greet Senator Lois de la Croix, an elegant woman, mid-sixties, five-foot-five-inches tall, with chemically colored auburn hair and tired eyes. She was a little on the heavy side, nothing a little lipo-sculpture wouldn't cure. Fay imagined de la Croix had most likely held "babe" status in her day, although Fay's mental image of the woman was more akin to that of the Queen of Hearts in "Alice's Adventures in Wonderland." Lois was a royal anal-retentive.

"Why, Faydra, it's a pleasure to see you again," Senator de la Croix said, extending her hand. There was little warmth in either de la Croix's face or her handshake. "How's your father?"

Fay firmly shook de la Croix's hand. "Afternoon, Senator," she responded. She hated to lie, but when it came to de la Croix, or any politician for that matter, lying was justified. "My father is well, and he sends his regards to the lady Senator from the sovereign state of Louisiana."

The senator's lips cracked into something resembling a smile. "Please, Faydra, I have a private room set aside for our meetin'." She gestured toward a hallway to Fay's left. "This way."

The meeting room was small but comfortable. Senator de la Croix offered her a seat, then spoke. "Lieutenant Commander Green, let's cut to the chase. You're investigatin' the accidental death of Seaman Gregory Rodman aboard the U.S.S. *Jonathan Carr.*"

Fay nodded. *No need to answer; Senator de la Croix has the facts.* She could tell from the onset this would be a one-sided conversation. Senator de la Croix would lecture; Fay would learn.

"Frankly, I don't necessarily care where y'all seem to think you're headin' with this investigation. Nor do I particularly care to know what you think you know regardin' it."

Mercy, that was a mouthful. Fay chuckled to herself. *No wonder this woman got elected. Political doubletalk is her forte.* She remained silent. *Senator de la Croix has been a politician a little bit too long apparently, or perhaps she just needs to get laid.*

"Seaman Rodman's death, while unfortunate," de la Croix said, "was accidental and nothin' more."

So, the old bat knew all about this and decided an accident was what it was.

"You're a bright woman," de la Croix continued. "In fact, I've heard you're on a fast track to becomin' one of the youngest lady admirals in the history of the U.S. Navy. I would hate for your illustrious career path to take an unfortunate wrong turn somewhere along the way."

Threaten me!? A basic white girl who has not had her coffee fix today!? Fay nodded and remained silent. She had not liked de la Croix from the first time she had met her. She enjoyed her even less now. *Ah, what the hell, may as well fire one across the old scow's bow.* "Senator de la Croix, career path or no, I must investigate this incident, regardless of whose toes I may step on," Fay spoke up; it was something her dad would have said at a time like this.

Her impertinent response quickly drew the ire of de la Croix. The Senator's nostrils flared; her eyebrows arched. "You listen to me, little lady, and you listen well." Her open palm smacked the surface of the conference table as she demonstratively drove her point home.

This woman comes to anger quickly. Maybe this is where she bellows, "Off with her head." It was something the Queen of Hearts would have said at a time like this.

"I don't need to hear of your platitudes on duty to God and country. I know duty. I began servin' your country while you were still in diapers, Missy," the Senator snapped.

One more time with this little lady/missy bull crap and de la Croix will be missin' her own damn head, Fay thought. At times, it was hard to remain respectful with one whom you had so much disrespect for.

Senator de la Croix leaned forward to emphasize her following statement. "I don't give a flyin' rat hump whose fair-haired daughter you are…or on which admiral's pillow you're currently layin' your head. But I know all hell is about to break loose here in Korea. I also know a scandal regardin' any branch of the military would not rest well with any senior officer or the American public at this juncture."

Senator de la Croix continued to lecture while glaring directly into Fay's eyes. A weaker woman would have looked away from de la Croix. Not Faydra Green.

She wondered which admiral de la Croix had her sleeping with and what the heck a "flying rat hump" was. *Lois is not only belligerent, but she has her facts all screwed up. And they send these people on fact-finding missions?*

"They don't give a frickin' flip right now," de la Croix continued. "What they care about is a war and not much else. Am I makin' myself clear, Missy?"

Fay straightened in her chair. Clearing her throat, she said, "Crystal clear, Senator de la Crow." The mispronunciation of her name would not have gone unnoticed, but de la Croix retained her composure. Fay respected her for that.

"I would consider your next move very carefully, girl. I might add an arrest warrant, even for a simple traffic violation, may turn into an ugly mess, should the wrong people get involved with it." Senator de la Croix glanced at her wristwatch. "This meetin' has concluded. Think about what I've said." A slight smile came to her face, and her eyes took on a hint of softness; she said, "Nice to see you again, Faydra. Have a pleasant day."

Holy crap and mercy, de la Croix knows all about the speeding ticket. At least she has one of her facts right. But who is this admiral de la Croix has me sleeping with? Who the hell yanked de la Croix's chain? Fay knew the answer to her question. *She is right; the Navy does not want or need a scandal, not with the threat of war imminent. Accident or not, obviously, they want Rodman's death to be an accident.*

Senator de la Croix was one of the most powerful Democrats in the nation. Some felt she had what it took to be the first female President of the United States. Senator de la Croix had a lot at stake. Not only a ticket to the primaries, but several choice defense contracts for the shipyards in her home state of Louisiana hung in the balance. Whatever the reasons were, someone had pushed de la Croix's buttons hard and had left it to her to deliver the message to Fay. She had little finesse—it was obvious—yet Fay did appreciate her directness. It saved a lot of time anyway.

Fay returned to the Park Hyatt, concerned about her ordeal with Lois de la Croix. There was a message for her at the front desk to contact Major Kim ASAP. She went immediately to the house phone and dialed his room. He sounded distressed and asked to meet her right away.

Shortly after, Major Kim arrived in the lobby. He looked as distressed as he had sounded on the phone. Immediately he spoke. "I've received some disturbing news. Captain Nevada was found dead in his room, late this morning."

"What?!" Fay quickly collected her thoughts. "I'm stunned. Next time you might prepare me before you break the news like that to me." She did feel faint. Unsteady, she walked to a nearby chair and sat. After catching her breath, she said, "Details, please, Jangho."

He sat in a chair adjacent to her. Softly he said, "He was murdered. The hotel staff found him on the floor with his hands cuffed behind his back with a single bullet wound in the back of his head. His room was ransacked. It was either a robbery, or someone was looking for something."

"They were searching for the information I retrieved from Nevada's stateroom," Fay offered. "And now it's on me."

Kim replied, "We are fortunate in that regard. No

one knows you retrieved any information from the *Carr*."

"If I had a penchant for cursing, which I do not, I'd say 'Oh shit' right now. But I will not say it." Fay slowly shook her head. So much had happened in the past several hours. She quickly regained her composure. Her game face was back on. With a measure of frankness in her voice, she said, "Major Kim, my investigation has concluded. It's time I went home."

Kim looked relieved. "I'll make the necessary arrangements for you," he said. "I'll contact you later this evening with the details."

She patted Jangho on the shoulder. "Thank you. You have proven to be a loyal friend."

Fay returned to her room. Pearce was waiting patiently for her. Without so much as a "hello," Fay snapped, "Come on. Contact Mr. Winslow and pack up; the investigation has ended."

"I don't understand, ma'am. I thought we was onto somethin'?"

Fay could understand the puzzled look on Pearce's face. Still, without giving her an explanation, she simply responded, "I guess not. Rodman's death was an accident."

Pearce would know better; she also knew when to remain silent.

Fay felt compelled to explain her reasons. "JP, I want—" She was interrupted mid-sentence by a ringing phone.

Chapter 26

Captain Fletcher stood on the bridge of the *Nalon Vet*. He should have been to Hawaii and back by now. But this was Captain Moore's ship now, and he was but a passenger. Jeffrey was there, too. "Mr. Striplin, will you join me in a cigar?" Fletcher asked, reaching into his shirt pocket.

"Aye, aye, sir." Striplin smiled as Fletcher handed him the small cigar.

Egan looked out over the shimmering light blue ocean at the evening's hovering sun. He could not help but wonder if he would ever see a day like this again. By tomorrow night, he and his band of pirates would be aboard the Russian man-of-war, Rapunzel. Or they would be just another part of naval history.

"Hurricane, it's time," Captain Moore said as he patted Egan on the shoulder. Captain Moore sounded like a warden telling a condemned man his date with the hangman had come. "Mr. Striplin," Captain Moore ordered. "Come left to course one-eight-zero."

"Left to one-eight-zero, aye," Striplin replied.

"Full ahead," Moore ordered. "X-O, please alert the *David Ray* we're underway, heading one-eight-zero. Flank speed."

"Ahead flank, sir," reported the sailor who operated the engine control console.

"Goodnight, Adrian," Egan said to Moore. "I'm

going below." He saluted the watch as he departed for his quarters.

As Egan left the bridge, he glanced toward the U.S.S. *Bon Homme Richard,* the mission's support ship. She lay about three thousand yards to the *Vet's* portside. He wondered how Miss Pearce and Fay were faring.

****

Admiral Brandon May spoke to Vern Towsley via secure phone from the *Bon Homme Richard* bridge. "Who's minding the kids?"

"Kim is taking care of it."

"And Gifford Champion?" the Admiral asked.

"Kim, sir."

"You know, Vern, if Kim screws up, the old man will hang us out to dry."

"Understood, Admiral. I assure you, Kim is the best at what he does. There won't be any slip-ups," Towsley promised.

"Pray your assessment is correct."

****

Fay thought she had heard the last of Jangho Kim for the day. But he was now calling with an urgent request to meet with her. She agreed.

Twenty minutes later, she and her team were waiting patiently in the hotel lobby for Major Kim.

Kim arrived carrying an expensive black eel skin briefcase.

He greeted the trio, quickly sat down, and opened the briefcase. Kim produced a manila envelope, like the one Fay had received Paul Charma's service records in, and said, "Thank you for meeting me, Lieutenant Commander, Miss Pearce, Mr. Winslow. I understand you are leaving Seoul tomorrow." He offered Fay the envelope. "I was asked to deliver this to you."

A quizzical look came to her face. Fay took the envelope from Kim and promptly opened it. As she reviewed each page of the envelope's contents, the concerned look on her face deepened. She then handed each page to Pearce and Winslow for their perusal. Not a word was spoken.

When Pearce handed the envelope's contents back to her, Fay asked, "How did you come by this, Mr. Kim?"

"An anonymous source," he said. "Literally. I found the envelope in my mailbox this afternoon with instructions to review it and then forward it on to you."

"This is Admiral May's doing," Fay said. "I am sure of it."

Kim probably knew, but he was not going to admit to it. Kim furrowed his brow as if he were making a more concerted attempt at connecting the dots.

Then, surprise! Fay was wrong.

"Wait a minute," Kim said. "Admiral V. Brandon May headed up the Eastern Pacific Airways crash recovery effort last month. You think May is the anonymous source?"

"I do." Fay had not heard of the airliner crash. She scanned the documents. "I'm puzzled, Jangho. These are Gregory Rodman's service records, the man who drowned when the *Carr* sank, although these are not the identical records I reviewed the other day. If these are Rodman's actual records, then Gregory Rodman was an Air Force major and not Navy as we first believed."

"It would explain why Rodman couldn't find his way off the ship," Winslow remarked. "He wasn't a sailor. And it would explain why the entire crew was accounted for, as Nevada claimed. Rodman was not on the crew list. Rodman was on the passenger list."

"Thank you, Mr. Winslow," Fay said.

"His service record didn't indicate his duty assignment," Kim said.

"I've been running into a lot of that lately," Fay remarked. "It means Major Rodman's purpose was over-the-top secret. 'Eyes only,' as they say." Her logical mind was looking for a scenario, but she could not find one. "What part do you play in this, Jangho?"

He shrugged his shoulders. "I sometimes wonder myself. Rodman would be the person recovered from *Jonathan Carr*. My suggestion is to contact Gifford Champion. He will have more information on the airliner crash."

When Fay and her team returned to her room/office, she placed a call to Gifford. She told him she wanted to know about the Eastern crash. He agreed to meet her in her room within an hour.

Forty-five minutes passed before there was a knock at her door. It was Champion, with wine and cheese!

Fay reviewed with Gifford what she felt she was allowed to. She asked, "What can you tell us about the Eastern Pacific Airways crash?"

"I know a lot about the crash. I covered the story," Gifford informed her. "I store detailed information on the stories I cover on my computer's hard drive. I was searching my database on my way over here in the cab. I ran across a note I made to myself." He reopened his briefcase. "A curiosity, really." He withdrew a sheet of paper and handed it to Fay.

She reviewed the paper. "This speaks of two SEALs. Both men were injured during the search and recovery operation of an Eastern Pacific Airways airliner downed in the Yellow Sea last month. One SEAL named David Rodman."

"Yes, I searched my database for the name Rodman and came up with this," Gifford explained. "I've covered several airline mishaps for NCC. I was assigned to the EPA crash. It's my custom to hang around the hospital/morgue. The real stories are the people—the victims of the crash, their families, and the personnel involved in the recovery operation."

"What connection does Navy SEAL David Rodman have with Gregory Rodman? Are they related?" Fay asked.

"It wasn't so much the men's similar names that piqued my curiosity, Fay, but rather SEAL David Rodman himself," Gifford replied. "I talked to David Rodman at the EPA crash site when he was brought into the infirmary with a nasty slice on his leg. The jagged metal those crashes create is treacherous. As I spoke with Rodman, it occurred to me that I'd seen him before. I didn't immediately recall where, but it came to me later. It was several years earlier. I had covered the crash of a Trans Global Airlines 787, which went down off New York's coast. The scenario was the same. A jumbo jet explodes in mid-air and falls into the ocean. In the case of the Trans Global incident, the investigation team concluded a fuel tank had exploded."

"I recall the crash," Fay said. "How tragic."

Gifford nodded in agreement. "On the second day of the TGA recovery operation, I was milling around the infirmary. An injured diver was brought in. What struck me as odd and made the memory of the event so lasting in my mind was the diver was under constant guard for the entire time he was in the infirmary. No one could approach him except, of course, the medical staff. I did get a good look at the man's face but didn't speak to him."

"The diver was David Rodman?" Fay guessed.

"One and the same."

"Sounds like a coincidence."

"Fay, I don't believe in coincidence. The security surrounding the diver at the TGA crash site got my attention. I wondered, why all the fuss? After the diver was discharged from the infirmary, I snooped around. I was looking for a name, anything on which to build my story," Gifford stated.

"And?" Fay asked. Gifford could not tell his story fast enough.

"The diver at the EPA crash site was the same man as the diver at the TGA site, only his name had changed. The man I met last month was David Rodman. The man I saw in New York was a man named Paul Charma."

"CHARMA!" Fay exclaimed.

Pearce and Winslow were aghast.

"You sound like you know Charma," Gifford replied.

Fay tried to respond to Gifford, but the best she could muster was a gasp. When she felt she could speak, she turned to Pearce and asked, "Miss Pearce, will you do a couple of things for me? You and Don download anything regarding the Eastern Pacific Airways and the Trans Global Airlines disasters. Also, call the front desk and tell them we are not leaving tomorrow. And leave a message for Major Kim. Tell him we have changed our plans and will be staying on for a few more days."

Without hesitating, Winslow and Pearce stood.

"Aye, aye, ma'am," Pearce responded. She smiled at Gifford Champion. "Goodnight, Mr. Champion."

He smiled and said, "Goodnight."

As Pearce walked away, Fay called after her. "See if you can locate Bart Hay. And leave a message for him. I would like to meet with him at his earliest convenience." Fay thought for a moment. "Oh, and find out for me what a 'flyin' rat hump' is."

"What?" Pearce hesitated while apparently processing Fay's instructions. "You got it, ma'am," she said and gave Fay the thumbs-up signal and a wink.

Something less than fifteen minutes passed before Pearce called Fay. She had found Bart Hay.

"Quick work, Miss Pearce. How did you find him so fast?" Fay asked.

"He's a man," Pearce replied. "It's dinnertime. I figured he would be either in the coffee shop or in a topless bar. Lucky for me, he was in the coffee shop."

Fay chuckled. "See if he will wait for Gifford and me. We will be right down."

"You got it," Pearce replied.

Fay and Gifford arrived at the coffee shop and quickly found JP and Bart.

"Good evening, and I believe you have met Mr. Champion, Bart? I wonder if you would help us?" Fay asked.

Bart nodded. "Sure."

"I'd like to know everything you can tell us about the *Goddess of the Dawn*," Fay requested.

"The *Aurora*? Sure. I will tell you what I am allowed to. I'm on my way out. Ace and I broke our jet. We're gonna ferry from Osan to Gimpo for repairs." Bart looked at Pearce. "I'd just asked Miss Pearce if she would join us. Unfortunately, she seems to be busy."

Fay shifted her gaze from Bart to Pearce. Pearce had a pleading look in her eyes.

Fay thought for a moment and then said, "Tell ya what. Winslow can download the information; JP, you go with Bart and see what you can learn about the *Aurora*. And how long will you be gone?"

"Maybe four hours? Give or take," Bart estimated.

Pearce displayed a large grin, and without waiting for any further instructions from Fay, she grabbed Bart by the arm and said, "Come on, Bart, we got a plane to catch. Hold up! Wait here. I gotta run to my room and grab a coat."

Fay's gaze followed Pearce and Bart as they disappeared into the lobby. Then she said, "JP's father taught her how to fly. Her dream was to be a naval aviator like her dad. Sadly, it did not work out for her. This short flight with Bart will make her happy."

"I would imagine," Gifford said. "I have some additional information regarding the crashes you might find useful. I'd be happy to make it available to you if you like."

"I would like," Fay confirmed.

"What do the Rodman brothers have to do with *Aurora* and the sinking of the *Carr*?" Gifford asked.

"Air Force Major Greg Rodman was aboard the *Carr*, which means one of two things," Fay explained. "He was either an advisor involved with the recovery of the *Aurora*, or he was *Aurora's* pilot. Although, I had heard the pilot died." She looked at Gifford. "Either way, it's something I want to pursue."

"I don't mean to be presumptuous, Faydra, but

would you like some help with your project this evening?"

She smiled. "Looking for a story, Mr. Champion?"

"Always."

"You, sir, have a deal!" Fay exclaimed.

Chapter 27

Late that night, as he lay in his bunk, Egan could hear the steady hum of *Nalon Vet's* numerous electronics systems as the *Vet* made its way across the East China Sea. Even though he was experiencing deep trepidation about the upcoming mission, his last conscious thought was of his beloved son, Kristian, before he slipped off into a well-earned sleep.

****

Fay, Don, and Gifford managed to download more information on the two airliner crashes than they could possibly digest, even in a week. They were looking for any reference that would link the two mishaps. The three people worked quietly for most of the night. Occasionally, they would converse on personal subjects, getting to know one another better as individuals in the process. Fay told Gifford the details of her investigations, starting with the death of Paul Charma, a.k.a. David Rodman, and concluding with her conversation with Senator de la Croix. She withheld any information she deemed classified.

Gifford listened with interest but remained silent.

When Fay finished her dissertation, Gifford said, "It came to light recently the National Reconnaissance Office misplaced a two-billion-dollar slush fund. Because it was a highly classified fund, even the nation's top intelligence officials had no control over it. Usually, classified slush funds are earmarked for our government's various black projects."

"Two billion bucks seems like a lot of cash," Fay said. "I'd suppose many of those black budget slush funds exceed even that amount."

"They do. However, this fund couldn't be accounted for. The money disappeared," Gifford said. "Almost twenty cents of every tax dollar go to military spending. The various branches squander close to one hundred fifty billion dollars each year, so to misplace two billion is a drop in the bucket to them."

"I had no idea."

"The intelligence-industrial complex generates tens of billions of dollars per year in highly profitable government defense contracts," Gifford went on. "These contracts go to a handful of the nation's largest contractors, with a grateful return of campaign funds from the contractors to the acquiescent politicians."

"Senator de la Croix?" Don asked.

Gifford chuckled. "You did not hear it from me, lad."

"Is any of this illegal?" Fay asked.

"Oh, there's nothing illegal about it. It's a common and accepted practice."

"Thank goodness," she said. "You mentioned politicians."

"The members of the HPSCI, the House Permanent Select Committee on Intelligence, are responsible for awarding those contracts."

"I would assume Senator de la Croix has a large influence over the committee."

"Big-time," Gifford said.

"It would explain why she implored me to back off

from the Rodman investigation. Somehow, Senator de la Croix, the *Aurora* crash, Nevada's death, and the Rodman brothers' deaths are linked."

Gifford nodded and continued, "Only a select handful of legislators and their staffs are privy to the intelligence appropriation process. A scandal related to any black project would cause a freeze in intelligence spending. The defense contractors would lose profits, and the politicians would lose campaign money. And to some extent, the American economy, in some parts of the country, would tank."

"And you believe," Winslow asked, "the TGA and the EPA air disasters are included in this mix?"

"A SEAL told me Charma died for what he knew," Fay replied. "The man adamantly warned me not to pursue the truth, or my life would be in danger as well."

"For some reason, Charma decided to tell his secret," Gifford said. "Probably because his brother, at the time, was being held and charged as a spy in North Korea. His killer, aware of his decided indiscretion, silenced him before he could reveal it."

****

The glow from the jet's instrument panel cast an amber ambiance over Bart's face. He had not said much to Pearce since they had first buckled into their seats in the *C-40*'s cockpit fifteen minutes earlier. Bart and Ace were busy with their routine preflight procedures, communicating with the air traffic controllers, and attending to their endless supply of instructions and information. Also, the *C-40* was temperamental.

Typically, when the pilot applied power to the jet's twin engines via the thrust levers, thrust was delivered equally to both of its engines. Unique to this *C-40* (hence the need for a service check), the thrust levers were out of sync, causing each engine to produce thrust at different levels. Needless to say, it made it difficult for Bart and Ace to control the plane.

Once the plane reached its cruising altitude, Bart became less frantic.

Sensing he could now converse, Pearce said, "I wanted to be a *Blue Angel* when I joined the Navy. They didn't allow women to fly with the *Angels* at the time. What's the cruisin' speed of this puppy?" she added.

"Our C-Forty is a military knockoff of a civilian passenger jet, flown by many airlines. Its cruising speed is nine hundred thirty-eight knots," Ace replied. "Around five hundred eighty-three miles per hour. It's actually slow for a jet. Navy fighter jets fly two and a half times faster."

Ace was not telling her anything she did not already know. But Pearce reasoned having him tell her this was good for his ego. "I like to go fast," she offered. "My friend, Winslow, told me his motorcycle is capable of doing one hundred fifty miles per hour. I didn't believe him. I got it up to one hundred thirty before I chickened out."

Both men laughed.

"So, I guess he was right. If I was wearin' a helmet, I could have breathed better and have gone faster. Then it wouldn't have seemed as scary to me. And the bugs wouldn't have stung when they hit my face either," Pearce continued.

Bart laughed again. "I seriously doubt I'd have the cajones to go much past seventy on a motorcycle, JP."

She asked Bart to tell her about his assignment with the *Blackbird* spy plane.

He explained, "With the advent of the CIA's *Invision* and the military's *Milstar II* surveillance satellites, *Blackbird* was destined for retirement. Several have been redesigned for special-purpose use. A new spy plane has been developed; naturally, it is classified top-secret."

"The aircraft known as *Aurora*?" JP asked.

"The name was derived from a documentation mix-up. I was told an accounting office inadvertently left the name on a budget line item. As a result of the clerical error, the project was dubbed *Aurora* by the general public," Bart explained.

"Y'all miss recon, don't ya?" Pearce asked.

"*Blackbird* is an awesome aircraft," Bart said, with a hint of sadness evident in his voice. "Flyin' at three times the speed of sound, three thousand two hundred feet per second, powered by two engines producin' enough thrust to power the *Queen Mary*." He quit speaking while receiving navigational instructions from the Osan air traffic controller. "*Blackbird's* roof is ninety thousand feet," he continued.

"I heard the titanium for her skin was purchased from the Russians," Ace said.

"It seems ironic to me," replied Bart. "The Russians sellin' us the metal to build the plane we spy on them with. In one ten-hour flight, *Blackbird* can photograph up to one hundred thousand square miles of the earth's surface."

"Ninety-thousand feet high," JP repeated thoughtfully. "Solves one age-old military objective: seize the high ground. Doesn't it?"

"That it does, JP," Ace replied.

"How'd we get the titanium from Boris?" she asked.

"The story goes the CIA set up several small companies." Ace said. "They bought the titanium in small amounts, so's the Commies wouldn't notice."

"Tricky," Pearce replied.

"I'm told the *Aurora* travels at a speed of somewhere near four thousand miles per hour," Bart informed her. "If you can imagine it."

"Faster than a speedin' bullet," Pearce remarked.

"*Aurora* is one of those black projects y'all don't hear much about," Bart added. "Most are thought to be based at Area 51, Groom Lake, Papoose Lake, all in Nevada, and another secret base in Utah."

"*Aurora* is powered by a pulse detonation wave engine, I understand," Pearce added.

"Y'all been holding out on us, Buckwheat," Bart said. "It would seem y'all know somethin' about *Aurora*."

"Somethin', Hayseed," Pearce said coyly. "Why didn't you continue on into the *Aurora* project as a pilot?"

"It's a young man's game. To fly a jet at four thousand miles per hour takes someone with reflexes quicker than those of a mongoose."

"You're right," she said. "Didn't consider it. How do they do it?"

"As you know, eye-hand coordination dominates reaction time," Bart explained. "The eye registers the situation and sends the message to the brain. The brain records the message and sends an impulse to the muscle required to carry out the appropriate reaction. It's a prolonged process - too slow to control an aircraft travelin' at *Aurora's* velocity. Suppose an *Aurora* was required to take evasive action. In that case, a hesitation of anythin' less than the blink of an eye could prove fatal. To fly an aircraft like an *Aurora* requires a pilot with much the same physical attributes as a triathlete or a pro football player - a large, strong heart, tremendous stamina, that sort of thing. There are few pilots with those attributes. In an emergency, and if an evasive reaction were required, no human could command the reaction time it takes to maneuver an object travelin' at four thousand miles per hour."

"A computer could do it," Pearce offered.

"True," Bart replied, "but a computer has a weakness. Computers are fast at processin' information, but they are incredibly dumb. They lack cognitive psychology. On the other hand, the human brain is incredibly slow at processin' information but highly intelligent."

"It would take a human, armed with a calculator, ten million years to process the same information a super-computer can calculate in one second," Ace chimed in. "The human brain supplies the cognitive psychology. The computer and the human brain are a powerful match for those reasons."

Pearce snickered. "Y'all went to MIT, didn't you, Ace? Somehow, they've figured out how to mate the pilot's brain to *Aurora's* computer to control the aircraft."

"It's what I suppose they've done," Ace replied. "*Aurora* is flown by the thought process."

"It makes sense," Bart said. "Because when they eliminate one step in the reaction process, instead of eye-brain-hand coordination, you have eye-brain coordination. This is made possible by the onboard computer. However, there's one problem."

"What's that?" JP asked.

"As you know, the human mind is easily bored, hence easily distracted. Suppose the pilot, say, should start dreamin', thinking about a problem back home, or any situation other than payin' attention to his plane. In that case, he could still run into trouble."

"How do ya suppose they get around it, Bart?"

"Somethin' I've heard. I don't know this for a fact, JP, but it makes sense to me. The Systems Officer, the pilot who naturally flies backseat on *Aurora*, would not only be responsible for monitorin' reconnaissance systems but is also responsible for juicin' the pilot," Bart stated.

"They juice him?!" Pearce exclaimed.

"That's what I understand," he said. "The driver is flyin' an extreme machine. He needs to be on edge with his aircraft at all times. I'd imagine a narcotic of some sort would not only keep him focused on the task at hand but take his reflexes to the edge of human capabilities."

"It sounds like science fiction stuff," Pearce said.

"Anythin' spawned by those Skunks Works engineers is science fiction," Bart replied.

****

It was 03:15 hours when Fay heard the handle of her room door rattle.

"I don't mean to spoil this evening with an excursion into the realm of paranoia, guys," Fay whispered to Champion and Winslow while moving quickly to her bed, "but someone is lurking near the door." She slid open the drawer of the nightstand next to her bed. It was her habit to place the LM4 derringer and mace in the nightstand drawer each night, whether she was at home or on the road.

Champion's eyes widened when Fay removed the small black derringer from the drawer and unlocked the safety. She put her index finger to her lips and patted the spot next to where she sat on her bed. The two men quickly moved from their chairs, placed in line with the door, to the bed, thereby placing them out of view from the door.

Fay stood up and inched closer to the door, listening intently as she moved like a cat across the floor. She paused, listening for any sound coming from near the door.

She heard Pearce's voice say, "Goodnight," as the door swung open. Fay eased the tension on the weapon's trigger, breathed a sigh of relief, and said, "Hi, Sissy."

JP glanced at the gun she had expected Fay to be holding, and without missing a beat, chirped, "Y'all been interfacin' with one another? Why, Mr. Champion, you look like ya seen a ghost."

He nodded but remained silent.

Fay, not knowing how to take her sister's inference, laughed. "Well, darlin', y'all caught us red-handed," she said, feigning embarrassment. "Actually, Gifford has been helpin' Winslow and me download the reference material from the plane crashes."

Pearce looked at Champion. Some color had returned to his face. "I hope the reference material is the only thing he downloaded," she giggled. Turning her attention back to Fay, she asked, "Y'all havin' any luck?"

"I think we are," Winslow replied.

"Who were you talking to in the hallway?" Fay asked Pearce.

"I was talkin' to Major Kim."

Fay glanced at her wristwatch. Noting it was 03:30, she remarked, "Jangho is up and about kind of early. Or up and about kind of late."

"I guess," Pearce responded. "I saw him at the end of the hall, near the stairs. I guess he uses them rather than the elevator?"

"I suppose," Fay said. "Hey, tell us about your flight with Bart!"

"Ma'am, I was livin' high in the cotton. Thrillin' would be a better choice of words. We had fun, and I did remember to get the information y'all wanted."

Pearce spent something close to thirty minutes downloading her research regarding the *Aurora*, then asked, "Would y'all like some help?"

Fay wrinkled her brow, giving Pearce one of those *are you sure?* looks. "If you feel up to it. It's getting late."

Pearce eagerly agreed. Fay handed her a stack of computer pages.

Approximately five minutes had passed when Pearce announced, "Here's somethin'." All stopped what they were doing and directed their attention toward her.

"I don't know if this is anythin' or not, but I notice the law firm who was representin' the victims of both crashes is the same. Rothchild, Barrymore, and Gain," Pearce observed.

"Does it mean anything to you, Fay?" Gifford asked.

"Rothchild, Barrymore, and Gain is a law firm based near the JAG headquarters in Falls Church. We used them several times when I was stationed there." Fay thought for a moment, then said, "Make a note of it, JP. It may mean something after all."

Fay knew the law firm of Rothchild, Barrymore, and Gain specialized in government litigation, primarily for the military. It was not a coincidence Rothchild, Barrymore, and Gain had ended up representing the families of the victims of both airliner crashes. "Gifford, when you spoke with the victims' families, did they mention who their legal representatives were?" Fay inquired.

He thought for a moment. "Not as I recall."

"We have two dead servicemen, a sunk naval vessel, and a crashed spy plane. Plus, an intelligence black budget two-billion-dollars light and two crashed airlines," Fay said. "Not to mention several hundred dead airline passengers. I have the feeling these occurrences are all linked together. Did I leave anything out?"

"The impending doom, ma'am," Pearce said.

"Not to mention, we have ringside seats for the war of the century," Fay added. "Thank you, Miss Pearce." She was about to suggest they brainstorm a few possible scenarios, but one glance into Champion's glazed-over eyes told her otherwise. "Let's call it a morning, Gifford. I'd like to continue this later this afternoon. You game?"

He gave her a weak nod, then stood and walked zombie-like toward the door. He managed a feeble, almost inaudible, "Goodnight," as the door closed quietly behind him.

Chapter 28

The 06:00 reveilles awakened Egan. It would be a busy day for E-Team, planning and rehearsing for their imminent rendezvous with the Russian cruiser Rapunzel. He ate a hardy breakfast; he was surprised he had an appetite at all. At 09:00 hours, he joined the team for their final planning session.

Everyone appeared to be in good spirits. The team members' adrenaline began to flow in earnest. The atmosphere was a mixture of excitement and reverence. Peter "Kimo" Wu was smiling, as usual. Philip "Dah Vee" De Vinsone was putting on his game face—the one-thousand-yard stare was back. Andrew "Timmy" Lawrence was talking a mile a minute. The two Russian operators, Irina Sergeevna and Viktor Pavlodar, were not talking. The Russians were very calm, relaxed— professional—as they prepared for the mission. It seemed as if the Russians did this sort of thing every day; it was likely they did. It went without saying every team member felt the same anxiety Egan Fletcher felt at that moment.

The team would travel light. Egan took an inventory. He would carry a Colt .45-caliber automatic, with a small flashlight attached to the underside of the weapon's muzzle. His Kevlar vest was jampacked with ammunition. He also had a Ka-Bar knife. The team members would communicate via the AN/PRC-126, a lightweight, short-distance radio with attached Rascal headset. Since this was a night strike, each team member had a set of night-vision goggles. Each member would wear a black flight suit and a black ski mask.

Irina and Viktor's gear was essentially the same as Egan's, except for the weapons. The two Russians preferred the polymer-framed GSh-18 pistol. Philip, Peter, Valentine, Simon, Andrew, and James carried the Heckler & Koch *HK416* assault rifle, along with a supply of flash grenades. At night, the grenades would be effective for causing confusion and temporarily blinding anyone who happened to be nearby. Rayzon would also operate the SATCOM system. With the satellite link, the team could communicate with the U.S.S. *Nalon Ve*t, the U.S.S. *David Ray*, or the two Russian ships, Rapunzel and Sister Golden Hair. By combining James's ability to speak Russian with Irina's knowledge of the Russian communication codes, they would tap into Rapunzel's communication network.

All equipment was checked and then rechecked. Any malfunction would prove fatal. As each team member reported to team leader Rayzon they were satisfied with their equipment, he checked it one more time. It proved to be a very tedious and time-consuming process.

Egan reviewed the overall plan, going over what precisely each team member's responsibility would be. Operation Caspar's goal was for the team to approach Rapunzel unnoticed, scale the moving ship's side, seize the ship, and sail it to the rendezvous. Next, they would grab the counterfeit U.S. currency before returning Rapunzel and her cargo of missiles to the Russians. Then they would deliver the greenbacks to the

Treasury Department and return to *Bon Homme Richard*, leaving Irina and Viktor in command of *Admiral Moskva,* code-named Rapunzel.

"James," Fletcher explained, "will act as our interpreter and as the mission director. Once aboard Rapunzel, I will assume command of the ship. I'll be responsible for all decisions relating to the operation of the ship, much like I would aboard an American ship. Irina's assignment is to secure Rapunzel's communication center. Her knowledge of the Russian communication codes will ensure a well-meaning warning message is not transmitted, either to the North Koreans or Rapunzel's escort ship, Sister Golden Hair."

Viktor Pavlodar said, "My job will be to rally the crew and solidify them as soon as E-Team relieves rogue officers of their commands."

He did not admit it, but Egan knew Viktor was a military hero in the eyes of the Russian people. The Russian crew would follow him.

"*David Ray*," James explained, "will act as our Q-ship, the decoy. As we near Rapunzel, the *Ray* will close on Rapunzel's position, forcing Sister Golden Hair to intercept the *Ray*. With Sister Golden Hair distracted, we will be able to slip close enough to Rapunzel for us to board her."

Egan said, "We assume Rapunzel will slow while she waits for Sister Golden Hair to intercept our *David Ray*, thus allowing us to overtake Rapunzel with our Bat Boats. I don't know how all of you feel about scaling the side of a moving ship, but with Rapunzel slowed, it will be easier for an old geezer like me to climb her hull."

Egan's declaration coaxed a chuckle from Simon

Linn. "Yeah…right, Hurricane!"

"Once we're aboard, the *Ray* will stand down and leave the area. Any questions?" James asked.

No one responded.

"When the *Ray* leaves the area," Egan said, "it will appear to the Russians the U.S. Navy has little interest in their activities. If we pull this off, Sister Golden Hair won't know we are in command of Rapunzel. If Sister Golden Hair were to discover the plan, she would alert the North Koreans, and our mission would end in a disaster. We believe Sister Golden Hair will probably not make an aggressive move. However, the North Koreans would be frightened away."

Viktor said, "Because the mission will take place after twenty-three hundred hours, most of Rapunzel's crew will be in their bunks. The skeleton crew will be easier for us to deal with."

Everyone had one common concern—who could they trust? The Americans did not trust the Russians. The Russians did not trust the North Koreans, the Americans, or themselves, for that matter.

James had assured the American team Irina would perform, since the Russian *Spetsnaz* had sent someone to watch her daughter. That thought alone would keep her locked onto her mission goals without fault. It was James's duty to keep his eye on Viktor. His fluent Russian and AN/PRC-126 weapon would ensure Viktor responded appropriately.

The team reviewed the strike one final time.

Peter slipped a small packet into one of his pockets.

Andrew pointed at the packet and asked, "Kimo, what is it, man?"

"Caffeine, actually a caffeine pill," he replied. Peter

reached back into his pocket, drew out the packet, emptied a small white caplet into the palm of his hand, and flicked it to Andrew. "Every caplet contains the equivalent of a double shot of a high energy booster. I take one just before an op—my body goes berserk. It's kick-ass stuff. One of these babies and I guarantee you I'll be up the side of the ship before any of you can say, 'Where did he go?'"

Peter must have done an excellent job selling the stuff to the others, as every team member wanted him to share his pills.

Egan stood next to James, both looking down at the tiny pills in the palm of their open hands. "If one of us," he said, "makes it back alive, they should tell Faydra about these."

James said, "I think the Caffeine Queen played a major role in the FDA's testing of this."

****

Brandon May hovered near one of the many computer consoles located in the *Bon Homme Richard's* massive Tactical Logistics Center (TACLOG). There, he would observe Operation Caspar as it unfolded.

"They're away," Admiral May said to Marine Colonel Higgins, the TACLOG officer.

"The *Vet's* captain, Captain Moore, is waiting for a communications check from team leader Rayzon," Higgins said. "When Rayzon confirms the satellite linking codes with Moore, Moore will forward them to me."

By 23:05 hours, Admiral May could hear James Rayzon's voice loud and clear over the TACLOG intercom system. A shiver raced up his back as he listened to James conduct a series of test messages. May headed for a nearby coffeemaker. He could not remember ever feeling so anxious about anything in his life. He could only imagine how Hurricane Fletcher must feel at the moment.

****

The Pacific was relatively calm. The night sky was partially cloudy, allowing for some starlight, but there was no moon—the less light, the better. Having night vision goggles would only be an advantage if there was not much ambient light. The powerful twin engines of the two bat boats moved the small crafts across the ocean's surface with ease. E-Team would encounter the Russian Rapunzel in less than fifty minutes.

James radioed the *Vet*. The *Vet's* radar confirmed Sister Golden Hair was moving to intercept the *David Ray*. The *Vet's* crew advised him they had spotted a small fishing boat or cargo ship in the area. It was common at this time of year for fishing boats to populate the area. The TACLOG aboard the *Bon Homme Richard* was curious why there was not more activity than was indicated on the Plan Position Indicators.

Unfortunately, Rapunzel had not slowed as anticipated. The team had counted on her slowing while Sister Golden Hair intercepted *David Ray*. Only twenty minutes into the op, and something had already gone wrong.

Phillip pointed out he had not been on a strike where everything had gone as planned.

"Rapunzel's failure to reduce her speed poses a problem for us," Egan advised the team. "It will not only take longer for our boats to reach Rapunzel but climbing up the side of the fast-moving ship will be difficult at best."

****

"They have a problem," May said. "Rapunzel didn't cut her speed as we expected her to do. E-Team has to run her down. That'll take more time."

"Is there anything they can do?" Colonel Higgins asked.

"This is a lot like a chess match. A strategy move would help them right now."

"It sounds like you have an idea."

"I do. A seasoned ship's captain like Fletcher will have a plan B as well. I'm sure he has an idea, as does the *David Ray* captain. Rayzon back on," May stated. The two officers listened to team leader Rayzon communicate with the *David Ray*.

Fletcher did have a plan. He reasoned if the *Ray* were to challenge Sister Golden Hair, Rapunzel would feel obliged to cover her sister ship in a show of support.

James asked for the *Ray* to press Sister Golden Hair, like a matador testing a bull with his cape.

May smiled. "Fletcher is a smart man," he said. "He's a bit of a riverboat gambler as well. If *David Ray* presses too hard, Sister Golden Hair will open fire."

Minutes later, the *Ray* changed course, as indicated on May's monitor. Positioning her bow toward Sister Golden Hair, *David Ray* came to flank speed and charged.

All held their collective breath as Sister Golden Hair's captain presumably assessed his situation in terms of probability and outcome. No response came from James Rayzon.

Then May heard the *David Ray's* captain's voice on

the TACLOG's speaker. "Sister Golden Hair has turned broadside to *David Ray*," Captain Miles informed them.

May said, "Sister Golden Hair is defensive-posturing, indicating she is preparing her deck guns or anti-ship missiles for an attack."

The captain of *David Ray* thought it best to back down. "Hold your course for another minute, Mike," May told Captain Miles.

David Ray held her course. Then came the report from Captain Miles: "Rapunzel new course, heading zero-niner-zero."

"Rapunzel has turned toward *David Ray*," May said to Higgins. "More importantly, Rapunzel has reduced her speed by half. Fletcher's plan worked."

Colonel Higgins took a handkerchief from his shirt pocket and dabbed at the perspiration that had formed on his forehead.

"The second bit of luck has developed," Admiral May said. "Not only did Rapunzel slow, but when she changed course, our objective turned toward our pursuing strike boats. The strike team's travel time will shorten if Rapunzel stays on the course. The small fishing vessel changed course as well."

David Ray backed down. May and Higgins could hear the communication between the *David Ray* and the *Nalon Vet*. Captain Adrian Moore on the *Nalon Vet* asked Captain Mike Miles on the *David Ray,* "What's your take on the fishing boat, Mike?"

"We can't figure them out, Adrian. Our radar sweep is showing you as a small vessel as well, not completely invisible as we had hoped. *David Ray* is doing strange things to our radar. We think the second vessel could be an echo or radar shadow from *Nalon Vet*," the other captain replied.

Shortly afterward, the *David Ray*'s captain reported, "The fishing vessel has disappeared from our radar screen."

The strike craft continued to close in on their objective: Rapunzel. The report was received that Rapunzel had almost slowed to a stop.

As May and Higgins huddled around the ops tracking station, they could hear James Rayzon speaking with the *Nalon Vet*. He assured the *David Ray* that the team was well and had spotted Rapunzel.

Chapter 29

E-Team was not benefitting from a bright moon, which made for reduced visibility.

Viktor slipped his night vision goggles on for a better look. "Something's not right," he said to Egan. "Rapunzel is riding too low in water."

Egan took a look. "She wouldn't be drawing that much water, even with the weight of the missiles," he said to Viktor. Egan asked, "James, will you run a check on our position, then feed it to the *Nalon Vet*? Ask them to match our position with that of Rapunzel."

"Aye, sir," James replied.

Within minutes, James reported to Egan, "They say we are eight klicks from Rapunzel." He noticed the quizzical look on Egan's face. "Four and a half nautical miles, Captain."

"What do you think, Viktor?" Egan asked. "This isn't Sister Golden Hair either."

Viktor studied the dark hulk and then shook his head in disbelief. "I think, my friend, what we have found is in my country—how you Americans say— an 'insurance policy.'"

"This is the fishing vessel they were talking about," Egan said.

"I'm afraid so, comrade," Victor replied. "It seems we Russians have ghost ship of our own. Irina, do you know what ship?"

"If you maneuver us to side of the ship so I can see silhouette," she responded, "I tell you."

The strike boats repositioned so Irina could identify the mystery ship. "Is guided-missile destroyer *Besstrashny*," she reported.

"*Besstrashny* further complicates our op," Egan told the team. "Either *Besstrashny* is shadowing Rapunzel with Rapunzel's knowledge or shadowing Rapunzel without her knowledge. Either way, *Besstrashny* is someone's insurance policy, but whose?"

"James," Egan said, "inform the *Nalon Vet* they have company out here. *Besstrashny* may not be aware of *Nalon Vet*. We don't want to run the risk of a collision."

Egan spoke to the entire team again. "If the Russian good guys have dispatched *Besstrashny*, she could be aware of *David Ray* and her purpose. *Besstrashny* will keep a safe distance and allow the scenario to play itself out. If we fail to seize Rapunzel, the captain of *Besstrashny* will blast the Koreans out of the water, thus ending the transaction."

James added, "If we fail to turn Rapunzel over to the Russians, *Besstrashny* will sink Rapunzel. The Russians will lose their missiles now but will return later to salvage them."

Egan's money was on the pro-Russian option.

Andrew asked, "If the Russians have a ship like *Nalon Vet*, why wouldn't they run this mission themselves?"

"The Russians have the problem of trust," James replied. "What would prevent the crew of *Besstrashny* from changing their minds and joining Rapunzel? After all, the billion-dollar cargo could be very tempting for a crew who has not seen a paycheck for a few months. Because *Besstrashny* is here as our ally tonight doesn't mean she won't be our enemy come tomorrow morning, even if the mission goes as planned."

****

00:35 hours

Rapunzel's dark hull loomed over the team as they moved along the Russian cruiser's port, searching for the rope ladder "a friend" was to have left for them. It was difficult to spot the ladder in the dark. Viktor feared because they were behind schedule, it might have been withdrawn or discovered. They moved slowly along; James huddled with Simon Linn. He hoped Simon's experience as a MEU trainer might help them develop a method of scaling the ship's side, should they not find the ladder.

"Rapunzel, Rapunzel, let down your golden hair," James murmured as he gazed at *Admiral Moskva*. James's humor coaxed a chuckle out of a few E-Team members.

The team worked their way to Rapunzel's bow, then drifted back toward the stern.

Then Viktor said, pointing to the ladder, "There! Ladder is parallel with second stack."

The two small boats drew up to the ladder. It had now become a leap of faith for the team. E-Team had no way of knowing if a greeting party awaited them topside. If the Russian crew discovered the ladder, the Russians would be waiting to blast the first person who poked his head above the rail.

The mission planners had predetermined James

would be first up. After all, he was the leader, and he spoke Russian. Simon would follow him, then Philip, Peter, Valentine, and Andrew. The five men would secure the immediate area. Irina, then Viktor, would follow, and finally, Egan.

Without hesitation, James grasped the bottom rung of the ladder. He gave Egan a thumbs-up, popped one of the caffeine pills into his mouth, and scurried up the ladder. Thirty seconds later, Simon grabbed the ladder and began climbing. Philip, estimating James should have just reached the ship's deck, mounted the ladder and disappeared up into the darkness.

"We haven't heard any gunfire at least," Egan said.

James' voice came over the Rascal headset. "On deck—all clear. Not a creature is stirring, not even a mouseski," he whispered.

Viktor said to Egan, "I will cut ladder and boats. Go ahead. I will meet you."

Irina knew her job and disappeared toward the comm center, armed with the combination to the room's door. Her challenge would be to get to the room without being seen. Once inside the comm center, she would have to convince the comm center personnel to cooperate. The timing was such that she needed to succeed in her task first. Otherwise, a warning call from the bridge would funnel through the comm center and out to Sister Golden Hair.

As the team neared the bridge, Irina reported reaching the comm center. Approximately thirty seconds had passed before Irina was back on the headset. "I try combination—it no work." She made a second attempt. "No luck. Combination changed." Irina had no way to enter the room. "I shoot lock."

"Only as a last resort, Irina," James cautioned her in Russian. He had another idea. "Try knocking on the door. Take off your Nomex hood and unzip the top half of your suit. Show whoever looks through the peep you're a woman who has had a little too much vodka and is ready to party." He then said to Egan, "I told her to unzip the top of her black gear."

"Unzip her suit?" Egan asked.

"Sex sells," James said. He seemed unruffled.

Several minutes passed, then, "Clear," Irina chirped.

"She's in," James said. "Must have worked. Men are suckers for a beautiful woman."

It was time to storm the bridge. Intelligence reports had estimated as many as ten officers and crew would be on the night watch. Engaging in a firefight with the Russians was not an option. Except for a handful of rogue officers, the crew was innocent.

"Go! Go!" James whispered.

Viktor moved quickly through the door of the bridge with his weapon drawn. He said in his native Russian, "Good evening, comrades. My friends and I are here to commandeer your ship."

The rest of the team burst onto the bridge. The crewmembers present were as surprised as those in the communications room must have been. They quickly placed their hands behind their heads. Most looked relieved.

James ordered the Russians to move to the back of the bridge and sit on the floor. Viktor quickly found those officers identified as the perpetrators and established three out of the total eight were present. James then contacted Irina to tell her they had assumed the bridge's command. She stood by while the team members searched for the rogue officers.

The easiest and safest method to apprehend the remaining officers was to call them one at a time and invite them to the bridge. Viktor accomplished this with a few urgent calls, including one to the captain. As the officers appeared on the bridge, they were apprehended.

Valcov, *Rapunzel's* captain, seemed to know Viktor. The two spoke briefly, then Valcov approached Captain Fletcher.

A short man with gray hair and a beard, Valcov stopped just short of Fletcher, saluted, and said, "Captain Fletcher, I am Valcov of Russian Navy. I understand you have seized my ship under orders of my country. I formally surrender ship and crew to you. You will have my full cooperation and that of my crew." Valcov looked understandably sad.

"Captain Valcov, you have my word you and your crew will be treated with dignity and respect while I'm in command of this vessel," Egan assured him. He extended his hand to Valcov. The Russian shook Egan's hand, lingered for a moment as if he had something else to say, and then shook Egan's hand once again and took his place with the rest of his crew.

Viktor and Kimo escorted the Russian officers to their quarters. It had been preplanned that once Fletcher was in control of the ship, he was to signal his success by indicating a course change. On the hour, he would change Rapunzel's course by ten degrees—a signal to *David Ray* that all was well. On receiving his signal, *David Ray* would leave the area.

Captain Fletcher asked James to inform the Russian quartermaster to change course by ten degrees to port. When he inquired about Valcov and his rogue officers,

Egan learned Valcov and his officers were missing. Egan had left Victor to attend to the ladder and boats.

****

"Admiral," Colonel Higgins aboard the *Bon Homme Richard* said, "*Nalon Vet* reports Rapunzel has changed course on the hour. It's the first part of our indication that the team is in command of the ship."

"We'll know the rest in nine minutes," May said. "How's our coffee supply?"

****

At 02:09 hours, Captain Fletcher asked James to inform Rapunzel's quartermaster to change course by ten degrees to starboard and increase to flank speed.

****

David Ray confirmed Captain Fletcher and the team were in command of Rapunzel.

The span between course changes was nine minutes. Egan Fletcher was to have deducted one minute for each team member lost. If they had had one casualty, they would have changed course in eight minutes instead of nine.

The departure of *Nalon Vet* allowed the Russian escort destroyer, Sister Golden Hair, to change course. Sister Golden Hair was now heading back to rejoin Rapunzel for the remainder of their voyage. The Russian ghost ship, *Besstrashny*, the spirit in the night, did nothing.

Chapter 30

The sun spilled over the horizon. A few hours earlier, the blue-black waters had given way to a turquoise sea blushed with the reflection of the orange morning sky. It had been twenty-four hours since anyone had last slept. The adrenaline and Kimo Wu's caffeine pills had worn off long ago. Every team member was exhausted, with a full day ahead of them before their rendezvous with the North Koreans.

Egan asked Viktor to relieve Irina in the comm center. It was her turn to catch a short four-hour nap. She and Viktor alternated with one another on the communications watch. Simon, Valentine, and Kimo rested, relieved by Andrew and Philip. Egan caught a catnap, leaving James in command of Rapunzel. There was no one to relieve James; he was the only one who could communicate with the Russians on the bridge. Viktor announced to Rapunzel's crew the visitors were part of the deal and to respect their presence.

****

Fay was up by 07:00, showered, dressed in her uniform, and ate breakfast in her room. Then, she placed a call to Gifford Champion. They agreed to meet in her room at noon.

Gifford proved to be a patient and understanding listener when Fay told him she had second thoughts about continuing her investigation.

Gifford asked, "What does your heart tell you to do?"

Fay thought for a moment and then said, "The citizens of the United States of America employ me to do a job. I am to defend their homeland and their families from tyranny and aggression. I have a sworn duty to defend and protect the rights and privileges given to them by the United States Constitution. And I do my duty to my death, if necessary. And I will serve my superior officers without question."

"Then, you go on."

"Yes." Fay grabbed her investigation notes from a nearby table and dropped the neatly stacked pages into Champion's lap. "Where do we start?"

"Galaxy Friendship Association."

"Galaxy Friendship Association? Who are they? I have not heard of them," Fay questioned.

"You won't either, unless the GFA are caught at what they are doing. The GFA is a group of some of the nation's largest defense subcontractors—those companies who routinely bid on the defense contracts awarded by the government to major defense contractors," Gifford explained.

"The major defense contractors would be the aviation and aerospace defense companies of the world?" Fay asked.

"Correct," Gifford confirmed. "But understand, only the subcontractors are a party to this activity, not the prime contractors. When a major contract is put out for bid, the GFA meets. As a group, they decide who will win the bid and the bid price. Each GFA member submits a bid higher than the agreed-on bid. Once the contract is awarded, the winning subcontractor splits up the work, giving a slice of the pie to the losing companies."

"Illegal," she said. "No wonder forty-nine-cent wing-nuts cost the taxpayers that and another thirty-nine dollars."

Gifford laughed. "By that time, your wing-nut has been renamed a feathered appendage clamp or something similar."

Fay chuckled and said, "Why hasn't something been done about this?"

"It's going to take one of the GFA insiders to come forward with an offer to expose the Association. So far, none have."

"How did you find out about the GFA?" Fay asked.

"I was approached by one of the Association members who agreed to expose the scam. She died after our first series of meetings."

"Mercy."

"An accident. The woman was canoeing on a lake in front of her home," Gifford said. "The canoe overturned, and she drowned."

"More like a mechanic in scuba accidentally grabbed her and held her under until she drowned."

"Your version is probably correct. The woman died, and her story died with her."

Fay slowly shook her head. "Should one of those black budget projects go sideways, the result would be a massive freeze in the lucrative defense-spending process. The defense subcontractors would lose money. The black budget money would stop flowing, and the campaign funds to the Senator de la Croixs of the world would cease and desist."

"Exactly," Gifford replied.

"The black budget projects, such as the spy

ship *Nalon Vet* and *Jimmy Carter*, and aircraft like the *Aurora* would disappear. Much to the chagrin of the Navy, Air Force, NSA, NRO, CIA, politicians, and the list goes on and on," Fay stated.

Gifford shook his head. "The power behind this is awesome."

"The crashes of the EPA airliner and *Aurora,*" Fay said, "occurred at approximately the same time. You knew it."

"Well, not right away. But, yes, eventually I did piece it together," Gifford asserted.

"When you saw David Rodman, whom you also knew as Paul Charma, you suspected the military was interested in the two airline crashes," Fay went on.

"Right again," he replied.

"You doubt the National Transportation Safety Board's explanation that a fuel tank explosion brought down the TGA 787, do you?" Fay asked him.

"I think, in both the TGA and the EPA crashes, something else brought those airliners down," Gifford responded.

"A missile, perhaps?" She thought for a moment. "Or an *Aurora*."

"What do you need me for, Fay? I think you know what's going on here."

"With your prompting, I think I do. The public learns an errant and out-of-control spy plane, a plane driven by a pilot high on drugs, brings down two commercial airliners. The plane, traveling at something over four thousand miles per hour, clips a wing or horizontal stabilizer, perhaps, and down comes the liner. Hundreds are killed. The public outrage, spawned by the mishap, exposes and kills the *Aurora* program. All of the

283

parties mentioned would lose big money," Fay theorized.

"And in Senator de la Croix's case, a shot at the White House," Gifford elaborated.

"The Rodman brothers knew this," Fay said. "David, the SEAL, knew because he was at both crash sites. He was involved in recovering the airliners' black boxes; the boxes would indicate the collision with another aircraft. The top-secret *Aurora* project risked exposure. Someone not willing to take a risk replaced the black boxes with ones indicating a mechanical failure."

"Greg Rodman knew because he was one of the *Aurora* pilots who flew into the EPA jet which went down in the Yellow Sea," Gifford said.

"What about the *Carr's* captain, Matt Nevada?" Fay wondered.

"I don't know about him. It's possible Greg Rodman confided in him or gave him something for safekeeping. I suppose we'll never know for sure why Nevada was assassinated."

"Nevada took a couple of unanswered questions with him to his grave," she said. "Which leaves us with who actually killed these men."

"Any ideas?" Gifford asked.

"The *federales* often come off as being the ones unfairly accused of blowing people away in their attempts to cover up their various conspiracies. Although my hunch is one or more mechanics employed by the Galaxy Friendship Association were responsible for the deaths," Fay remarked.

"The GFA members had much to lose," Gifford said. "They would be my guess, too."

"Which means the second person in the alley on the

night of Paul Charma's death was the assassin. A GFA hitman." Fay sank back into her chair. No sooner had she done so when the sweet scent of aftershave filled her nostrils. She bolted upright. "Rodman!" she said. "Dr. Henry told me Greg Rodman's system was clear. No trace of any substances. But if he was an *Aurora* pilot, according to what Bart Hay told JP, then he would have a trace of a narcotic in his bloodstream."

"The *Aurora*'s systems officer was Greg Rodman."

"That's right. Greg was *Aurora's* SO. He was a crewmember and a pilot," Fay replied. "Hay said the *Aurora* pilots need to keep themselves in top physical condition. Like pro athletes. What business does Rodman have smoking cigarettes? There wasn't any trace of nicotine in his bloodstream. The missing cigarettes from the pack found on his body would indicate he had smoked several of them. And yet…and yet, as I recall, no matches were missing from the matchbook. So how did he light those cigarettes he didn't smoke?"

Fay leaped across the room to where she had left the Rodman evidence bag. She withdrew the pack of cigarettes and tossed them to Gifford. As the box flipped end over end through the air, she said, "See if I'm right."

He caught the pack. Grasping it firmly in his left hand, he carefully tore off the pack's open end, exposing the remaining cigarettes. He studied the pack contents for a moment and then inverted the box, allowing the cigarettes to spill out onto the table in front of him. "Seven cigarettes and a piece of paper rolled to imitate the size and shape of a cigarette," he said.

"See?" Fay said, pointing at the jumbled pile of cigarettes.

Gifford picked up the small tube of paper and unrolled it. "I see." He studied it for a moment, frowned, and then handed it to her.

Fay examined the paper. "Is it a code?"

"It could be."

Fay turned the paper upside down and held it up to a nearby light. "I don't really know." She read the inscriptions out loud, "PE0304111F, PE0207248F, and PE927424." She thought for a moment.

She stood up again and walked to the computer. "I'm going to have Winslow take a look at this. Winslow is excellent with research. Let's see what he comes up with," Fay decided.

She typed out a short e-mail to Winslow. "There," Fay said as she clicked the "send" icon on the screen. She consulted her wristwatch. "Want to buy me lunch, Champion?"

Chapter 31

Following a nap, Captain Fletcher was on back on the bridge. Viktor relieved James so James could rest for a few hours.

In the evening, a helicopter buzzed Rapunzel, then turned away.

"Probably a scout," Egan said to Viktor, "sent by the North Koreans to check on us—to see if all is going as planned."

"How far out are they, sir?" Philip asked.

"We're showing a group of several ships about five klicks ahead," Egan said. "We count one large ship and four smaller ones. *Nalon Vet* is positioning to the north of the group. She will act as a net if the North Koreans should get nervous and try to run."

"What about our spirit?" Philip asked.

"We presume *Besstrashny* is astern. She won't stray far from the action. We should be seeing the lights of the freighter *Serra Angel* soon. You men should get into position now."

Philip's smile had no warmth. "How ironic. The warrior angel carrying the devil's cargo." He motioned to Andrew, Simon, Valentine, and Kimo. "Time to go, lads." The men left the bridge without a word being spoken.

James relayed Egan's message: a Russian lookout had reported seeing *Serra Angel's* lights. He ordered Rapunzel's engines reduced to one-third. Sister Golden Hair followed suit. The next move was up to the North Koreans.

"Irina," Egan said, "will you send a cryptic message to *Nalon Vet*? Tell them the North Koreans have been sighted."

Irina was doing an excellent job of keeping Sister Golden Hair informed but unaware.

Irina updated Egan that she had received a message from *Serra Angel*. "They are waiting for a response code from Rapunzel," she said. Irina then responded with the proper code.

A North Korean helicopter would deliver a team to preview Rapunzel's cargo. It would be up to Viktor, posing as Captain Valcov, and James, posing as his X-O, to give the Koreans the grand tour. Once the Koreans were satisfied the missiles were indeed present and accounted for, Viktor and James would proceed to *Serra Angel* to repeat the process and to view the greenbacks.

Egan heard the thumping sound of a helicopter rotor as it approached Rapunzel. He ordered Rapunzel's stern helicopter landing pad to be illuminated.

Valentine, who was positioned near the stern, reported the helicopter's approach and touchdown. "Four bodies aboard, plus the pilot," Valentine advised. "Each body packing an automatic weapon."

Viktor and James met the four men as they ran from the chopper. One of the four was a Korean who spoke Russian. Putting brief formalities behind them, the party proceeded to the ship's hold. A brief inspection of the missiles was all that was needed to satisfy the Koreans.

The group returned to the helicopter pad. It was time to spring the trap.

While the Koreans inspected the missiles, with *Nalon Vet* in position north of *Serra Angel*, Viktor ordered Sister Golden Hair to take position south of the action. The maneuver was supposedly at the request of Captain Valcov. Rapunzel was positioned east of *Serra Angel*, which left the west as the only possible escape route. The North Koreans could escape toward the shore, but they would not get far. *Serra Angel* was not going anywhere. She was too big, too slow, and only lightly armed. The smaller and faster patrol boats accompanying *Serra Angel* would be harder to corral.

The exchange took place along the remote coastline of China, several hundred miles south of Shanghai. Egan received a report Chinese destroyers *Shenzhen* and *Harbin* were active in Shanghai harbor. Still, the two ships did not indicate they were interested. There were no Chinese ships or aircraft in the immediate area. The nuclear spy submarine *Jimmy Carter* hunkered down into the mud at the Shanghai harbor entrance. Should Shenzhen or Harbin show an interest in the shindig to the south, then *Jimmy Carter* would ensure they did not join the party as uninvited guests.

One team member went ashore to scout the nearby jungle for Chinese army patrols as a further safety measure. Andrew Lawrence had drawn the assignment, one he relished. His instructions were to respond every fifteen minutes with a status check.

James and Viktor were ready to board the Korean helicopter for the flight to *Serra Angel*. Simon, Philip, and Kimo were in position with their sniper rifles trained on the aircraft and the Koreans. As soon as Viktor and James subdued the Koreans aboard Rapunzel, *Nalon*

Vet would round up the Koreans aboard *Serra Angel* and those aboard the small patrol boats. *Nalon Vet* would fire a warning shot at *Serra Angel*. Immediately, Irina would radio the crew to ask for their surrender. *Nalon Vet* had two anti-ship missiles ready for Sister Golden Hair and two for the *Besstrashny*. Just as in an Old Western shootout, everyone had everyone else covered.

Egan gave the order. He heard a soft thud come from the general direction of *Nalon Vet*, then saw the ocean explode in a column of water near the bow of *Serra Angel*. The activity distracted the Koreans aboard Rapunzel. James and Viktor drew their weapons and subdued the bewildered Koreans.

The sting went as planned. Egan directed Irina to contact Sister Golden Hair, apprise the captain of the situation, and order him to hold his position or face the consequences.

Nalon Vet arrived on the scene. Several small boats, filled with Marines from the *Nalon Vet*, combed the waters. They were looking for those Koreans who had jumped ship and decided to take their chances with the sharks rather than be captured by the Marine Corps.

The last of the Koreans were rounded up, and then E-Team waited until the light of dawn to board *Serra Angel*. The Koreans were brought aboard *Nalon Vet* and jailed. Simon, Valentine, Kimo, James, and Philip traveled from Rapunzel by boat to *Serra Angel*.

In the meantime, two crafts loaded with Marines traveled from the *Nalon Vet* to *Serra Angel* to secure the ship and its cargo of counterfeit currency. *Serra Angel* would be towed to the Yokosuka Navy Base. The greenbacks would be turned over to the Treasury Department.

Besstrashny appeared, drifting nearby, her guns trained on everyone. Even though Irina was in contact with him, her captain was not committed. *Besstrashny* remained neutral for the moment.

"The *Besstrashny* should be flying the Swiss flag instead of the Ensign of St. Andrew," Egan said to Viktor.

Viktor and Irina would return to Russia aboard Rapunzel, the ship now crewed by loyal officers and crew. Sister Golden Hair was given no choice but to follow; the *Besstrashny* would see to it. E-Team would return to the *Nalon Vet.* At some point, E-Team would be picked up by an *Osprey* tilt-rotor aircraft and flown to *Bon Homme Richard.*

With a team of Treasury agents aboard, *David Ray* returned to the scene to watch over the abandoned cargo ship. Once a sea tug arrived, *David Ray* would escort *Serra Angel* and the sea tug back to Japan.

Whether the missile came from Viktor on Rapunzel, Captain Moore on *Nalon Vet,* or *Besstrashny*, no one would admit. Egan watched as the bow of *Serra Angel* rose skyward, hung motionless for a moment, and then slipped beneath the surface of the Pacific Ocean.

"I'm concerned," Egan said to James. "The last report we received from Timmy was over an hour ago." Andrew had reported seeing a group of men, fifteen in number, in a small encampment about two hundred yards inland. He had surmised they were either smugglers or drug runners and had advised he would hold his position until further notice. E-Team would not leave the area without Andrew Lawrence.

It was 12:00 hours when Hurricane Fletcher found himself racing across the water, surveying the distant shoreline.

Their faces painted with foliage camouflage greasepaint, E-Team sat quietly, checking and rechecking their equipment.

Fletcher could not decide if the anxiety he felt for Timmy Lawrence's safety was more significant than the anxiety he had felt before the Caspar mission. It unsettled him not to have a game plan. Unlike the elaborate ruse devised for the Caspar mission, this had to be played by ear.

The high-speed run from *Nalon Vet* to the beach objective took thirty minutes. As the boat neared the shore, Fletcher resolutely watched the looming shoreline, looking for anything unusual.

The boat ran up onto the deserted beach, and James gave the order to hide the craft in the undergrowth and fan out into the jungle. "When Timmy is located, everyone reconvenes on that location," he told the team.

Not more than ten minutes had passed when Matthew Valentine reported sighting their objective. The rest of the men quickly joined him at his location.

Egan observed the activity from his vantage point near the clearing edge. He estimated there to be approximately fifteen men. Egan noted three dogs, two jeeps, a cargo truck, and a twin-engine airplane. Andrew was spotted sitting near the center of the clearing near a corrugated metal shed, his hands bound behind him. No one seemed to be paying much attention to him.

Lying prone on the jungle floor, Egan thought of his life over the past week. *What is a fifty-year-old sea captain doing hiding in the bushes?* He brushed a giant

ant off of the back of his right hand and hoped he had not chosen to lie atop an ant nest.

"How's it going, Hurricane?" Simon whispered into his Rascal.

"I'm covered in ants."

"Lie still, Hurricane. A dog is heading toward you."

Egan looked through the tall grass toward the encampment, spotted the dog, and said, "You mean the one dragging his handler towards me?"

An alert German Shepherd had sensed something and was guiding his handler directly toward Fletcher. He watched the dog work its way through the tall grass bordering the clearing, the dog's ears erect as it moved purposefully toward him. "I have the man in my sight," Fletcher whispered. "You take the dog, Simon."

"Got him," Simon confirmed. "You say when, sir."

As the dog drew near, Egan held his breath, not daring to move. The Shepherd was now twenty paces away from him. Fletcher's finger tightened on the trigger of his weapon; he knew even the slightest movement would be noticed by the dog. He resisted the temptation to brush away the ants that had found their way to his face.

The dog stopped in its tracks. Suddenly, a small animal darted from a spot just in front of the dog and disappeared into the jungle in James's direction. The handler apparently realized the dog had picked up the animal's scent. Pulling sharply on the leash and issuing a command in Chinese, he retreated back toward the clearing.

"Close call," Egan whispered and frantically brushed off a small herd of ants from his face and neck. "I gotta get out of this ant hotel before these little guys decide it's dinnertime."

James was curious about the ants. "Those small ants or large ants?"

"Big ones."

"Are they black or red?" James quizzed.

"Ah…hold on," Egan replied. "Little ants, big ants, black ants, purple, I don't know…you think I'm some kind of entomologist or something, James?"

Four minutes passed, then Simon whispered, "One of those mutts is on to me, now." This one hurried through the tall grass, heading directly for him. "I've got the man, Hurricane," he said. "The dog is yours."

Egan did not respond. "You all right, Captain?" Simon asked.

"These goddamn ants are driving me nuts," Egan said as he brushed at the back of his neck. "I'm with you, Simon."

Egan disliked the thought of having to shoot an innocent animal. In this case, he had no choice. When the dog reached ten paces from Simon's position, Egan squeezed the trigger. The dog and the handler dropped dead, almost in the same instant, without a sound. No one in the clearing noticed.

"Fall back," ordered James Rayzon.

"Too late," Kimo barked, "we've been spotted."

Chapter 32

The message light on Fay's room phone was flashing, and so was the "e-mail-waiting" icon on her monitor. She called the front desk first to retrieve her messages. There was one message for her from Jangho Kim. He had asked she call his room ASAP. It would be good news, his message promised.

Fay called his room. His words brought a smile to her lips. Following a brief conversation, she hung up the phone.

Fay turned to Gifford and announced, "Good news. The tension between North and South Korea is subsiding. The threat of war has passed." Fay thought his response would have been to beat a hasty retreat to the nearest phone with the news tip of the year. While he did look happy to hear the news, he did not display any urgency to convey the information to anyone, such as his employer, NCC. "Gifford, don't you have to call someone?" Fay prompted.

"It's not my assignment," he replied.

"What is your assignment?" She thumped herself in the forehead with the heel of her hand and said, "Champion, you bastard. I'm your assignment. I'm your story."

He sheepishly nodded.

"DAMN!" Fay groaned as she glowered at him. "Can't I trust anyone?" she muttered to herself as she stalked to the window. She looked through angry eyes out over the tops of the office buildings at the gathering storm front as she felt hurt and rage welling in her gut and said, "Son-of-a-bitch." She then turned and glowered, again, at Gifford Champion. "This is bull…" She abruptly stopped speaking.

Gifford swallowed hard. "The bull you fed me about the *Carr* when we first met doesn't make us even?" he asked weakly.

"Not…even…close."

"I thought we made a pretty good team," he said softly.

Fay remained silent for a moment. A sly smile slowly formed on her lips. "You're right. We do make a good team. You get a good story, Champion?"

A look of relief came to Gifford's face. "We make a great team…and yes, I'm getting a great story. Although as it turns out, it may never be written."

Fay realized she had one more bit of communication to attend to: the e-mail. She retreated to the PC and brought up her e-mail. "Come look," she beckoned.

"Hi," she read the words displayed on the screen out loud, "I'm sorry this took so long. I had a difficult time figuring this one out. The three items you asked about are Air Force budget line items. Run an Internet search on the U.S. Air Force's annual expenditures; it's public knowledge. Good luck, Winslow."

Gifford stepped back from the computer. "The lad is good."

Fay moved to the phone to call Winslow. "Don, I need you, pronto. And call your buddy; I need her too."

"We're across the street, in the park," Winslow responded. "We'll be right up."

While waiting for her dynamic duo to arrive, Fay entered the required input needed to prompt the Air Force's complete annual expenditures database. The process took less than a minute.

"Okay, let's see what we have." Fay reviewed the various budget line items.

"There," Gifford said, pointing to a line item that had captured his attention.

Fay focused her attention on three-line items in the budget. "All of these expenditures are black budget items."

A knock at the door. "Winslow and Pearce. Will you let them in, Gifford?" Fay asked.

Winslow and Pearce entered.

"What were you kids doing in the park?" Fay inquired, "Or need I ask?"

Pearce replied, "Feedin' the squirrels, ma'am."

"It would seem, darlin', and y'all managed to bring a couple of them back with you. Make yourselves at home."

"Afternoon, Miss Pearce, Mr. Winslow," Gifford added.

Fay read the line Gifford had noticed. There were three items, and she read each one aloud. "'0304111F, *Special Activities*—nine hundred million dollars, Rothchild, Barrymore, and Gain—classified. PE 0207248F—five hundred million dollars, *Special Evaluation Program*—classified. PE 0207424, *Special Evaluation and Analysis Program*—six hundred million dollars—classified.' The line items don't mean anything to me," she finished.

"The sum of the three-line items does mean something, though," Winslow observed. "It totals slightly over two billion dollars. The *Special Activities* designation is the Air Force's name for their 'Black Projects.'"

"The line item referring to the law firm of Rothchild, Barrymore, and Gain is interesting," Fay noted. "The Air Force paid them a sizable amount of cash in the past year. It makes me wonder. I need to get into Gain's billing records."

"Wouldn't you need a password?" Gifford asked.

"Well, I do have some contacts at the NSA. They employ the best hackers in the world. But no. Hacking is illegal," Fay stated. "In a criminal trial, primary evidence, illegally obtained, is inadmissible under the Due Process Clause of the Fourteenth Amendment. Subsequently, such evidence can potentially taint legally obtained secondary evidence. It's a doctrine we refer to as 'fruit of the poisonous tree.'" She thought for a moment. "Tell ya what. There's a guy at Gain who owes me a favor. He knows I would never compromise him, no matter what I found in their records. He will probably help me out."

The keyboard keys clicked as Fay typed out an e-mail to her friend at Rothchild, Barrymore, and Gain. The clicking stopped. "Send," she said as she clicked the appropriate icon on the screen. "Let's see what Jerry can do for us."

****

Someone had grown suspicious when the dog and his handler did not return. The two remaining dogs were now heading toward Simon. He fired a shot at the dogs but missed. Egan knew Simon—all of the team members, for that matter—were trained to repeatedly hit a target the size of a quarter from a distance of a quarter of a mile away. It was called a "quarter shot." Simon had missed on purpose.

The dogs turned and ran. Seeing the fleeing dogs, two smugglers opened fire in Simon's direction. It seemed evident some of the smugglers were either terrible shots or blinded by the intense sunlight.

James and Simon worked their way forward through the tall grass from opposite directions, toward the opposing fire. Egan kept his gaze on Andrew and swatted at the many ants covering his body.

Suddenly a bullet caught Andrew in the side of his body. He slumped forward in the grass.

"Timmy's down!" Egan yelled. "I'll get him, cover me!" He worked his way forward on his belly. He found the going slow and the return gunfire incessant.

In a moment, Valentine, James, Kimo, and Philip joined in a terrific volley of fire. They managed to keep the pressure up as they all took turns maneuvering toward Andrew and Egan's position.

Simon was the first to reach Andrew. "Timmy is shot bad," he reported to the others.

The smugglers retreated into the edge of the jungle, leaving the twin-engine plane unprotected.

"I don't think Timmy's going to make it back to the ship," Simon said. "Let's get a chopper in here."

"There's not enough time," Egan said as he wrestled off his bug-ridden jacket and Kevlar vest. "I can fly the plane over there. You guys cover me. I'll taxi to this side of the clearing. I'll pick you up there. Watch out for the propellers."

The five team members pulled out everything they had in a tremendous assault. Egan made the dash across the clearing and, in what seemed like one quick motion, got the door open and jumped inside the plane. For a moment, the aircraft sat silently, then suddenly, the engines roared to life. He turned the tail of the airplane toward the smugglers. Advancing the throttle and holding the brakes, he sent a storm of sand, debris, grass, and smoke in the props blast. The plane pulled away.

"Go! Go!" James barked.

Egan watched the action from his vantage point in the plane's cockpit as Simon and Kimo gathered up Andrew. At the same time, Philip, Valentine, and James attended to the smugglers. The team retreated into the jungle to meet the plane further along the clearing. The men carried Andrew through the brushy cover's protection and then emerged into the open, farther away than smaller targets. Everything went as hoped, and the men scrambled out of the underbrush to the waiting plane with no more casualties.

Simon and Kimo jumped through the rear door, still carrying Andrew. The two big men made it look easy.

James climbed into the copilot seat. They were just pulling the doors closed when Egan started the plane down the grass runway.

"All right," James said with a note of relief in his voice.

"I have to assume the beach is at the end of this runway - if you can call it that," Egan said as they bumped along the grass strip, picking up speed.

"I hope we have enough runway," James said quietly.

"We got lucky there," Egan said. "This is a *Shrike Commander*—good for grass strips and lots of power, the preferred method of transportation of many drug runners. Drugs and money don't weigh much, but armed men do."

Egan was experiencing blurred vision as the plane roared down the clearing toward the beach. He had not taken the time to tell the team that he, too, had been shot. "James, watch the airspeed for me. Tell me when we reach seventy-five knots." He then said, "See if you can find something that I can stuff into my T-shirt to stop this bleeding."

James quickly glanced at the growing red stain on the front of Egan's shirt. "Anyone see a towel back there?"

Simon found several clean mechanic's rags and passed them forward to James, who hastily packed them up under the front of Egan's shirt.

"Can you make it, sir?" James asked Egan.

"I'm having trouble focusing." Egan looked at James, then rubbed the red wet area on his upper left chest.

"Seventy-five knots, Hurricane," James said matter-of-factly.

Egan pulled the wheel back. The twin-engine *Commander* lifted off quickly. But only an instant after they were airborne, they saw the surf zone flash by underneath them. No one said a word as the plane climbed steadily into the bright afternoon sky.

Chapter 33

Two hours had passed before Fay noticed the "you have mail" icon flashing on her monitor. She clicked on the icon to retrieve the message waiting for her. *Hi, baby, long time no hear,* his e-mail read. *I will call you on your cell.* Fay smiled as she read. *And next time you are in Falls Church, let's do dinner. You owe me, now. And my job offer still stands. Let me know when you tire of the Navy life and want to earn some real money. Love, Jerry.*

Shortly after, Fay's cell rang. It was Jerry. She asked him to call her back on the secure phone line and gave him the number. When he called back, she told him what she needed. He said he would fax it to her.

Next, Fay deleted Jerry Gain's message from both the inbox and trash folders of her email account. Gifford, Pearce, and Winslow had taken a break. She told them she would call them when she had something.

When Jerry's fax arrived. Fay called her crew to advise them her documents had arrived. She was scanning the law firm's billing records when she heard a knock at the door. She moved to the door, checking through the peep hole to ensure it showed the familiar faces she had been expecting: Pearce, Winslow, and Gifford.

As they entered the room, Fay asked, "Where were you guys? Don't answer!" she teased as they filed through the doorway. "You were in the park feeding the squirrels! Come see what I have."

They followed her to the PC.

"So, your friend came through for you," Gifford commented.

"He's one of the partners." Fay pointed at the screen. "See. I've passed through the main menu and into their billing records."

"Want some coffee?" Gifford asked.

Fay nodded. "Black."

Gifford poured two cups and set one of the cups down next to her. "It's hot," he warned.

She smiled and said, "Take a load off while I search these records."

"Okay," Gifford said as he slipped off his shoes, grabbed a newspaper, and flopped down in a chair near the window. He chuckled. "Let me know if you need anything."

"Yes, dear," she said in a melodious tone.

Gifford had a curious expression on his face when he asked Winslow, "I heard you met President Lee Ka Eun, lad? I am impressed!"

Winslow's ego was at an all-time-high. "Alex is an impressive lady."

"Alex!" Gifford repeated.

"Only her closest of friends call her Alex. It's the name she used when she attended university in the United States," Winslow explained.

Except for the constant click of the keyboard keys and the occasional crunch of the newspaper as Gifford turned its pages, the room was silent. The rhythmic sound created by Fay's typing and the lack of inspired reporting by the staff of the paper he was reading must have been too much for Gifford. Soon, he was fast asleep.

"There it is," Fay said, loudly enough to wake Gifford from his slumber. But he did not stir. "Yo, Sleeping Beauty!" she barked. "I found what we were looking for."

****

"James, contact the *Vet*," Egan said. "Tell them we'll be there in about seven minutes."

"Aye, aye, sir," James said. "How are you going to land?"

"The water," he said and winced. "But first, we have to get there."

Seven minutes later, James reported, "There's the *Nalon Vet*, sir."

"Too bad it's not a carrier." Egan looked down at the dark silhouette of the *Vet* and said, "We're going to ditch."

No one spoke. The plane droned on for another minute.

"Call the *Vet*, tell them what's up," Egan said. "They'll know what to do. They'll stand by to pick us up."

James spoke briefly to Captain Moore aboard the *Nalon Vet*. They agreed to ditch the plane ahead of the ship on the port.

"Do you have life jackets?" Captain Moore asked.

James turned to Simon, who had made a thorough search of the rear compartments.

"Two," Simon called out.

"Affirmative, two," James confirmed.

"We've alerted the crew. The ship is stopped. Rescuers are standing by, and *Bon Homme Richard* is sending two medical evac-choppers." Captain Moore's voice sounded reassuring. "We're waiting for you, gentlemen."

There was no discussion about who would wear the lifejackets. Simon tossed one to James, who intended to wrestle Egan Fletcher into it the first chance he had. Andrew would wear the other one; Simon and Philip would see to it.

"Okay, this is all we have to do." Egan's voice was weak. "We'll come down to their port. Plan to set down ahead of the ship. I'm going to cut the engines. Then I'll feather the props—we don't want them digging into the water and flipping the plane. The surface of the water might be a little hard to find. We should gauge where the surface is as we watch the ship, but we want to hold it just off the water, as close as we can get, and stay there until we just stop flying. James, make sure the gear is up and locked, and the minute I cut the engine, shut the fuel off. Everybody, get out as fast as you can. This being a high-wing airplane is to our advantage. The belly will act like a boat, but remember, the elevators are back there. If you jump when we're going too fast and they hit you, they'll kill you. The plane will probably sink quickly." Egan took a deep breath. "Are we clear on this?"

"Yes, sir," all but Andrew responded in unison.

"The rest is up to the Lord," Egan replied under his breath.

The men sat quietly as James helped Egan carry out his plan. The *Nalon Vet* loomed ahead, a dark blank spot in the turquoise ocean, as they descended past the level of the deck. The plane glided, seemingly in slow motion, past the bow of the ghost ship. Suddenly, Egan felt very small.

The plane continued to descend—the water rushing

by only inches beneath the plane's wings for what felt like a very long time. Just when it seemed as if perhaps they could continue in that position indefinitely, suddenly the ocean grabbed them, dragging the plane into its dark belly.

****

Gifford woke with a start and groaned as he lifted himself from a chair. To Fay, he looked more drunk than tired. She wondered if the poor man had gotten any sleep over these past few days.

"What did we find?" Gifford asked as he stretched and then stifled a yawn.

"We found two separate four hundred fifty-million-dollar payments to Rothchild, Barrymore, and Gain from the Air Force," Fay replied.

"It totals the nine hundred million dollars the Air Force budget showed as being paid to Rothchild, Barrymore, and Gain," Gifford said.

"Here's what's interesting," Fay said as she scrolled through the billing records. "Here, look at this." She again pointed at the screen. "On this one day, June twenty-fourth, two hundred thirty individual checks were written for one million dollars each." She looked at Gifford. "Does the number ring a bell?"

Gifford shook his head. "It must be late. I'm not following you."

"You covered the story."

"Two hundred thirty passengers and crew died on TGA Flight Eighty," Gifford replied.

Winslow whistled. "Two hundred thirty settlement checks at the rate of one million per. Wow."

Fay scrolled again. "Now look," she said, pointing at the screen. "Two weeks ago. Same thing. How many died on the EPA flight?"

"Two hundred twenty." He studied the screen. "Two hundred twenty individual checks written for one million dollars each." Gifford looked at Fay. "The goddamned Air Force settled with the families of the victims of both crashes."

"Every last one of them settled, too," Pearce noted. "I find it interesting."

Gifford commented, "The settlement seems low. Libya offered ten million dollars restitution for each of the two hundred seventy passengers killed aboard the Pan Am flight which crashed at Lockerbie. This settlement seems unusual."

"Why would they settle?" Pearce asked.

"I doubt if any one of the victim's families would have done as well in litigation," Fay said. "You know, as well as I do, the Death on the High Seas Act not only applies to ships at sea, but to airliners that crash into the sea. The Act denies damages, including lawsuits stemming from these crashes, if the crash occurs in international waters."

"With damage awards limited to as little as one million per surviving family for pecuniary losses," Gifford said, "one million looks like a tempting offer."

"Add in the time a lawsuit would take and the legal fees the families' individual lawyers would charge them for their services," Fay replied.

"The victims' families get squat," Winslow commented.

"This was a deal too good for anyone to pass up," Fay said.

"Jesus," Gifford said. "I don't suppose any of the recipients knew the settlements came from the Feds."

"I doubt they did," Fay replied. "The payouts were laundered through Rothchild, Barrymore, and Gain."

"Okay, it accounts for roughly twenty-five percent of the NRO's missing budget money. Where's the other seventy-five percent?" Gifford asked.

"Right here," Fay said as she scrolled down the screen again.

Gifford scanned the screen. "Will you look at this!"

"I don't know what an airliner costs these days, Gifford, but it appears the U.S. government bought each airline a new jet. Or reimbursed them for estimated lost revenues as a result of bad publicity," Fay remarked.

Gifford responded, "When the black boxes were switched, blame was taken from the Air Force and *Aurora* and placed on the manufacturer of the two airliners."

"Possibly they received a few choice defense contracts as throw-ins," Pearce said. "Everyone comes out of this clean."

"Everyone, except for the people who died," Fay said.

"Of course," Gifford replied. He walked from where he had been standing to the window. He looked out over the city. "What's next?"

"I was just thinking the same thing," Fay replied. "The conclusion I've come to is we do nothing."

"Let sleeping dogs lie, as they say?" Pearce asked.

"Precisely, JP." Fay sat down. "We do have proof; I'll give us that. I fear, should we take this story public, it will draw a lawsuit from any one or all of the many parties involved." Fay sat back in her chair. "You know the story of the old man and the sea."

"Hemingway," Pearce confirmed. "He caught the

grandmother of all fish," she explained. "Tied the big fish to his boat and dragged it back to his home. By the time he got home, the sharks reduced his prize catch to a skeleton."

"We'd be labeled as 'whistle-blowers,'" Fay explained. "We'd be dragged into court for a costly and lengthy trial. It would be brought to the court's attention our proof was obtained dubiously. It would damage our credibility. And I have to consider what exposure this could potentially bring to Rothchild, Barrymore, and Gain."

"The Navy and NCC would hang us out to dry," Winslow said thoughtfully.

"Our careers would be ruined, our finances would be decimated, our reputations would be trashed," Fay said. "This is not something I want to risk or something I want to experience."

"Nor I," said Gifford.

Fay looked at everyone in the room and flicked off the computer. "Done," she said. She thought for a moment. "I'd still like to castrate those bastards at the Galaxy Friendship Association."

"Before you overdose on caffeine," Gifford cautioned, "think it out, Faydra."

She thought for a moment. "Give me a hint."

"The Galaxy Friendship Association comprises several military defense subcontractors—people who are apparently not opposed to murdering anyone who threatens their business. Let's say, for the sake of argument, two of those subcontractors are companies owned by an enterprising government agency."

"Our friends, the Christians in Action?"

Gifford remained silent for a moment. "You have a

death wish, don't you? But yes, the CIA."

"So I have been told. Anyway, I changed my mind. I don't want to know which agency," Fay stated.

Gifford remained noncommittal. "You might decide to move on the Galaxy Friendship Association if you first find a way to warn said government agency. Give them time to distance themselves from the Association. In light of the recent events, I understand this agency may not be opposed to terminating its GFA membership. Otherwise, you might ensure your last will and testament is up to date."

Chapter 34

Egan Fletcher had been in the Yokosuka Naval Hospital for three days after being transferred from the hospital facility aboard *Bon Homme Richard*. The surgical staff on the *Richard* could have removed the bullets from his chest, even though they had not done so. The flight from the jungle to the *Nalon Vet* and the crash landing in the Pacific had added to the toll the bullets had taken on his chest. By the time James had pulled Egan free of the wreck, he had lost consciousness. It was all James and Dah Vee could do to keep him afloat and hoist him into the bobbing medivac sled lowered by *Richard's* helicopter. By the time the doctors had examined him, their main concern was to stop the bleeding and replenish lost blood. He had presented with symptoms of shock and had been unconscious. Fearing a head injury, the chief medical officer had ordered a CT scan but had found no significant cranial damage, though Captain Fletcher did have a concussion. The staff had decided to postpone surgery until after he had been stabilized. He had spent two days on the *Richard*. He had then been transported to the Naval Hospital, where the bullets had been removed, followed by a recovery period.

Altogether, he had been hospitalized for almost seven days, a new record for Hurricane Fletcher. He was not good at bed rest. However, each time he moved, the pain reminded him why he was still there. As he adjusted the automatic hospital bed to a more upright position, he noticed a small bouquet of roses on the bedside table. He did not remember seeing them the last time he was awake. He had been losing track of time, coming in and out of consciousness for a few days. But he thought he was over it. Now, he just felt dreadful. He was sure about the flowers, though.

A young orderly came bustling into the room. "Good morning, sir," he chirped.

"Good morning," Egan said. He knew this would be what he called the health drill. It was similar to the sanity drill. When an elderly person was asked who the President was or what day of the week it was, they had better come up with the correct answer—the sanity drill. When an orderly or nurse said, "Good morning," say "Good morning" back. No matter what. Even if you do not know what they are talking about at first - the health drill. If you want to get out of the hospital, pass the health drill. "Fine," Egan said, without being asked a question.

"Captain Fletcher," the orderly said, "I think you're still a little groggy." The orderly tended to his duties, refilling the water pitcher and straightening the covers. Egan had been thrashing a little.

Egan struggled to clear his head and again looked at the bouquet. It was then he noticed a book on the stand next to the flowers. "What's this?" he asked as he picked up *Alice's Adventures in Wonderland.*

"Your book, sir," the orderly answered.

"Ah…good," Egan said thoughtfully. "I can still read."

The orderly must have realized he just stated the obvious. "Sorry, sir. The tall lady has been reading it to you." He pointed to the flowers. "I'm sure those are from your wife, too."

"My tall wife?"

"I'm sorry, sir. I assumed she was your wife. She told me she was Native American when I asked about her tan. She's nice, and if you don't mind me saying so, beautiful, sir. You're a lucky man."

"I'm a lucky man," Egan said. His head was definitely clearing, but he had no idea what the man was talking about. He decided to wait. He would see what his mind told him once the fog had lifted entirely.

The orderly started to leave. "Oh, one more thing," Egan said.

"Yes, sir."

"Is there a toothbrush somewhere?"

"Sir, the lady brought a kit bag for you. I believe it's in the closet." The orderly opened the door of the closet to check. "Yes, right here." He set the small leather zippered bag on Egan's bed within his reach. "I will have your nurse stop by. Anything else, sir?"

"No, thank you." The orderly left.

"Nice kid," Egan said to no one. He struggled out of bed and into the bathroom. He was a tough guy, so he was not up to asking for help with a shower. Instead, he managed to shave and brush his teeth. He noticed a marked improvement in how he felt. *Maybe that's all that's wrong with me now*, he thought. *I just need cleaning up.*

With his left arm in a sling and his chest bandaged, he used only his right hand and managed to wash his hair before feeling nauseated from the pain in his chest. He hobbled back to his bed. Lying down seemed to ease the pain.

"Mornin', Captain," a familiar voice said as a knock came on the open door. "Permission to come aboard, sir?"

"Granted." It was the first time Egan could remember seeing Petty Officer Pearce since the impromptu dinner and evening they had spent together in Seoul. It seemed like a very, very long time had passed, although he did recall the long and passionate goodnight kisses they shared that night.

Pearce hugged him gently. She seemed happy to see him awake and looking well. "You've been a sick cowboy," she said. "We've been worried." She looked as if she might cry. "Don't ruin the moment by makin' a scene," she reminded herself out loud.

At that moment, a nurse entered the room. "Excuse me, sir. But we need to get you ready for President Ross's visit."

"President Ross?"

"Yes," the nurse said. "We discussed it yesterday."

"Oh…yeah, right." Egan smiled and then adjusted his bed to a more comfortable position. "Refresh my memory, sailor."

"Sir," the nurse patiently replied, "President Ross will be here in one hour to visit with you and Petty Officer Lawrence. And to present the two of you with your Purple Heart medals."

"That's right." This was the first he had heard of it. "I'm up to speed now. Thanks." Egan then rolled his head to the side of the bed on which Pearce sat. "How's Andrew doing?"

"I just left his room. Had a nice chat with him and his parents. He is doing great!"

A thankful smile came to Egan's lips. Picking up the

book, he said, "Where did this come from?"

"It's Faydra's book, Captain," Pearce explained.

His eyes searched the room as if he were looking for Faydra. Egan leaned slightly over the side of his bed, pretending to look under it. "Is she here?"

"No, sir, she returned to Bremerton several days ago."

"I see," he said. "I've enjoyed hearing Alice's adventures, JP." He was lying. Still, he did not want to run the risk of hurting her feelings. "You know," Egan said, "we didn't finish it." He handed the book to her.

"Not now, sir. The President is comin'," Pearce insisted.

"I want you to read. The President will just have to wait."

Pearce took the book from him. With a small amount of bravery in her voice, she said, "Sir, I don't think so. You really need to meet with President Ross." She paused. "So, you were a naval aviator like my father."

She was clumsy, but she was brilliant. Pearce picked the one topic other than his son that was near and dear to Egan's heart: flying. "Go ahead," he encouraged, "tell me about your father."

"Well," Pearce was radiant, "I don't know if you know this, but my father was a Navy pilot." She scooted her chair closer to the bed. "He flew *Shadowhawks* during the Persian Gulf War aboard the U.S.S. *Theodore Roosevelt*. He was a squadron commander. After he retired…" Suddenly, she seemed to hit a painful block. "Afterward…it was a while…well…a lot happened." She was struggling.

"It's okay, you don't have to explain. Maybe

another time."

"It's just hard to put into words. My dad is such a great man. He taught me about aerobatics—about life, really."

Egan wanted to see where she was headed. "Really?"

"Oh, yes. Y'all probably noticed," JP said, bringing her fingertips of her right hand up to the long scar on her cheek, "or maybe ya didn't, but I was in a car wreck when I was little. I was thrown through the windshield of the car. I got filleted by the jagged glass."

Egan carefully studied her face. "I see some lipstick, some eyeshadow, two bright and sensitive blue eyes, a little blush in the cheeks.... can't tell if it's cosmetic or natural." He winced as he leaned toward her and lightly touched her scarred cheek with his fingers. "What scar?" he said. "I see a wonderful woman."

Pearce cupped his left hand in hers and gently kissed his hand. "After that, I was afraid to even ride in a car," she said as she continued to hold his hand. "I was that way for years. Then one day, my dad said he should take me flyin'."

Her eyes looked distant, but there was no pain in her expression. At first, Egan could not read it; the look seemed out of place. Finally, he realized what it was: tenderness.

"He had a *Stearman* he bought, salvaged, and restored," Pearce continued. "He and his plane were inseparable. He taught me a lot about aerobatics. He said I'd be safer if I knew how to get out of any situation, recover from any attitude." She looked a little embarrassed. "Listen to me go."

"I asked. Remember?" Egan reminded her.

"Well, one thing he told me, time and again, was how to get out of an inadvertent spin," Pearce went on. "He said that's one thing I needed to know how to do. It's how people die doin' aerobatics. They get into a spin they didn't plan. They react instinctively and yank back the stick, unwittingly holdin' the plane in the spin all the way to the ground. Dad said, 'Remember two things: let go of the stick and push the rudder opposite of the spin.' Can you imagine? To pull out, y'all have to let go and push in the opposite direction?"

"Seems paradoxical, doesn't it?"

"That's just how it seemed to me. It's how I knew it to be true," Pearce said. "I thought about it a lot. I wanted to do it right if it ever happened to me. Then, one night I was lyin' in bed and realizin' I was in a spin. I'd been livin' in fear, not acceptin' the changes that occurred in my life. My mother was dead, two mothers I mean, and I'd been badly injured in a car wreck. I knew what I had to do to recover was to let go and push in the opposite direction. Before long, my entire outlook changed. Afterwards, I guess I came out of my shell." She looked at Egan's face. "I love flyin'. In a way, it saved my life."

Egan was listening intently.

"I'm pretty out of my shell now, don't ya think?" Pearce laughed self-consciously. She appeared embarrassed.

Egan realized his life, too, had been in an inadvertent spin since the death of his wife. Pearce had sensed it in him and had found a way to express it to him in terms he could understand. She was indeed an elegant woman.

The orderly came through the doorway. "The arrangements are all finished," he said. "I just checked in on Petty Officer Lawrence. It's good to see him back to his old self." The orderly was beaming with excitement.

"The President will be here soon, Egan," Pearce said. "Is there anythin' y'all need me to do?"

"No, thanks. But I would like to get dressed."

"Egan, do ya think you're up to it?" JP asked, her brow wrinkled with concern.

"Sweetheart," he smiled at her, "this is probably the only time in my life I'm going to meet the President, and I'm going to do it with my pants on."

Both Pearce and the orderly laughed. The orderly opened the closet once more. "Your son brought this by yesterday," he said, producing Egan's uniform.

"Kristian is here?"

"Yes. The Navy flew him in from Seattle the moment we learned of your condition. We discussed it yesterday too, sir."

"I must have missed a good day yesterday," Egan said. "This is good news. Where is he?"

"He's comin' over with President Ross," Pearce said.

"Have you met Kristian?" Egan asked her.

"Yes, sir. He and I have done a lot of prayin' together these past few days," Pearce replied.

"Praying for me?"

"Well, sir…actually," she drew closer to him and whispered, "Kristian and I split a lottery ticket. We was prayin' we'd become millionaires."

Egan clutched his chest and roared with laughter. He felt an uncomfortable pain in his chest, but the pain was well worth the humor. He regained his composure, wiped the tears from his eyes with the fingers on his good hand, and said, "Now, if you…" he caught himself, "if y'all would excuse me, Miss Pearce…I need to get my pants on. The President is coming."

Chapter 35

Faydra sat at her desk with a giant smile on her face. She had just finished speaking with her sister on the phone. Pearce was very excited to tell her sister she would be accompanying Egan Fletcher and his son to Hawaii. She would spend one week there, doing her part nursing him back to health, then she would fly to Pensacola to visit with her father for the remainder of her four-weeks leave of absence. Faydra was elated. Yet, she was left wondering how she could have been so self-absorbed not to have noticed the budding romance between Pearce and Egan Fletcher, one that had quietly sprouted and taken bloom under her very nose. She did recall two days in Seoul where Pearce had not been around.

Fay, too, would take a well-earned leave of absence. Unlike Pearce's, her plans were devoid of any significant event and avoided any important ones. She had considered spending her leave on the beach at her summer home on the Hood Canal, reading. Or perhaps she would start the novel she had always threatened to write. In light of her recent experiences, she felt she had enough material for a great mystery story. Fiction, of course. Or she could write her memoirs if she could remember anything.

The voice of Petty Officer Winslow interrupted her

daydream. "Lieutenant Commander Green, there's a gentleman here to see you," he said.

Fay could tell by the look on Winslow's face this was no ordinary gentleman caller. As she opened her mouth to ask who, the gentleman entered through the doorway. Had her mouth not already been open, she would have opened it to gasp.

Fay sprang from her chair, so quickly and with such force, it sent her chair sailing halfway across the room on its casters. "Why, sir," she said, "I'm surprised. Welcome." It was about all her mind could come up with at the moment. She found herself at a loss for words.

"I'm sorry for coming unannounced, Commander," the gentleman said. "I was in town, and I felt as if I owed you an explanation."

Winslow quietly dismissed himself. He actually retreated from the room backward.

"An explanation, sir?" Fay vaguely gestured toward one of the chairs facing her desk and said, "Have a seat.

The gentleman seemed as if he were very weary. *And well he should be*, Fay thought. "Can I get you a cup of coffee, sir? Or a soda perhaps?"

"A soda would be fine," the gentleman said.

Fay, who had not yet retrieved her chair, walked to a nearby refrigerator, opened the door, and extracted a familiar red can. She carefully chose a bone-china mug from a cupboard near the small refrigerator. The cup was embossed with the words "Go Navy" in gold leaf. She poured the drink with a trembling hand, then returned with the refreshment to the gentleman and rolled her chair back to its proper spot behind her desk and sat. The act of serving the soda had bought her enough time to regain her composure.

"So, Admiral," Fay said, "if I understood you correctly, you said we have some unfinished business?"

"If you would allow me to explain. There is so much I have to tell you," he said.

She waved her right hand in a dismissing manner. "Just tell me, sir, I was not deceived, misled, or taken advantage of. Lie to me if you have to."

"None of it happened, Commander."

"Commander, sir?" She glanced at the nameplate to confirm it read "Lt. Commander Green."

"That was one of the things I came to tell you," Admiral May replied. "Vern and I signed the request today for your promotion to Commander. Congratulations."

"Thank you, sir! I am at a loss for words." Fay regained her composure and asked, "What brings you back to Bremerton, sir?"

"It would be fine with me if you would call me Brandon."

"Brandon, it is then."

Brandon smiled. "I came to pay my respects to Mrs. Rodman. She's burying her sons tomorrow at Tahoma National Cemetery."

"Oh," she said softly. "How sad. Tomorrow, sir?"

Brandon nodded. "I hope you and Petty Officer First Class Winslow will accompany me?"

"My Winslow!? Also promoted!?" Fay cried.

"Winslow, your sister, there were several promotions granted as a result of the missions," May said. "Also, two special promotions for your two friends as well."

"Which friends?" Fay asked.

"Juliet and Romeo."

"WHAT!? No frickin' way! How does that work, Brandon?" she exclaimed.

"All Navy dolphins hold a rank at one grade higher than their handler. There was a ceremony for them when they received their promotions," Admiral May explained. "For saving a life, they were awarded the Navy Distinguished Service Medal. I understand there was a large photo of you placed in the pen during the ceremony."

Fay could no longer contain herself and began to cry. When she regained her composure, she fanned her face with her hand and said, "I am so sorry, sir. I do not cry. Ever!"

Brandon snatched a Kleenex from her desk and handed it to her. "I think, Faydra, if nothing else, the Navy owed one to you."

Fay dabbed at the tears in her eyes, sniffed, and softly blew her nose. "I am ecstatic, sir! I declare, this news is the best! Mr. Winslow and I would be honored to accompany you." A grin came to her face. "Whew! This has been one day I would not want to wish on anyone!"

"Well, whatever it was, you earned it. And then some," Brandon remarked.

"I have placed you on the wrong team, Admiral," Fay noted.

"I was hoping to set the record straight."

She looked at her wristwatch. "Are you married, Brandon?"

"No. I'm a single man."

"I'll bet it's been a while since you have had a home-cooked meal."

"Longer than I care to admit, Commander."

Fay shrugged her shoulders and sighed. She stood, moving around her desk. She sat down next to Brandon and placed her hand on his arm. "It seems like I have been through a lot lately. I wanted to make a difference…" Her voice trailed off. She refreshed the smile that had drained from her face and continued, "I was considering, just this morning, hanging up my uniform. Trading my roadster in for an SUV. Perhaps starting a small private practice here in the Northwest. Adopting a child. Quitting talking to my cat." Fay frowned and emitted a heavy sigh. "In light of all that has happened today, I've decided I'm traveling to Florida later this week to see my dad. And… well, it's been a long time."

"I was hoping you had one more battle left in you," the admiral said.

Fay thought for a moment. "You're talking about the Galaxy Friendship Association, aren't you?"

Admiral May nodded. "The NCIS and the FBI are preparing to go after them. The NCIS asked me if I knew of anyone who might be qualified to head up the operation."

She smiled. "Me, a Terminator? Sounds dangerous."

"Not for the faint of heart, I'm afraid," the Admiral confirmed.

"Huh," Fay said. "Tell the NCIS you know of two people who are qualified to head up their operation."

"You and Gifford Champion?"

Fay chuckled. "Yeah. Champion. If that old spook is up for it, then count me in."

"That 'old spook,' as you call him, is a highly decorated CIA operative," Brandon stated.

She grinned. "I was right."

"When I talked to Champion about the GFA, he said the same thing about you."

Fay frowned. "Champion called me old?"

The Admiral laughed. "No. He said he was in if you were in."

"Outstanding! Ah, Brandon, I have a question, if I may?"

"Sure."

"Major Kim. What of my friend?" she asked.

"Your visit with President Lee Ka-Eun," May replied.

"Girl talk, sir. I did mention to her my undying admiration for Jangho Kim," Fay answered.

"Whatever you two discussed, Major Kim is now Colonel Kim and Special Military Attaché to President Lee."

"Holy kimchee! Man! And the hits just keep on comin'! I will call Jangho this evening!" Fay exclaimed.

Brandon reached into his briefcase. "Sometimes, we make a larger impact on the lives of those around us than we realize. I was asked to present this to you." He retrieved a small, plain-wrapped package and handed it to her. "The guys asked me to deliver this to you."

Fay took it from him. "What is it, Brandon?"

"The custom is to unwrap it and find out."

Although the object was crudely wrapped in what appeared to be brown butcher paper, Fay carefully peeled away the tape that was holding the wrapping together. She lifted the thing—a nicely framed photograph—from the wrapper and admired it.

"It's a photo of seven scruffy, yet obviously happy-looking men standing on the fan-tail of a ship," Fay said as she described the photo to Brandon. "Two of the men are holding an ensign - Saint Andrew, I think? And while I do not understand the significance of the Russian flag, I do know the faces of the men in the photo." She said each name as her finger lightly touched each face. "Andrew, Philip, Peter, James, Mathew, Simon, Egan." She looked up from the photo with a quizzical look in her eyes.

"E-team," Brandon said.

Fay remembered Andrew Lawrence had told her his team was training for a ship seizure. The photo could only have been taken after she had last seen the E-team aboard the *Nalon Vet* and before Egan and Andrew had been wounded. She recalled the Russian military jet she had seen entering the hanger at Chinhae.

"The data I found on *Jonathan Carr* had nothing to do with the *Aurora* and everything to do with this Russian ship. The North Koreans sank the *Carr* and killed Greg Rodman and Matt Nevada for the information the data contained," Fay put together.

"That's an interesting theory, Fay. I didn't notice any mention of it in your report." An appreciative look formed on Brandon's face. "You could have reported so much more than you did."

Fay knew he could neither deny nor confirm her theory. The information would be classified as a national defense secret. "As I prepared my report, sir, I was reminded of something someone once said. 'In every operation, there is an above the line and a below the line.' - John Le Carre."

His eyes brightening, Brandon answered, "Above the line is what you do by the book. Below the line is how you do the job."

"It is how it see it, sir," Fay confirmed.

"On occasion, I, too, will follow that line of reasoning. I'd be interested in hearing more of your theory… over dinner? And just because I'm curious, how did you arrive at this theory of yours?" Brandon asked.

"Conan Doyle, sir. 'When you have eliminated the impossible, whatever remains, however improbable, must be the truth.' It was a guess. And one who guesses will probably guess wrongly. So, I'm probably wrong," Fay remarked.

She smiled slyly and then returned her gaze to the photograph. Fay squinted and brought the photo closer to her face. It was similar to the one she had seen in Simon's home.

"There is something written on the flag." Fay squinted again and finally reached into her pocketbook, carefully removed her glasses from their case, and slipped her reading glasses on. "It says, 'Hear ye, one. Hear ye, all. Hear ye and know the talk. That by…'" Her throat tightened. She could no longer speak. Several tears raced down her cheeks. She tried again to say, "That…."

Admiral May wiped a tear from his left eye, cleared his throat, and proudly said, "Hear ye, one. Hear ye, all. Hear ye and know the talk. That by this way…a hero did walk."

A word about the author…

Except for time spent in military service I live in the Pacific Northwest with my legal-beagle son K-K. and seven large tropical fish from the Amazon River. I am a second-generation Seattleite (that's what they call those of us who dwell in the shadow of Mr. Rainier). I have had the opportunity to travel our planet many times over. My stories are created from my memories of my personal experiences, the places I have visited, and the people and friends I have known.

Thank you for purchasing
this publication of The Wild Rose Press, Inc.

For questions or more information
contact us at
info@thewildrosepress.com.

The Wild Rose Press, Inc.
www.thewildrosepress.com

CPSIA information can be obtained
at www.ICGtesting.com
Printed in the USA
BVHW040922271221
624880BV00017B/781